THE
AVENGING
CHANCE

THE AVENGING CHANCE

AND EVEN MORE MYSTERIES
FROM ROGER SHERINGHAM'S
CASEBOOK

ANTHONY BERKELEY

EDITED BY TONY MEDAWAR
AND ARTHUR ROBINSON

Crippen & Landru Publishers
Norfolk, Virginia
2024

The Avenging Chance and Other Mysteries From Roger Sheringham's Casebook

By ANTHONY BERKELEY

EDITED BY TONY MEDAWAR AND ARTHUR ROBINSON

Third edition enlarged

ISBN: 978-1-936363-80-3

Crippen & Landru Publishers
P.O. Box 532057
Cincinnati, OH 45253 USA

Website: www.crippenlandru.com

Email: info@crippenlandru.com

Contents

The Master of the Final Twist

ANTHONY BERKELEY COX (1893-1971) was a versatile author who wrote under several names. As A.B. Cox, he wrote humorous novels, political commentary, and even comic operas. As Francis Iles, he wrote the groundbreaking psychological novels of murder *Malice Aforethought* and *Before the Fact.* And as Anthony Berkeley, the name by which we shall refer to Cox throughout this introduction, he wrote fourteen detective novels, many of which feature Roger Sheringham, a novelist whose hobby is criminology. Roger works sometimes with Chief Inspector Moresby of Scotland Yard and the two also appear, together or separately, in several short stories. Except for "The Avenging Chance," an acknowledged classic, these stories are little known today and hard to find. This collection is therefore long overdue; it is the first to include all of the stories about Roger Sheringham and the Chief Inspector known to have been published in Berkeley's lifetime. Importantly, the collection includes a novelette and two short stories which were rediscovered only recently and have not previously been collected or published in any form since their original appearance over eighty years ago. Several of the other stories have only been published in book form once before and then only in a strictly limited edition of ninety-five copies, *The Roger Sheringham Stories* (Pledge Limited Editions for Subscribers only, by Thomas Camacki, 1994).

Various people have played a part in one way or another in bringing this collection to fruition and we would like in particular to thank Geoff Bradley of *CADS* magazine, Ayresome Johns for his thoughtful studies of Berkeley's papers, John McLaughlin, Paul Moy for his pioneering research on Berkeley, the late John Warmington, Librarian of Sherborne School, the staff of the BBC Written Archives Centre, and, of course, the Greene family and Jeffrey Marks at Crippen & Landru.

In a sense, Anthony Berkeley *was* Roger Sheringham but at the very least the two have much in common. Roger, like his creator, was the son of a doctor, "born in a small English provincial town."[1] Both went to public school and, later, to Oxford; Berkeley achieved a third in classics, Roger a second

---

[1] "Concerning Roger Sheringham," preface to Berkeley's Dead Mrs. Stratton (New York: Doubleday, 1933).

in classics and history. Both served in World War I; Berkeley
was invalided out of the army with his health permanently
impaired, while Roger "was wounded twice, not very seriously." Each tried his hand at business after the war, then
turned to writing. Roger became a best-seller with his first
novel, but generally speaks disparagingly of his fiction —
though he is annoyed when others criticise his books.[2] Berkeley
appears to have treated writing as merely a means to an
end. Against this background, his remark that Roger Sheringham was "founded on an offensive person I once knew"[3]
is likely to have been an example of his often-noted peculiar
sense of humour.[4] Indeed there is ample proof that Berkeley
often called on his own experiences and circle of friends when
writing[5] and on more than one occasion characters comment

---

2 Roger Sheringham also seems to have shared some of his creator's
experiences with American reviewers. In Murder in the Basement,
Roger quotes to Moresby the reviews his last book received from three
American periodicals; the comments are taken verbatim from the same
publications' reviews of books by Berkeley. And in Panic Party, Roger
is annoyed when someone tells him that Alexander Woollcott has described him as "a writer of pot-boiling thrillers." Woollcott had in fact
described Berkeley in precisely these words (New Yorker, 4 February
1933). Berkeley has his revenge in Roger's retort that a "distinguished
American critic" would never have used such a "gratuitously offensive
and vulgar phrase."

3 Howard Haycraft, "Anthony Berkeley Cox," Wilson Library Bulletin,
December 1939.

4 In an article published shortly after Berkeley's death, Julian Symons
commented that his fellow crime writer "could be touchy and crotchety
when he felt his dignity was called into question, yet he was a most engaging companion particularly sympathetic to the young. Perhaps they
appreciated his sense of humour" (Sunday Times, 14 March, 1971).
While Berkeley's sense of humour may have been unusual, it is unclear
whether he shared Roger Sheringham's mild misogyny and distinctly
un-mild anti-Semitism or was merely, reflecting in his character some
of the prejudices of his generation — either way some of the sentiments
expressed in the novels are distinctly regrettable.

5 As an example, Berkeley served with the Seventh Service Battalion
of the Northamptonshire Regiment, as did the murderer in one of the
novels. In another novel the name of one character 'Elaine Delamere'
echoes that of E. M. — "Emmie"— Delafield, a writer to whom Berkeley
dedicated both The Wychford Poisoning Case and the final lies novel As
for the Woman (1939); Delafield was at one time suspected in the press
of being Francis lies. And the murderers in The Silk Stockings Murders
and The Poisoned Chocolates Case share their unusual names — pre-

that the easiest way to create fictional characters is to base them on someone real.[6]

Roger Sheringham makes his debut as a detective in *The Layton Court Mystery,* published anonymously in 1925 (the title page gave the author's name as "?").

> In appearance, he is somewhat below the average height, and stockily built; with a round rather than a long face, and two shrewd, twinkling grey eyes. The shapeless trousers and the disreputable old Norfolk jacket he is wearing argue a certain eccentricity and contempt for convention that is just a little too self-conscious to be quite natural without going so far as to degenerate into a pose. The short-stemmed, big-bowled pipe in the corner of his mouth seems a very part of the man himself. Add that his age is over thirty and under forty; that his school had been Winchester and his university Oxford; and that he had (or at any rate professed) the profoundest contempt for his reading public, which was estimated by his publishers at a surprisingly large figure — and you have Roger Sheringham, Esq., at your service.[7]

During a house party Roger's host, Victor Stanworth, is found dead in a room locked on the inside and with a gun in his hand. Although the police seem satisfied that this is a clear case of suicide, Roger suspects murder and decides to investigate. He appoints a young friend, Alexander Grierson, as Watson to his Holmes. Grierson, unlike Watson, does not shower the amateur investigator with the reverential admiration he craves and for good reason, not least because Roger's suspicions fall on one person after another before he *finally* determines what really happened. Berkeley

sumably only their names — with two of Berkeley's schoolboy contemporaries, as does one of the suspects in the latter novel, while another shares his surname with one of Berkeley's teachers.

6 In Top Storey Murder a writer of newspaper serials comments "Lionel is useful to me. Well, so is John for that matter. I've used them both a dozen times, under different names. That's the best of my kind of work, you know; stick a new name on, and you get a different person; no bother about character, or anything like that."

7 The Layton Court Mystery, Chapter I.

maintained that he wrote *The Layton Court Mystery* "for pure amusement,"[8] and it is indeed an entertaining parody of country house mysteries. However, the novel is also very much a fair-play detective story, with all the evidence given to the reader. The first chapter, which seems to be merely humorous and expository, contains important clues, and although the solution is startling it is also, in retrospect, obvious. Like such later masters of the genre as John Dickson Carr and Edmund Crispin, Berkeley presents clues fairly but does so in comic scenes to distract the reader from their significance. The novel was a great success and one reviewer, noting that "Roger's facetiousness is a trial to the reader," also commended Berkeley for "his skill in construction and for the remarkable ingenuity of his plot."[9]

Ingenuity in the plotting is common to all of Berkeley's novels and while many other writers at the time concentrated on finding ever more incredible means of dispatching victims and ever more implausible "least likely suspects," Berkeley focused on turning established conventions upside down. Thus the explanation of the locked room in *The Layton Court Mystery* is absurdly straightforward. In another novel the official detective is right and the amateur wrong. In another, the last person known to have seen the victim alive *is* after all the murderer. On more than one occasion it is argued that the victim deserved to die and murderers are allowed to go free because their crime was justifiable or simply for want of evidence. And, most atypically, death may occur not by accident, murder or suicide but simply as a result of natural causes. Above all, facts uncovered by one of Berkeley's investigators are almost always capable of more than one explanation, and the first deductions drawn by his detectives, amateur and professional alike, are rarely entirely if at all correct. In this last respect, Berkeley clearly took some of his inspiration from certain historical crimes, particularly those whose solution has never been clear-cut and where the facts, such as there are, routinely afford of more than one possible explanation.

The second Sheringham novel, *The Wychford Poisoning Case* (1926), again published anonymously, is based on just

8 Introduction to The Poisoned Chocolates Case in The Crime Club Golden Book of British Detective Stories (New York: Doubleday, 1933), reprinted in this collection.
9 Times Literary Supplement, 5 March 1925.

such a case —in this instance the poisoning of James May-brick in 1889. Prompted by press reports of an apparently straightforward case of murder by arsenical poisoning, Roger concludes that the prime suspect must in fact be innocent. He persuades a friend, the editor of *The Courier* — a news-paper possibly based on the *Daily Express,* which published a few short pieces by Berkeley — to take him on as an "unof-ficial special correspondent," and he and Alec Grierson go down to Wychford to investigate. The novel is less effective than *The Layton Court Mystery* and the conclusion too abrupt and unconvincing. Berkeley returns to form in the third novel, *Roger Sheringham and the Vane Mystery* (1927), the first to be published as by Anthony Berkeley. On this occasion, Roger enlists his cousin, Anthony Walton, to act as his Wat-son, cheerfully informing him that he is indispensable as "the idiot friend" that all the best sleuths have. They travel to Ludmouth to investigate the death of a woman who has fallen from a cliff, leaving a far from inconsolable husband and a cousin who inherits her fortune. A policeman, Inspector Moresby, is already on the spot. Unlike the usual Scotland Yard man of fiction, he greets the amateurs with geniality rather than hostility, partly because he knows the publicity a 'journalist' can give him will help his career.

> Moresby was as unlike the popular idea of a great detective as can well be imagined. His face resembled anything but a razor, or even a hatchet (if it must be compared with something in that line, it was more like a but-ter-knife); his eyes had never been known to snap since infancy; and he simply never rapped out remarks — he just spoke them. "Let us not shirk the fact; a more ordinary-looking and ordinarily-behaved man never existed ... The Inspector was heavily-built, with a grizzled wal-rus moustache and stumpy insensitive fingers; his face habitually wore an expression of bland innocence; he was frequently known to be jovial, and he bore not the least malice to any of his victims."[10]

So much for appearances. Moresby is a first-rate police-man and not merely a foil for Roger, whose methods he

---

10 Roger Sheringham and the Vane Mystery, Chapter III

regards with sardonic amusement — "It's our business to deal in facts, not fancies." [11]Their styles contrast: Roger's is based mostly on psychology and close to what he believes is the French approach to the investigation of crime — "more used to considering characters than actions"[12] as one police detective puts it, while Moresby's relies on evidence, the English approach. Both have their successes and their failures and when, near the end of *Roger Sheringham and the Vane Mystery,* Roger reveals his solution — an ingenious one, similar to that of Edmund Crispin's *Swan Song* (1947) — it is Moresby who has the last laugh. After praising Roger for "as clever a bit of constructive reasoning as I've ever heard," he points out flaws in Roger's case, unmasks another character as the killer, and ends the book by observing kindly: "Do you know what's the matter with you, sir? You've been reading too many of those detective stories." This sort of final twist was to become a trademark and Berkeley later said that it amused him "to try to prove a complete case against the wrong person in the ante-penultimate chapter. Then I upset this in my last chapter."[13]

Roger gets revenge for this failure in Berkeley's next novel, *The Silk Stocking Murders* (1928)[14], by beating Moresby (now a Chief Inspector) to the solution and telling him: "Do you know what's the matter with you real detectives at Scotland Yard, Moresby? You don't read enough of those detective stories." However, for all his lightheartedness, Roger's reaction to defeat at the hands of the official force in *Roger Sheringham and the Vane Mystery* may be what leads him in later books to disturb crime scenes, to plant false evidence and conceal facts and, on one quite disgraceful occasion, to allow a callous murderer to go free on the basis that, having once been a small-time thief and more recently. Apparently attempted blackmail, the victim probably "deserved shooting."

We have already noted how Berkeley delighted in experimenting and in playing with the conventions of crime fiction,

11 Roger Sheringham and the Vane Mystery, Chapter XII

12 The Layton Court Mystery, Chapter IV.

13 Quoted in Basil Hogarth, Writing Thrillers for Profit (London: A. & C. Black, 1936), pp. 11&-117.

14 This novel may have been influenced by the "Silk Stocking Mystery," a crime widely reported in the London newspapers in 1926.

such as the detective's invariably drawing one conclusion from each clue, and always being right. As Moresby says in *Roger Sheringham and the Vane Mystery*, "when the known facts are so precious few, it's possible to make half a dozen sets of deductions from them, all quite different" Berkeley illustrates this masterfully in *The Poisoned Chocolates Case* (1929). In this *tour de force*, expanded from the short story "The Avenging Chance," Moresby invites the six members of the Crimes Circle, a club of amateur criminologists that Roger has formed[15], to investigate the murder of Joan Bendix, a case that Scotland Yard has been unable to solve. Each member comes up with a different solution, as Berkeley spoofs the various types of crime stories, from the dry puzzle that relies only on physical clues to the psychological story that disdains them. The results are surprising. For instance, one member of the Circle, a detective-story writer, using the techniques of his trade, establishes, twelve pointers to the criminal's identity, gets the others to agree that whoever fills all twelve of these conditions must be the culprit, and then proves logically that the murderer must be... himself.

Roger, the fourth to speak, presents the same solution as in "The Avenging Chance," but is proved wrong by the fifth speaker, who, after demolishing Roger's theory, presents a convincing and apparently unanswerable case. It is left to Mr. Ambrose Chitterwick, the last member to speak and a character that Berkeley used in two other books, to demonstrate how each of the five to go before him has made different deductions from the same clues. He then uses the clues that the others had misinterpreted to expose the real poisoner. It turns out that one of the earlier "solutions," which had been intended as a joke, was closer to the truth than anyone had realised. Again, humour is used to mislead the reader.

Chitterwick appears, without Roger Sheringham, in Berkeley's next book, *The Piccadilly Murder* (1929), where, with

---

15 The Circle therefore has much in common with the Detection Club, which Berkeley founded in 1929. It numbered among its early members G.K. Chesterton, Agatha Christie and Dorothy L. Sayers. Berkeley may also have had in mind the somewhat less well-known Crimes Club, which was formed in the early 1920s and counted Sir Arthur Conan Doyle, the creator of Sherlock Holmes, and several celebrated jurists among its membership.

a little help from Moresby, he solves a mysterious poisoning. Sheringham returns in *Top Storey Murder* (1931) but, as in *Roger Sheringham and the Vane Mystery,* it is Moresby who succeeds. Roger uncovers crucial clues to the identity of a woman's murderer but gives Moresby the evidence he has compiled without explaining where this has led him. As he explains in a later novel, "I don't care a bit about convictions. All that interests me is to get to the bottom of a problem and prove it to my own satisfaction. What happens to the murderer later isn't my affair or my concern."[16] This tendency sometimes leads to unfortunate consequences, none more so than in *Top Storey Murder* where Roger is in the act of giving his explanation to the person he suspects of the murder, whose identity he has kept from Moresby, when the Chief Inspector telephones to inform him that thanks to his help, the police are now able to charge the person they'd suspected all along! Roger is only just able to conceal his embarrassment and even manages to leave the person he has all but accused of murder convinced that he had never thought anything of the kind.

Roger Sheringham is thus the antithesis of the great detective rather than an archetype, much more so than E. C. Bentley's Philip Trent, with whom Roger is sometimes compared. His tendency to jump to conclusions and to make mistakes make him, in the words of Dorothy L. Sayers, "a refreshing change from the stock type of 'infallible sleuth.'"[17] Even so the scale of that fallibility is surprising. Roger's solutions turn out to be wrong in five of the ten novels in which he appears, and in two others his initial theory is incorrect, although he later gets on the right track. He is more successful in the short stories in this volume, although in one he again finds the right clues while suspecting the wrong person and lets the police think he had been on the right track all along.

Detective stories tend to tell the tale from the detective's point of view rather than that of the criminal and, consistent with this, most of Berkeley's early novels feature murderers who must stand by and witness Roger — or the police, or both — gradually discovering the clues that will lead to their exposure. The murderers' emotions are usually apparent only in the last chapter since the solution is not revealed until the end of the book. This was another

16 Murder in the Basement, Chapter XVIII.

17 Evening Standard, 28 August 1936, p. 24.

convention and, in *The Second Shot* (1930),[18] Berkeley attempts to turn it on its head. In his famous foreword to this novel, he quotes "the only reviewer of detective fiction whom we who write it can take seriously"[19] as advocating the development of character and atmosphere, and announces that in this book he is making an attempt at this. *The Second Shot* is not wholly successful — for one thing, the murderer seems more of a caricature than a character. Nevertheless, Berkeley stuck with the idea that a detective novel could be driven by characterization and tried again the following year, under a new name.

In *Malice Aforethought* (1931), using the pseudonym Francis Iles, Berkeley makes no secret of the murderer's identity as he depicts first the steps that lead a doctor to murder, then his reactions as the police track him down. *Before the Fact* (1932), the second Iles novel, takes the approach one step further and portrays the murderer from a new point of view that of the victim. The identity of "Francis Iles" remained a secret for over two years yet the Iles books contain many echoes of Berkeley's Sheringham novels as well as some striking differences. In ten of his fourteen novels as Berkeley, the author withholds the criminal's identity until the final chapter or an epilogue, and in two cases until the last sentence; but *Malice Aforethought* and *Before the Fact* reveal whodunit (or rather who'll do it) in the first paragraph.

Moresby, working without Sheringham, is the central character of the first part of the next Berkeley novel, *Murder in the Basement* (1932).[20] This book begins with a newlywed couple moving into their new home only to discover a body buried under the cellar floor — could this have given Dorothy L Sayers the idea of furnishing the Wimseys' new house with a corpse in *Busman's Honeymoon* (1937)? The corpse in

18 According to Berkeley's agent's records, the novel was originally entitled Murder at Minton Deeps.

19 This is evidently Margaret Cole; see The Roger Sheringham Stories, ed. Ayresome Johns (London: Pledge Limited Editions, Thomas Carnacki, 1994), pp. xiii-xiv.

20 Moresby does appear alone in one story by Berkeley, "Unsound Mind," which is reprinted in this collection for the first time since its original appearance in 1931. In one important respect, this extraordinary story prefigures the second Francis Iles novel Before the Fact (1932).

Berkeley's basement, a woman's, is unrecognisable, and the police doctor cannot even determine how long she has been dead. In anticipation of the police procedural novel, we follow Moresby as he unearths the meager clues, questions the neighbours, narrows down the time of death, painstakingly perseveres through several false trails, and finally succeeds in identifying the victim. Only then does he consult Roger who, by an extraordinary coincidence, taught briefly at the prep school where the victim had worked until shortly before her death.[21] Roger tells Moresby that he had been researching for a novel and that he produced several chapters, featuring characters based on the teaching staff, before abandoning the idea. The incomplete manuscript then forms the second part of the novel; effectively the reader is challenged to pick from among the characters not only the murderer but also the victim.

At the end of *Murder in the Basement,* Roger identifies the killer but elects not to give the name to Moresby. As Berkeley comments of his creation, "he has unbounded confidence in himself and is never afraid of making grave decisions, and often quite illegal ones when he thinks that pure justice can be better served in this way."[22] Indeed, in half of the Sheringham novels, Roger does not inform the police of his solution — though this does not matter so much in two of these, as his solution is wrong (although he never realises this).

Roger Sheringham went on to appear in two more novels. The first is the excellent *Jumping Jenny* in which a murder party and a murder and pretty much everything else as well go wrong. The second is *Panic Party* (1934), an intriguing and much-underrated novel that anticipates William Golding's *Lord of the Flies* (1954) by isolating a group of normal, respectable individuals and charting their psychological and moral decay, in Berkeley's book, as they suspect that a murderer is among them.

---

21 The school's name, Roland House, recalls that of Berkeley's own prep school, Rose Hill.

22 "Concerning Roger Sheringham," Dead Mrs. Stratton. Berkeley would appear to have had much the same view, seeking once to defend himself on a charge of having failed to stop at a halt sign on the grounds that, by ignoring the sign, he was in fact "driving to the public safety" (Daily Sketch, 14 October 1937). The defense was unsuccessful.

signed by lies because it is an "inverted" crime novel rather than a detective story, but Berkeley insisted in a 1947 radio interview that "*Trial and Error* is a detective story because the main interest which keeps the book going is the detection, although seen from a new angle." [23]The central character is Lawrence Todhunter, an eccentric bachelor who, after learning he has only a few months to live, decides to perform a final service for humanity by ridding the world of the most obnoxious person he can find, a sentiment that Berkeley uses to justify the actions of his murderers on other occasions too. We follow Todhunter as he seeks a suitable victim and then tries to devise the perfect crime. He studies detective stories, hoping to find pointers, but concludes from them that "so long as nobody saw you at the scene of the crime or near it, and you left neither incriminating evidence of any sort nor finger-prints, and had no possible motive for eliminating the victim, you were absolutely certain to be caught" The murder appears to come off successfully, but when an innocent person is arrested, Todhunter goes to Scotland Yard and tries to give himself up to Chief Inspector Moresby. To his outrage, neither the police nor his own lawyer will believe his confession. To save the person whom the police suspect, who is convicted and sentenced to death, Todhunter must turn detective and search for clues to the murder that he himself had planned, and then arrange for his own prosecution in a civil trial. Despite the potentially grim subject matter, the novel is often hilarious; it is dedicated to P.G. Wodehouse, who apparently helped Berkeley with at least one suggestion as he wrote it. But it is also suspenseful and at times, uncharacteristically for Berkeley, quite moving.

As illustrated by his expansion of "The Avenging Chance" suggestion as he wrote it. [24] But it is also suspenseful and at times, uncharacteristically for Berkeley, quite moving.

As illustrated by his expansion of "The Avenging Chance" into *The Poisoned Chocolates Case*, Berkeley liked to try different versions of the same plot, experimenting with his own ideas as well as with the genre. Two of the other stories in this collection show this too. "Perfect Alibi," originally published in 1930, is effectively a highly compressed version of

23 "Books and Authors," BBC Written Archives Centre, Radio Talks T67, 11 October 1947.

24 Ayresome Johns, The Anthony Berkeley Cox Files (London: Ferret Fantasy, 1993), p. 29.

the novel *The Second Shot* and, as in *The Poisoned Chocolates Case*, the solution in the short story is one of those put forward and discarded in the novel. "The Mystery of Horne's Copse" (1931) also resembles *The Second Shot* in some details, such as the narrator's needing help from Roger, an acquaintance from his youth, to clear him of suspicion, but the problem and solution are different The solution of the mystery does however have something in common with one of the wrong solutions to the problem propounded in *The Poisoned Chocolates Case.*

"The Wrong Jar" (1940) is a variation on Berkeley's 1938 non-Sheringham novel *Not To Be Taken,* and "Mr. Bearstowe Says ..." (1943) is an adaptation of a radio play broadcast in 1940, "Red Anemones"; both may in fact be considered adaptations of "Razor-Edge," a short story apparently not published in Berkeley's lifetime. "Double Bluff" is especially unusual." Typescripts of this story and another, "Direct Evidence," were discovered among Berkeley's papers after his death. These are essentially the same story but told differently and with different solutions. For this collection, we have selected "Double Bluff," as this appears to be the later of the two.[25]

In addition to the twenty-four books he published between 1925 and 1939, Berkeley was a prolific contributor to periodicals under his various names. Between 1922 and 1939 he published more than 300 stories, sketches, and articles in about thirty periodicals, not counting book reviews for *Time and Tide,* the *Daily Telegraph,* and *John O'London's Weekly.* Most were brief comic sketches in humorous magazines such as *Punch, The Humorist, London Opinion,* and *The Passing Show*[26] although several reflect Berkeley's interest in criminology. He also wrote a few serious crime-related stories in the 1920s, including one important early short story, "Over the Telephone."[27] This recently rediscovered story concerns

25 Malcolm J. Turnbull, Elusion Aforethought: The Life and Writing of Anthony Berkeley Cox (Bowling Green, Ohio: BowlingGreen University Popular Press, 1996), p. 46.

26 In Top Storey Murder, we learn that Roger contributed to The London Merryman and The Passer-By.

27 Truth, 17 February 1926.

a doctor who murders his wife. Not only does the approach foreshadow Berkeley's later crime novels as Francis Iles but several key elements of the plot, including the murder method, reappear in *Malice Aforethought* There was widespread speculation as to the identity of "Francis Iles" in the early 1930s*[28] but there would have been no mystery had anyone remembered "Over the Telephone," published under Cox's real name five years earlier."[29]

Berkeley also wrote several non-series criminous novellas, published in serial form under his own name. "The Wintringham Mystery"[30] is not so much a detective story as a comic thriller and was revised by Berkeley and published in 1927 as a novel, *Cicely Disappears*, under yet another pseudonym, A. Monmouth Platts. Two other previously unrecorded light thrillers appeared as twelve-part serials for *Home and Country,* which published the Sheringham novelette "The Mystery of Horne's Copse." These were "The Manoeuvres of Mary" (1928) and "The Man with the Twisted Thumb" (1933) which, despite the tide, does not have any Sherlockian connections.[31] Berkeley's final novels, *Not To Be Taken* (1938) and *Death in the House* (1939), neither of which feature Roger Sheringham or Moresby, also appeared first as serials, in *John O'London's Weekly*[62] These are fairly routine and unremarkable myster-

---

28 Johns, The Anthony Berkeley Cox Files, pp. 30-32, reviews the debate. Francis Iles's identity is described as "one of the best-kept literary secrets of the present time" in the Daily Telegraph, 27 October 1933. Some sources have wrongly suggested that Cox refused to admit his identity as Iles for many years, but the title page of Berkeley's quasi-political tract O England! (1934) stated clearly that A. B. Cox was Francis Iles.

29 Another story apparently written in the 1920s, "It Pays To Look Soulful," contains several passages that reappear verbatim in Malice Aforethought. This story survives in typescript (signed "A. B. Cox"), but may never have been published.

30 Daily Mirror, 1 March to 6 April 1926. Reprinted, with introduction by Tony Medawar (Collins Crime Club, London, 2021).

31 A fourth serial, "Village Wooing," also signed A. B. Cox, appeared in Home and Country in 1936. This is not a crime story, but an expansion of the short story "A Sense of Humour," published as by Francis Iles in Strand Magazine, October 1935.

32 Some of Berkeley's other novels may also have appeared originally in serial form — the dedication of Panic Party states that it had been

ies though the Parliamentary setting of the latter is unusual. After 1939, no more books appeared under any of Berkeley's names, although a few short stories appeared during the Second World War and, as Francis Iles, he continued to review books,[33] covering crime fiction for the *Sunday Times* between 1951 and 1956 and for the *Manchester Guardian* from 1956 until September 1970, shortly before his death on 9 March 1971.

Although Anthony Berkeley Cox is still hailed as a pioneer of the modern crime novel for his work as Francis Iles, his "straight" detective fiction as Anthony Berkeley has fallen into undeserved neglect. Happily, this tendency has been reversed in recent years with the reprinting of most of his detective novels.[34] This is a welcome development and fitting given Berkeley's popularity between the wars when he was praised by critics and other mystery writers alike. It, therefore, seems appropriate to close this introduction with the words of his peers. To Agatha Christie, Berkeley was "Detection and crime at its wittiest — all his stories are amusing, intriguing and he is a master of the final twist, the surprise denouement.[35]

Dorothy L. Sayers also admired him and has Harriet Vane, in *Have His Carcase* (1932), describe Berkeley's "twistiness" thus: "There's the Roger Sheringham method, for instance. You prove elaborately and in detail that A did the murder, then you give the story one final shake, twist it round a fresh corner, and find that the real murderer is B."[36] Another giant of the genre, John Dickson Carr, wrote after Berkeley's death of his "dazzling ingenuity" and said that he shared equal honours with Ellery Queen as "the

"rejected by a leading popular magazine" — but the publication of these remains untraced.

33 Two reviews were published, as by Francis Iles, in 1963 in The Shiburnian, the magazine of Sherborne School at which the Francis Iles Prize is awarded annually for clear and accurate English.

34 Details are given in the bibliographical note at the end of this book.

35 "Detective Writers in England." This was first published in Russian but further details are not known.

36 Have His Carcase, Chapter 33.

world's best practitioner" of the detective story."[37] The last word can be left to Christianna Brand, a near neighbour of Berkeley's who, reminiscing about the Detection Club, commented: "Sometimes I have thought he was really the cleverest of all of us."[38]

Tony Medawar
and Arthur Robinson
Cyberspace, 2003

---

37 'The Jury Box," Ellery Queen's Mystery Magazine, July 1972.
38 Introduction to The Floating Admiral (Boston: Gregg Press, 1979).

Concerning Roger Sheringham

ROGER SHERINGHAM was born in 1891, in a small English provincial town near London where his father practised as a doctor. Roger therefore grew up in a familiar atmosphere of drugs and medical talk. He was an only child, and was educated in the usual English way for the sons of professional men; that is to say, he went first to a local day school, then at the age of ten as a boarder to a preparatory school, in Surrey; then at fourteen he won a small scholarship at one of the ancient smaller public schools which despise Eton and Harrow just as thoroughly as Eton and Harrow ignore them; and finally, in 1910, he went up to Merton College, Oxford, where he failed to win a scholarship. At Oxford he read classics and history, and took a second class in each, but distinguished himself more conspicuously by winning his blue in his last year for golf; he played rugby football for his college but did not shine at it, and he lazed most of his summer terms away in a punt on the Cherwell. He was just able to take his degree before the war shut Oxford down like an extinguisher.

Roger served from 1914 to 1918 in a sound line regiment, was wounded twice, not very seriously, and though recommended twice for the Military Cross and once for the D.S.O. was awarded nothing, which privately annoyed him a good deal.

After the war he spent a couple of years trying to find out what nature had intended him to do in life; and it was only after spasmodic interludes as a schoolmaster, in business, and even as a chicken farmer, that by the merest chance he bought some pens, some ink, and some paper, and at enormous speed dashed off a novel. To his extreme surprise, the novel jumped straight into the best-selling ranks both in England and America, and Roger had found his vocation. He exchanged his pens for a typewriter, engaged a secretary, and got down to it. He was always careful to treat his writing as a business and nothing else. Privately he had quite a poor opinion of his own books, combined with a horror of ever becoming like some of the people with whom his new work brought him into contact: authors who take their own work with such deadly seriousness, talk about it all the time, and consider themselves geniuses beside whom Wells and Kipling and Sinclair Lewis are just amateurs. For this reason he was always careful to keep his hobbies well in the front of his mind; and his chief hobby was criminology, which appealed not only to his sense of the dramatic but to his feeling for character.

It had never occurred to him that he himself might have any gifts as a detective, though a love of puzzles of all kinds had been handed down to him by his father, so that when on a visit to a country house called Layton Court in 1924 his host was discovered one morning dead in his library, in circumstances pointing to suicide, it did not occur to Roger at once to make any investigations on his own account. It was only when certain points struck him as curious that his inquisitive nature asserted itself. The same thing happened at a town called Wychford, which was in a ferment over the arrest of the French wife of one of its leading citizens on a charge of poisoning her husband. The woman and her husband were both complete strangers to him, but Roger on the evidence in the newspapers decided that she was innocent and really more for his own gratification than anything else set out to prove it. This case brought him the recognition of Scotland Yard and a certain amount of publicity; with the result that his hobby developed and he was soon in a position to lake an active part in any case which interested him.

Just as Roger-the-novelist had determined to avoid becoming like the worse specimens of that profession, so Roger-the-detective was anxious not to resemble the usual pompous and irritating detective of Action — or rather, one should say, of the Action at the time when he began his career, for the fashion in detectives has since altered considerably. He knew that he could never pose as one of the hatchet-faced, tight-lipped, hawk-eyed lot, while his natural loquaciousness would prevent him from ever being inscrutable. As a result, he went perhaps too far to the other extreme and erred on the side of breeziness. In matters of detection, Roger Sheringham knows his own limitations. He recognizes that although argument and logical deduction from fact are not beyond him, his faculty for deduction from character is a bigger asset to him; and he knows quite well that he is not infallible. He has, in point of fact, very often been quite wrong. But that never deters him from trying again. For the rest, he has unbounded confidence in himself and is never afraid of making grave decisions, and often quite illegal ones, when he thinks that pure justice can be served better in this way than by twelve possibly stupid jurymen. Many people like him enormously, and many people are irritated by him beyond endurance; he is quite indifferent to both. Possibly he is a good deal too pleased with himself, but he does not mind that either. Give him his three chief interests in life, and he is perfectly happy criminology, human nature, and good beer.

The Avenging Chance

WHEN HE WAS able to review it in perspective Roger
Sheringham was inclined to think that the Poisoned Chocolate Case, as the papers called it, was perhaps the most
perfectly planned murder he had ever encountered. Certainly,
he plumed himself more on its solution than on that of any
other. The motive was so obvious, when you knew where to
look for it — but you didn't know; the method was so signif-
icant, when you had grasped its real essentials — but you
didn't grasp them; the traces were so thinly covered, when
you had realised what was covering them — but you didn't
realise. But for the merest piece of bad luck, which the murderer could not possibly have foreseen, the crime must have
been added to the classical list of great mysteries.

This was the story of the case, as Chief Inspector Moresby
told it one evening to Roger in the latter's rooms in the
Albany a week or so later. Or rather, this is the raw material of Moresby's story as it passed through the crucible of
Roger's vivid imagination:

On Friday morning, the fifteenth of November, at half-past
ten in the morning, Graham Beresford walked into his club
in Piccadilly, the very exclusive Rainbow Club, and asked
for his letters. The porter handed him one and a couple of
circulars. Beresford walked over to the fireplace in the big
lounge to open them.

While he was doing so, a few minutes later, another member entered the club, a Sir William Anstruther, who lived in
rooms just round the corner in Berkeley Street and spent
most of his time at the Rainbow. The porter glanced at the
clock, as he always did when Sir William entered, and, as
always, it was exactly half-past ten to the minute. The time
was thus definitely fixed by the porter beyond all doubt.
There were three letters for Sir William and a small parcel,
and he also strolled over to the fireplace, nodding to Beresford but not speaking to him. The two men only knew each
other very slightly and had probably never exchanged more
than a dozen words in all.

Having glanced through his letters Sir William opened
the parcel and, after a moment, snorted with disgust. Beres-

ford looked at him, and Sir William thrust out a letter which had been enclosed in the parcel, with an uncomplimentary remark, upon modern trade methods. Concealing a smile (Sir William's ways were a matter of some amusement to his fellow members), Beresford read the letter. It was from a big firm of chocolate manufacturers, Mason and Sons, and set forth that they were putting on the market a new brand of liqueur chocolates designed especially to appeal to men; would Sir William do them the honour of accepting the enclosed two-pound box and letting the firm have his candid opinion on them?

"Do they think I'm a blank chorus-girl?" fumed Sir William. "Write 'em testimonials about their blank chocolates, indeed! Blank 'em! I'll complain to the blank committee. That sort of blank thing can't blank well be allowed here." Sir William, it will be gathered, was a choleric man.

"Well, it's an ill wind so far as I'm concerned," Beresford soothed him. "It's reminded me of something. My wife and I had a box at the Imperial last night and I bet her a box of chocolates to a hundred cigarettes that she wouldn't spot the villain by the end of the second act. She won. I must remember to get them this morning. Have you seen it, by the way — *The Creaking Skull*—? Not a bad show."

"Not blank likely," growled Sir William, unsoiled. "I've got something better to do than sit and watch a lot of blank fools with phosphorescent paint on their faces popping off silly pop-guns at each other. Got to get a box of chocolates, did you say? Well, take this blank one. I don't want it."

For a moment Beresford demurred politely and then, most unfortunately for himself, accepted. The money so saved meant nothing to him, for he was a wealthy man; but trouble was always worth saving.

By an extraordinarily lucky chance neither the outer wrapper of the box nor its covering letter were thrown into the fire, and this was the more fortunate in that both men had tossed the envelopes of their letters into the flames. Sir William did, indeed, make a bundle of wrapper, letter and string, but he handed it over to Beresford with the box, and the latter simply dropped it inside the fender. This bundle the porter subsequently extracted and, being a man of orderly habits, put it tidily away in the waste-paper basket, whence it was retrieved later by the police. The bundle, it may be said at once, comprised two out of the only three material clues to the murder, the third of course being the chocolates themselves.

Of the three unconscious protagonists in the impending tragedy, Sir William was without doubt the most remarkable. Still a year or two under fifty he looked, with his flaming red face and thick-set figure, a typical country squire of the old school, and both his manners and his language were in accordance with tradition. There were other resemblances too, but always with a difference. The voices of the country squires of the old school were often slightly husky towards late middle-age, but it was not with whiskey. They hunted, and so did Sir William. But the squires only hunted foxes; Sir William was more catholic. Sir William, in short, was no doubt a thoroughly bad baronet. But there was nothing mean about him. His vices, like such virtues as he had, were all on the large scale. And the result as usual, was that most other men, good or bad, liked him well enough (except a husband here and there, or a father or two) and women openly hung on his husky words.

On comparison with him Beresford was rather an ordinary man, a tall, dark, not unhandsome fellow of two-and-thirty, quiet and reserved; popular in a way but neither inviting nor apparently reciprocating anything beyond a rather grave friendliness. His father had left him a rich man, but idleness did not appeal to him. He had inherited enough of the parental energy and drive not to allow his money to lie softly in gilt-edged securities and had a finger in a good many business pies, out of sheer love of the game.

Money attracts money. Graham Beresford had inherited it, he made it, and, inevitably, he had married it too. The daughter of a late ship-owner in Liverpool, with not far off half a million in her own right. That half-million might have made some poor man incredibly happy for life, but she had chosen to bring it to Beresford, who needed it not at all. But the money was incidental, for he needed her and would have married her just as inevitably (said his friends) if she had not a farthing.

She was so exactly his type. A tall, rather serious-minded, highly cultured girl, not so young that her character had not had time to form (she was twenty-five when Beresford married her, three years ago), she was the ideal wife for him. A bit of a Puritan, perhaps, in some ways, but Beresford, whose wild oats, though duly sown, had been a sparse crop, was ready enough to be a Puritan himself by that time if she was.

To make no bones about it, the Beresfords succeeded in achieving that eighth wonder of the modern world, a happy marriage.

And into the middle of it there dropped, with irretrievable tragedy, the box of chocolates. Beresford gave her the chocolates after the meal as they were sitting over their coffee in the drawing-room, explaining how they had come into his possession. His wife made some laughing comment on his meanness in not having bought a special box to pay his debt, but approved the brand and was interested to try the new variety. Joan Beresford was not so serious-minded as not to have a healthy feminine interest in good chocolates.

She delved with her fingers among the silver-wrapped sweets, each bearing the name of its filling in neat blue lettering, and remarked that the new variety appeared to consist of nothing but Kirsch and Maraschino taken from the firm's ordinary brand of liqueur chocolates. She offered him one, but Beresford, who had no interest in chocolates and did not believe in spoiling good coffee, refused. His wife unwrapped one and put it in her mouth, uttering the next moment a slight exclamation.

"Oh! I was wrong. They are different. They're twenty times as strong. Really, it almost burns. You must try one, Graham. Catch!" She threw one across to him and Beresford, to humour her, consumed it. A burning taste, not intolerable but far too strong to be pleasant followed the release of the liquid filling.

"By Jove," he exclaimed, "I should think they are strong. They must be filled with neat alcohol."

"Oh, they wouldn't do that surely," said his wife, unwrapping another. "It must be the mixture. I rather like them. But that Kirsch one tasted far too strongly of almonds; this may be better. You try a Maraschino too." She threw another over to him.

He ate it and disliked it still more. "Funny," he remarked, feeling the roof of his mouth with the tip of his tongue. "My tongue feels quite numb."

"So did mine at first," she agreed. "Now it's tingling rather nicely. But there doesn't seem to be any difference between the Kirsch and the Maraschino. And they do burn!

The almond flavouring's much too strong too. I can't make up my mind whether I like them or not."

"I don't," Beresford said with decision. "I shouldn't eat any more of them if I were you. I think there's something wrong with them."

"Well, they're only an experiment, I suppose," said his wife.

A few minutes later Beresford went out, to keep a business appointment in the City. He left her still trying to make up her mind whether she liked the new variety or not. Beresford remembered that conversation afterwards very clearly because it was the last time he saw his wife alive.

That was roughly half-past two. At a quarter to four Beresford arrived at his club from the City in a taxi, in a state of collapse. He was helped into the building by the driver and the porter, and both described him subsequently as pale to the point of ghastliness, with staring eyes and livid lips, and his skin damp and clammy. His mind seemed unaffected, however, and when they had got him up the steps he was able to walk, with the porter's help, into the lounge.

The porter, thoroughly alarmed, wanted to send for a doctor at once, but Beresford, who was the last man in the world to make a fuss, refused to let him, saying that it must be indigestion and he would be all right in a few minutes. To Sir William Anstruther, however, who was in the lounge at the time, he added after the porter had gone: "Yes, and I believe it was those infernal chocolates you gave me, now I come to think of it. I thought there was something funny about them at the time. I'd better go and find out if my wife's all right."

Sir William, a kind-hearted man, was much perturbed at the notion that he might be responsible for Beresford's condition and offered to ring up Mrs. Beresford himself, as the other was plainly in no fit state to move. Beresford was about to reply when a strange change came over him. His body, which had been leaning back limply in his chair, suddenly heaved rigidly upright; his jaws locked together, the livid lips drawn back in a horrible grin, and his hands clenched on the arms of his chair. At the same time, Sir William became aware of an unmistakable smell of bitter almonds.

Believing that the man was dying under his eyes, Sir William raised an alarmed shout for the porter and a doctor. The other occupants of the lounge hurried up, and between them, they got the convulsed body of the unconscious man into a more comfortable position. They had no doubt that Beresford had taken poison, and the porter was sent off post-haste to find a doctor. Before the latter could arrive a telephone message was received at the club from an agitated butler asking if Mr. Beresford was there, and if so would he come home at once as Mrs. Beresford had been taken seriously ill. As a matter of fact, she was already dead.

Beresford did not die. He had taken less of the poison than his wife, who after his departure must have eaten at least three more of the chocolates, so that its action in his case was less rapid and the doctor had time to save him. Not that the latter knew then what the poison was. He treated him chiefly for prussic acid poison, on the strength of the smell of bitter almonds, but he wasn't sure and threw in one or two other things as well. Anyhow it turned out in the end that he could not have had a fatal dose, and by about eight o'clock that night he was conscious; the next day he was practically convalescent As for the unfortunate Mrs. Beresford, the doctor arrived too late to save her and she passed away very rapidly in a deep coma.

At first, it was thought that the poisoning was due to a terrible accident on the part of the firm of Mason & Sons. The police had taken the matter in hand as soon as Mrs. Beresford's death was reported to them and the fact of poison established, and it was only a very short time before things had become narrowed down to the chocolates as the active agent. Sir William was interrogated, the letter and wrapper were recovered from the waste-paper basket, and, even before the sick man was out of danger, a detective inspector was asking for an interview just before closing-time with the managing director of Mason & Sons. Scotland Yard moves quickly.

It was the police theory at this stage, based on what Sir William and two doctors had been able to tell them, that by an act of criminal carelessness on the part of one of Mason's employees, an excessive amount of oil of bitter almonds had been included in the filling mixture of the chocolates, for that was what the doctors had decided must be the poisoning ingredient. Oil of bitter almonds is used a good deal, in the cheaper kinds of confectionery, as a flavouring. However, the managing director quashed this idea at once. Oil of bitter almonds, he asserted, was never used by Mason's.

The inspector then produced the covering letter and asked if he could have an interview with the person or persons who had filled the sample chocolates, and with any others through whose hands the box might have passed before it was dispatched.

That brought matters to a head. The managing director read the letter with undisguised astonishment and at once declared that it was a forgery. No such letter, no such samples had been sent out by the firm at all; a new variety of liqueur chocolates had never even been mooted. Shown the fatal chocolates, he identified them without hesitation as their ordinary brand. Unwrapping and examining one more closely, he called the inspector's attention to a mark on the underside, which he suggested was the remains of a small hole drilled in the case through which the liquid could have been extracted and the fatal filling inserted, the hole afterwards being stopped up with softened chocolate, a perfectly simple operation.

The inspector agreed. It was now clear to him that somebody had been trying deliberately to murder Sir William Anstruther.

Scotland Yard doubled its activities. The chocolates were sent for analysis, Sir William was interviewed again, and so was the now conscious Beresford. From the latter, the doctor insisted that the news of his wife's death must be kept till the next day, as in his weakened condition the shock might be fatal, so that nothing very helpful was obtained from him. Nor could Sir William, now thoroughly alarmed, throw any light on the mystery or produce a single person who might have any grounds for trying to kill him. The police were at a dead end.

Oil of bitter almonds had not been a bad guess at the noxious agent in the chocolates. The analysis showed that this was actually nitrobenzene, a kindred substance. Each chocolate in the upper layer contained exactly six minims, the remaining space inside the case being filled with a mixture of Kirsch and Maraschino. The chocolates in the lower layers, containing the other liqueurs to be found in one of Mason's two-pound boxes, were harmless.

And now you know as much as we do, Mr. Sheringham," concluded Chief Inspector Moresby; "and if you can say who sent those chocolates to Sir William, you'll know a good deal more."

Roger nodded thoughtfully. "It's a brute of a case. The field of possible suspects is so wide. It might have been anyone in the whole world. I suppose you've looked into all the people who have an interest in Sir William's death?"

"Well, naturally," said Moresby. "There aren't many. He and his wife are on notoriously bad terms and have been living apart for the last two years, but she gets a good fat legacy in his will and she's the residuary legatee as well (they've got no children). But her alibi can't be got round. She was at her villa in the South of France when it happened. I've checked that, from the French police."

"Not another Marie Lafarge case, then," Roger murmured. "Though of course there never was any doubt as to Marie Lafarge really being innocent, in any intelligent mind. Well, who else?"

"His estate in Worcestershire's entailed and goes to a nephew. But there's no possible motive there. Sir William hasn't been near the place for twenty years, and the nephew lives there, with his wife and family, on a long lease at a nominal rent, so long as he looks after the place properly. Sir William couldn't turn him out if he wanted to."

"Not a male edition of the Mary Ansell case, then," Roger commented. "Well, two other possible parallels occur to me. Don't they to you?"

"Well, sir," Moresby scratched his head. "There's the Molineux case, of course, in New York, where a poisoned phial of Bromo-seltzer was sent to a Mr. Cornish at the Knickerbocker Club, with the result that a lady to whom he gave some at his boarding-house for a headache died and Cornish himself, who only sipped it because she complained of it being bitter, was violently ill. That's as close a parallel as I can call to mind."

"By Jove, yes." Roger was impressed. "And it had never occurred to me at all. It's a very close parallel indeed. Have you acted on it at all? Molineux, the man who was put on trial, was a fellow member of the same club, if I remember, and it was said to be a case of jealousy. Have you made enquiries about any possibilities like that among Sir William's fellow members at the Rainbow?"

"I have, sir, you may be sure; but there's nothing in it along those lines. Not a thing," said Moresby with conviction. "What were the other two possible parallels you had in mind?"

"Why, the Christina Edmunds case, for one. Feminine jealousy. Sir William's private life doesn't seem to be immaculate. I daresay there's a good deal of off with the old light-o'-love and on with the new. What about investigations round that idea?"

"Why, that's just what I have been doing, Mr. Sheringham, sir," retorted Chief Inspector Moresby reproachfully. "That was the first thing that came to me. Because if anything does stand out about this business it is that it's a woman's crime. Nobody but a woman would send poisoned chocolates to a man. Another man would never think of it. He'd send a poisoned sample of whiskey, or something like that."

"That's a very sound point, Moresby," Roger meditated. "Very sound indeed. And Sir William couldn't help you?"

"Couldn't," said Moresby, not without a trace of resentment, "or wouldn't. I was inclined to believe at first that he might have his suspicions and was shielding some woman. But I don't know. There may be nothing in it."

"On the other hand, there may be quite a lot. As I feel the case at present that's where the truth lies."

Moresby looked as if a little solid evidence would be more to his liking than any amount of feelings about the case. "And your other parallel, Mr. Sheringham?" he asked, rather dispiritedly.

"Why, Sir William Horwood. You remember that some lunatic sent poisoned chocolates not so long ago to the Commissioner of Police himself. A good crime always gets imitated. One could bear in mind the possibility that this is a copy of the Horwood case."

Moresby brightened. "It's funny you should say that, Mr. Sheringham, sir, because that's about the conclusion I'm being forced to myself. In fact, I've pretty well made up my mind. I've tested every other theory there is, you see. There's not a solitary person with an interest in Sir William's death, so far as I can see, whether it's from motives of gain, revenge, hatred, jealousy or anything else, whom I haven't had to rule out of the question. They've all either got complete alibis or I've satisfied myself in some other way that they're not to blame. If Sir William isn't shielding someone (and I'm pretty sure now that he isn't) there's nothing else for it but some irresponsible lunatic of a woman who's come to the conclusion that this world would be a better place without Sir William Anstruther in it — some social or religious fanatic, who's probably never even seen Sir William personally. And if that's the case," sighed Moresby, "a fat lot of chance we have of laying hands on her."

Roger reflected for a moment "You may be right, Moresby. In fact I shouldn't be at all surprised if you were. But if I were superstitious, which I'm not, do you know what I should believe? That the murderer's aim misfired and Sir William escaped death for an express purpose of providence: so that he, the destined victim, should be the ironical instrument of bringing his own intended murderer to justice."

"Well, Mr. Sheringham, would you really?" said the sarcastic chief inspector, who was not superstitious either.

Roger seemed rather taken with the idea. "*Chance, the Avenger.* Make a good film title, wouldn't it? But there's a terrible lot of truth in it. How often don't you people at the Yard stumble on some vital piece of evidence out of pure chance? How often isn't it that you are led to the right solution by what seems a series of sheer coincidences? I'm not belittling your detective work; but just think how often a piece of brilliant detective work which has led you most of the way but not the last vital few inches, meets with some remarkable stroke of sheer luck (thoroughly well-deserved luck, no doubt, but *lucky,* which just makes the case complete for you. I can think of scores of instances. The Milsom and Fowler murder, for example. Don't you see what I mean? Is it chance every time, or is it Providence avenging the victim?"

"Well, Mr. Sheringham," said Chief Inspector Moresby, "to tell you the truth, I don't mind what it is, so long as it lets me put my hands on the right man."

"Moresby," laughed Roger, "you're hopeless. I thought I was raising such a fruitful topic. Very well, we'll change the subject. Tell me why in the name of goodness the murderess (assuming that you're right every time) used nitrobenzene, of all surprising things?"

"There, Mr. Sheringham," Moresby admitted, "you've got me. I never even knew it was so poisonous. It's used a good deal in various manufactures, I'm told, confectionery for instance, and as a solvent; and its chief use is in making aniline dyes. But it's never reckoned among the ordinary poisons. I suppose she used it because it's so easy to get hold of."

"Isn't there a line of attack there?" Roger suggested. "The inference is that the criminal is a woman who is employed in some factory or business, the odds favouring an aniline dye establishment, and who knew of the poisonous properties of nitrobenzene because the employees have been warned about it. Couldn't you use that as a point of departure?"

"To interrogate every employee of every establishment in this country that uses nitrobenzene in any of its processes, Mr. Sheringham? Come, sir. Even if you're right, the chances are we should all be dead before we reached the guilty person."

"I suppose we should," regretted Roger, who had thought he was being rather clever.

They discussed the case for some time longer, but nothing further of importance emerged. Naturally, it had not been possible to trace the machine on which the forged letter had been typed, nor to ascertain how the piece of Mason's notepaper had come into the criminal's possession. With regard to this last point, Roger suggested, as an outside possibility, that it might not have been Mason's notepaper at all but a piece with a heading especially printed for the occasion, which might give a pointer towards a printer as being concerned in the crime. He was chagrined to learn that this brilliant idea had occurred to Moresby as a mere matter of routine, and the notepaper had been definitely identified by Merton's, the printers concerned, as their own work. He produced the piece of paper for Roger's inspection, and the latter commented on the fact that the edges were distinctly yellowed, which seemed to suggest that the sheet was an old one.

Another idea occurred to Roger. "I shouldn't be surprised, Moresby," he said, with a certain impressiveness, "if the murderer never *tried* to get hold of this sheet at all. In other words, it was the chance possession of it which suggested the whole method of the crime."

It appeared that this notion had also occurred to Moresby. If it were true, it only helped to make the crime more insoluble than before. From the wrapper, a piece of ordinary brown paper with Sir William's name and address hand-printed on it in large capitals, there was nothing at all to be learnt beyond the fact that the parcel had been posted at the office in Southampton Street, Strand, between the hours of eight-thirty and nine-thirty p.m. Except for the chocolates themselves, which seemed to offer no further help, there was nothing else whatsoever in the way of material clues.

Whoever coveted Sir William's life had certainly no intention of purchasing it with his or her own.

If Moresby had paid his visit to Roger Sheringham with
any hope of tapping that gentleman's brains, he went away
disappointed. Rack them as he might, Roger had been unable
to throw any effective light on the affair.

To tell the truth, Roger was inclined to agree with the
chief inspector's conclusion, that the attempted murder of
Sir William Anstruther and the actual death of the unfortunate Mrs. Beresford must be laid to the account of some
irresponsible criminal lunatic, actuated by a religious or
social fanaticism. For this reason, although he thought about
it a good deal during the next few days, he made no attempt
to take the case in hand. It was the sort of affair, necessi-
tating endless enquiries, that a private person would have
neither the time nor the authority to carry out, which can
only be handled by the official police. Roger's interest in it
was purely academic.

It was hazard, two chance encounters, which translated
this interest from the academic to the personal.

The first was at the Rainbow Club itself. Roger was lunching there with a member, and inevitably the conversation
turned on the recent tragedy. Roger's host was inclined to
plume himself on the fact that he had been at school with
Beresford and so had a more intimate connection with the
affair than his fellow members. One gathered, indeed, that
the connection was a trifle closer even than Sir William's.
Roger's host was that kind of man.

"And just as it happened I saw the Beresfords in their
box at the Imperial that night. Noticed them before the cur-
tain went up for the first act I had a stall. I may even have
seen them making that fatal bet." Roger's host took on an
even more portentous aspect. One gathered that it was by
no means improbably due to his presence in the stalls that
the disastrous bet was made at all.

As they were talking a man entered the dining room and
walked past their table. Roger's host became abruptly silent.
The new comer threw him a slight nod and passed on. The
other leant forward across the table.

"Talk of the devil! That was Beresford himself. First time
I've seen him in here since it happened. Poor devil! It knocked
him all to pieces, you know. I've never seen a man so devoted
to his wife. Did you notice how ghastly he looked?" All this

in a hushed, tactful whisper, that would have been far more obvious to the subject of it, had he happened to have been looking their way, than the loudest shouts.

Roger nodded shortly. He had caught a glimpse of Beresford's face and been shocked by it even before he learned his identity. It was haggard and pale and seamed with lines of bitterness, prematurely old. "Hang it all," he now thought, much moved, "Moresby really must make an effort. If the murderer isn't found soon it'll kill that chap too."

He said aloud, somewhat at random and certainly without tact "He didn't exactly fall on your neck. I thought you two were such bosom friends?"

His host looked uncomfortable. "Oh, well, you must make allowances, just at present," he hedged. "Besides, we weren't *bosom* friends exactly. As a matter of fact, he was a year or two senior to me. Or it might have been three. We were in different houses, too. And he was on the modern side of course, while I was a classical bird."

"I see," said Roger, quite gravely, realising that his host's actual contact with Beresford at school had been limited, at the very most, to that of the latter's toe with the former's hinder parts.

He left it at that.

The next encounter took place the following morning. Roger was in Bond Street, about to go through the distressing ordeal of buying a new hat. Along the pavement, he suddenly saw bearing down on him Mrs. Verreker-le-Flemming. Mrs. Verreker-le-Flemming was small, exquisite, rich and a widow, and she sat at Roger's feet whenever he gave her the opportunity. But she talked. She talked, in fact, and talked, and talked. And Roger, who rather liked talking himself, could not bear it. He tried to dart across the road, but there was no opening stream. He was cornered.

Mrs. Verreker-le-Flemming fastened on him gladly. "Oh, Mr. Sheringham! *Just* the person I wanted to see. Mr. Sheringham, *do* tell me. In confidence. *Are* you taking up this dreadful business of *poor* Joan Beresford's death? Oh, don't— *don't* tell me you're not." Roger was trying to do so, but she gave him no chance. "It's too dreadful. You must — you simply *must* find out who sent those chocolates to that dreadful Sir William Anstruther. You are going to, aren't you?"

Roger, the frozen and imbecile grin of civilised intercourse on his face, again tried to get a word in without result.

"I was horrified when I heard of it — simply horrified. You see, Joan and I were such *very* close friends. Quite intimate. We were at school together — Did you say anything, Mr. Sheringham?"

Roger, who had allowed a faint groan to escape him, hastily shook his head.

"And the awful thing, the truly *terrible* thing is that Joan brought the whole business on herself. Isn't that *appalling,*?"

Roger no longer wanted to escape. "What did you say?" he managed to insert, incredulously.

"I suppose it's what they call tragic irony. Certainly, it was tragic enough, and I've never heard anything so terribly ironical. You know about that bet she made with her husband of course, so that he had to get her a box of chocolates, and if he hadn't Sir William would never have given him the poisoned ones and he'd have eaten them and died himself and good riddance? Well, Mr. Sheringham —" Mrs. Verreker-le-Flemming lowered her voice to a conspirator's whisper and glanced about her in the approved manner. "I've never told anybody else this, but I'm telling you because I know you'll appreciate it. You're interested in irony, aren't you?"

"I adore it," Roger said mechanically. "Yes?"

"Well — Joan wasn't playing fair!"

"How do you mean?" Roger asked, bewildered.

Mrs. Verreker-le-Flemming was artlessly pleased with her sensation. "Why, she ought not to have made that bet at all. It was a judgment on her. A terrible judgment, of course, but the appalling thing is that she did bring it on herself, in a way. She'd seen the play before. We went together, the very first week it was on. She *knew* who the villain was all the time."

"By Jove!" Roger was as impressed as Mrs. Verreker-le-Flemming could have wished. "Chance the Avenger, with a vengeance. We're none of us immune from it."

"Poetic justice, you mean?" twittered Mrs. Verreker-le-Flemming, to whom these remarks had been somewhat obscure. "Yes, it was, wasn't it? Though really, the punishment was out of all proportion to the crime. Good gracious, if every woman who cheats over a bet is to be killed for it where would any of us be?" demanded Mrs. Verreker-le-Flemming with unconscious frankness.

"Umph!" said Roger, tactfully.

"But Joan Beresford! That's the extraordinary thing. I

should never have thought Joan *would* do a thing like that. She was such a *nice* girl. A little close with money, of course, considering how well off they were, but that isn't anything. Of course, it was only fun, and pulling her husband's leg, but I always used to think Joan was such a *serious* girl, Mr. Sheringham. I mean, ordinary people don't talk about honour, and truth, and playing the game. Well, she paid herself for not playing the game, poor girl, didn't she? Still, it all goes to show the truth of the old saying, doesn't it?"

"What old saying?" said Roger, hypnotised by this flow.

"Why, that still waters run deep. Joan must have been deep, I'm afraid." Mrs. Verreker-le-Flemming sighed. It was evidently a social error to be deep. "I mean, she certainly took me in. She can't have been quite so honourable and truthful as she was always pretending, can she? And I can't help wondering whether a girl who'd deceive her husband in a little thing like that might not — oh, well, I don't want to say anything against poor Joan now she's dead, poor darling, but she can't have been quite such a plaster saint after all, can she? I mean," said Mrs. Verreker-le-Flemming, in hasty extenuation of these suggestions, "I do think psychology is so *very* interesting, don't you, Mr. Sheringham?"

"Sometimes, very," Roger agreed gravely. "But you mentioned Sir William Anstruther just now. Do you know him, too?"

"I used to," Mrs. Verreker-le-Flemming replied, with an expression of positive vindictiveness. "Horrible man! Always running after some woman or other. And when he's tired of her, just drops her — biff! — like that. At least," added Mrs. Verreker-le-Flemming hastily, "so I've heard."

"And what happens if she refuses to be dropped?"

"Oh, dear, I'm sure I don't know. I suppose you've heard the latest?" Mrs. Verreker-le-Flemming hurried on, perhaps a trifle more pink than the delicate aids to nature on her cheeks would have warranted. "He's taken up with that Bryce woman now. You know, the wife of the oilman, or petrol, or whatever he made his money in. It began about three weeks ago. You'd have thought that dreadful business of being responsible, in a way, for poor Joan Beresford's death would have sobered him up a little, wouldn't you? But not a bit of it; he-"

"I suppose Sir William knew Mrs. Beresford pretty well?" Roger remarked casually.

Mrs. Verreker-le-Flemming stared at him. "Sir William? No, he didn't know Joan at all. I'm sure he didn't. I've never heard her mention him."

Roger shot off on another lark. "What a pity you weren't at the Imperial with the Beresfords that evening. She'd never have made that bet if you had been." Roger looked extremely innocent "You weren't, I suppose?"

"I?" queried Mrs. Verreker-le-Flemming in surprise. "Good gracious, no. I was at the new revue at the Pavilion. Lady Gavelstoke had a box and asked me to join her party."

"Oh, yes. Good show, isn't it? I thought that sketch The Sempiternal Triangle very clever. Didn't you?"

"The Sempiternal Triangle?" wavered Mrs. Verreker-le-Flemming.

"Yes, in the first half."

"Oh! Then I didn't see it. I got there disgracefully late, I'm afraid. But then," said Mrs. Verreker-le-Flemming with pathos, "I always do seem to be late for simply everything."

Once more Roger changed the subject. "By the way, I wonder if you've got a photograph of Mrs. Beresford?" he asked carelessly.

"Of Joan? Yes, I have. Why, Mr. Sheringham?"

"You haven't got one of Sir William too, by any chance?" asked Roger, still more carelessly.

The pink on Mrs. Verreker-le-Flemming's cheeks deepened half a shade. "I — I think I have. Yes, I'm almost sure I have. But —"

"Would you lend them to me some time?" Roger asked, with a mysterious air, and looked around him with a frown in the approved manner.

"Oh, Mr. Sheringham! Yes, of course, I will. You mean — you mean you *are* going to find out who sent those chocolates to Sir William?"

Roger nodded and put his finger to his lips. "Yes. You've guessed it. But not a word, Mrs. Verreker-le-Flemming. Oh, excuse me, there's a man on that bus who wants to speak to me. *Scotland Yard,*" he hissed in an impressive whisper. "Good-bye." He dived for a passing bus and clung on with difficulty. With awful stealth, he climbed up the steps and took his seat, after an exaggerated scrutiny of the other passengers, beside a perfectly inoffensive man in a bowler hat. The man in the bowler hat, who happened to be a clerk in the

employment of a builder's merchant, looked at him resent-
fully; there were plenty of quite empty seats all round them.

Roger bought no new hat that morning.

For probably the first time in her life, Mrs. Verreker-le-
Flemming had given somebody a constructive idea.

Roger made good his opportunity. Getting off the bus at
the corner of Bond Street and Oxford Street, he hailed a taxi
and gave Mrs. Verreker-le-Flemming's address. He thought
it better to take advantage of her permission at a time when
he would not have to pay for it a second time over.

The parlor-maid seemed to think there was nothing odd
in his mission and took him up to the drawing-room at once.
A corner of the room was devoted to the silver-framed photographs of Mrs. Verreker-le-Flemming's friends, and there
were many of them. Roger, who had never seen Sir William
in the flesh, had to seek the parlor-maid's help. The girl, like
her mistress, was inclined to be loquacious, and to prevent
either of them getting ideas into their heads which might
be better not there, he removed from their frames not one
photograph but five, those of Sir William, Mrs. Beresford,
Beresford himself, and two strange males who appeared to
belong to the Sir William period of Mrs. Verreker-le-Flemming's collection. Finally he obtained, by means of a small
bribe, a likeness of Mrs. Verreker-le-Flemming herself and
added that to his collection.

For the rest of the day he was very busy.

His activities would have seemed, no doubt, to Mrs. Verreker-le-Flemming not merely baffling but pointless. He
paid a visit to a public library, for instance, and consulted
a work of reference, after which he took a taxi and drove to
the offices of the Anglo-Eastern Perfumery Company, where
he enquired for a certain Mr. Joseph Lea Hardwick and
seemed much put out on hearing that no such gentleman
was known to the firm and was certainly not employed in
any of their numerous branches. Many questions had to be
put about the firm and its branches before he consented to
abandon the quest. After that he drove to Messrs. Weall and
Wilson, the well-known institution which protects the trade
interests of individuals and advises its subscribers regarding investments. Here he entered his name as a subscriber,
and explaining that he had a large sum of money to invest,
filled in one of the special enquiry forms which are headed
STRICTLY CONFIDENTIAL.

Then he went to the Rainbow Club, in Piccadilly.

Introducing himself to the porter without a blush as connected within Scotland Yard, he asked the man a number of questions, more or less trivial, concerning the tragedy. "Sir William, I understand," he said finally, as if by the way, "did not dine here the evening before?"

There it appeared that Roger was wrong. Sir William had dined in the club, as he did about three times a week.

"But I quite understood he wasn't here that evening?" Roger said plaintively.

The porter was emphatic. He remembered quite well. So did a waiter, whom the porter summoned to corroborate him. Sir William had dined rather late, and had not left the dining-room till about nine o'clock. He spent the evening there too, the waiter knew, or at least some of it, for he himself had taken him a whiskey-and-soda in the lounge not less than half an hour later.

Roger retired.

He retired to Merton's, in a taxi.

It seemed that he wanted some new notepaper printed, of a very special kind, and to the young woman behind the counter he specified at great length and in wearisome detail exactly what he did want. The young woman handed him the book of specimen pieces and asked him to see if there was any style there which would suit him. Roger glanced through it, remarking garrulously to the young woman that he had been recommended to Merton's by a very dear friend, whose photograph he happened to have on him at that moment. Wasn't that a curious coincidence? The young woman agreed that it was.

"About a fortnight ago, I think my friend was in here last," said Roger, producing the photograph. "Recognise this?"

The young woman took the photograph, without apparent interest "Oh, yes. I remember. About some notepaper too, wasn't it? So that's your friend. Well, it's a small world. Now this is a line we're selling a good deal of just now."

Roger went back to his rooms to dine. Afterwards, feeling restless, he wandered out of the Albany and turned down Piccadilly. He wandered round the Circus, thinking hard, and paused for a moment out of habit to inspect the photographs of the new revue hung outside the Pavilion. The next thing he realised was that he had got as far as Jermyn Street and was standing outside the Imperial Theatre. The advertisements of *The Creaking Skull* informed him that it began at half-past eight. Glancing at his watch he saw that the time was twenty-nine minutes past that hour. He had an evening to get through somehow. He went inside.

The next morning, very early for Roger, he called Moresby at Scotland Yard.

"Moresby," he said without preamble, "I want you to do something for me. Can you find me a taximan who took a fare from Piccadilly Circus or its neighbourhood at about ten past nine on the evening before the Beresford crime, to the Strand somewhere near the bottom of Southampton Street, and another who took a fare back between those points. I'm not sure about the first. Or one taxi might have been used for the double journey, but I doubt that. Anyhow, try to find out for me, will you?"

"What are you up to now, Mr. Sheringham?" Moresby asked suspiciously.

"Breaking down an interesting alibi," replied Roger serenely. "By the way, I know who sent those chocolates to Sir William. I'm just building up a nice structure of evidence for you. Ring up my rooms when you've got those taximen."

He strolled out, leaving Moresby positively gaping after him. Roger had his annoying moments.

The rest of the day he spent apparently trying to buy a secondhand typewriter. He was very particular that it should be a Hamilton No. 4. When the shop people tried to induce him to consider other makes he refused to look at them, saying that he had had the Hamilton No. 4 so strongly recommended to him by a friend, who had bought one about three weeks ago. Perhaps it was at this very shop? No? They hadn't sold a Hamilton No. 4 for the last three months? How odd.

But at one shop they had sold a Hamilton No. 4 within the last month, and that was odder still.

At half-past four Roger got back to his rooms to await the telephone message from Moresby. At half-past five it came.

"There are fourteen taxi drivers here, littering up my office," said Moresby offensively. "They all took fares from the Strand to Piccadilly Circus at your time. What do you want me to do with 'em, Mr. Sheringham?"

"Keep them till I come, Chief Inspector," returned Roger with dignity. He had not expected more than three at the most, but he was not going to let Moresby know that. He grabbed his hat.

The interview with the fourteen was brief enough, however. To each grinning man (Roger deduced a little heavy humour on the part of Moresby before his arrival) he showed in turn a photograph, holding it so that Moresby could not see it and asked if he could recognise his fare. The ninth man did so, without hesitation. At a nod from Roger Moresby dismissed the others.

"How dressed?" Roger asked the man laconically, tucking the photograph away in his pocket

"Evening togs," replied the other, equally laconic.

Roger took a note of his name and address and sent him away with a ten-shilling tip. "The case," he said to Moresby, "is at an end."

Moresby sat at his table and tried to look official. "And now, Mr. Sheringham, sir, perhaps you'll tell me what you've been doing."

"Certainly," Roger said blandly, seating himself on the table and swinging his legs. As he did so, a photograph fell unnoticed out of his pocket and fluttered, face downwards, under the table. Moresby eyed it but did not pick it up. "Certainly, Moresby," said Roger. "Your work for you. It was a simple case," he added languidly, "once one had grasped the essential factor. Once, that is to say, one had cleared one's eyes of the soap that the murderer had stuffed into them."

"Is that so, Mr. Sheringham?" said Moresby politely. And yawned. Roger laughed. "All right, Moresby. We'll get down to it. I really have solved the thing, you know. Here's the evidence for you." He took from his note-case an old letter and handed it to the chief inspector. "Look at the slightly crooked s's and the chipped capital H. Was that typed on the same machine as the forged letter from Mason's, or was it not?"

Moresby studied it for a moment, then drew the forged letter from a drawer of his table and compared the two minutely. When he looked up there was no lurking amusement in his eyes. "You've got it in one, Mr. Sheringham," he said soberly. "Where did you get hold of this?"

"In a secondhand typewriter shop in St Martin's Lane. The machine was sold to an unknown customer about a month ago. They identified the customer from that photograph. By a lucky chance this machine had been used in the office after it had been repaired, to see that it was OK, and I easily got hold of that specimen of its work. I'd deduced, of course, from the precautions taken all through this crime, that the typewriter would be bought for that one special purpose and then destroyed, and so far as the murderer could see there was no need to waste valuable money on a new one."

"And where is the machine now?"

"Oh, at the bottom of the Thames, I expect," Roger smiled. "I tell you, this criminal takes no unnecessary chances. But that doesn't matter. There's your evidence."

"Humph! It's all right so far as it goes," conceded Moresby. "But what about Mason's paper?"

"That," said Roger calmly, "was extracted from Merton's book of sample notepapers, as I'd guessed from the very yellowed edges might be the case. I can prove contact of the criminal with the book, and there is a gap which will certainly turn out to have been filled by the piece of paper."

"That's fine," Moresby said more heartily.

"As for that taximan, the criminal had an alibi. You've heard it broken down. Between ten past nine and twenty-five past, in fact, during the time when the parcel must have been posted, the murderer took a hurried journey to that neighbourhood, going probably by bus or underground, but returning, as I expected, by taxi, because time would be getting short."

"And the murderer, Mr. Sheringham?"

"The person whose photograph is in my pocket," Roger said unkindly. "By the way, do you remember what I was saying the other day about *Chance the Avenger,* my excellent film-title? Well, it's worked again. By a chance meeting in Bond Street with a silly woman I was put by the merest accident in possession of a piece of information which showed me then and there who had sent those chocolates addressed to Sir William. There were other possibilities of course, and I tested them, but then and there on the pavement I saw the whole thing, from first to last. It was the merest accident that this woman should have been a friend of mine, of course, and I don't want to blow my own trumpet," said Roger modestly, "but I do think I deserve a little credit for realising the significance of what she told me and recognising the hand of Providence at work."

"Who was the murderer, then, Mr. Sheringham?" repeated Moresby, disregarding for the moment this bashful claim.

"It was so beautifully planned," Roger went on dreamily. "We were taken in completely. We never grasped for one moment that we were making the fundamental mistake that the murderer all along intended us to make."

He paused, and in spite of his impatience Moresby obliged. "And what was that?"

"Why, that the plan had miscarried. That the wrong person had been killed. That was just the beauty of it. The plan had *not* miscarried. It had been brilliantly successful. The wrong person was *not* killed. Very much the right person was."

Moresby gaped. "Why, how on earth do you make that out, sir?"

"Mrs. Beresford was the objective all the time. That's why the plot was so ingenious. Everything was anticipated. It was perfectly natural that Sir William would hand the chocolates over to Beresford. It was foreseen that we should look for the criminal among Sir William's associates and not the dead woman's. It was probably even foreseen that the crime would be considered the work of a woman; whereas really, of course, chocolates were employed because it was a woman who was the objective. Brilliant!"

Moresby, unable to wait any longer, snatched up the photograph and gazed at it incredulously. He whistled. "Good heavens! But Mr. Sheringham, you don't mean to tell me that — Sir William himself!"

"He wanted to get rid of Mrs. Beresford," Roger continued, gazing dreamily at his swinging feet. "He had liked her well enough at the beginning, no doubt, though it was her money he was after all the time. But she must have bored him dreadfully very soon. And I really do think there is some excuse for him there. Any woman, however charming otherwise, would bore a normal man if she does nothing but prate about honour and playing the game. She'd never have overlooked the slightest peccadillo. Every tiny lapse would be thrown up at him for years.

"But the real trouble was that she was too close with her money. She sentenced herself to death directly. He wanted it, or some of it, pretty badly; and she wouldn't part. There's no doubt about the motive. I made a list of the firms he's interested in and got a report on them. They're all rocky, every one of them. They all need money to save them. He'd got through all he had of his own, and he had to get more. Nobody seems to have gathered it but he's a rotten businessman. And half a million — Well!

"As for the nitrobenzene, that was simple enough. I looked it up and found that beside the uses you told me, it's used largely in perfumery. And he's got a perfumery business. The Anglo-Eastern Perfumery Company. That's how he'd know about it being poisonous of course. But I shouldn't think he got his supply from there. He'd be cleverer than that. He probably made the stuff himself. I discovered, quite by chance, that he has at any rate an elementary knowledge of chemistry (at least he was on the modern side at Selchester) and it's the simplest operation. Any schoolboy knows how to treat benzol with nitric acid to get nitrobenzene."

"But," stammered Moresby, "but Sir William — He was at Eton."

"Sir William?" said Roger sharply. "Who's talking about Sir William? I told you the photograph of the murderer was in my pocket." He whipped out the photograph in question and confronted the astounded chief inspector with it "Beresford, man! Beresford's the murderer, of his own wife." Roger studied the other's dumbfounded face and smiled secretly. He felt avenged now for the humour that had been taking place with the taximen.

"Beresford, who still had hankerings after a gay life," he went on more mildly, "didn't want his wife but did want her money. He contrived this plot, providing, as he thought, against every contingency that could possibly arise. He established a mild alibi, if suspicion ever should arise, by taking his wife to the Imperial, and slipped out of the theatre at the first interval (I sat through the first act of the dreadful thing myself last night to see when the interval came). Then he hurried down to the Strand, posted his parcel, and took a taxi back. He had ten minutes, but nobody was going to remark if he got back to the box a minute or two late; you may be able to find that he did.

"And the rest simply followed. He knew Sir William came to the Club every morning at ten-thirty, as regularly as clockwork; he knew that for a psychological certainly he could get the chocolates handed over to him if he hinted for them; he knew that the police would go chasing after all sorts of false trails starting from Sir William. That's one reason why he chose him. He could have shadowed anyone else to the Club if necessary. And as for the wrapper and the forged letter, he carefully didn't destroy them because they were calculated not only to divert suspicion but actually to point away from him to some anonymous lunatic. Which is exactly what they did."

"Well, it's very smart of you, Mr. Sheringham," Moresby said, with a little sigh but quite ungrudgingly. "Very smart indeed. By the way, what was it the lady told you that showed you the whole thing in a flash?"

"Why, it wasn't so much what she actually told me as what I heard between her words, so to speak. What she told me was that Mrs. Beresford knew the answer to that bet; what I deduced was that, being the sort of person she sounded to be, it was almost incredible that Mrs. Beresford should have made a bet to which she knew the answer. Unless she had been the most dreadful little hypocrite (which I did not for a moment believe), it would have been a psychological impossibility for her. *Ergo,* she didn't. *Ergo,* there never was such a bet. *Ergo,* Beresford was lying. *Ergo,* Beresford wanted to get hold of those chocolates for some reason other than he stated. And, as events turned out, there was only one other reason. That was all.

"After all, we only had Beresford's word for the bet, didn't we? And only his word for the conversation in the drawing-room — though most of that undoubtedly happened. Beresford must be far too good a liar not to make all possible use of the truth. But of course he wouldn't have left her till he'd seen her take, or somehow made her take, at least six of the chocolates, more than a lethal dose. That's why the stuff was in those meticulous six minim doses. And so that he could take a couple himself, of course. A clever stroke, that. Took us all in again. Though of course he exaggerated his symptoms considerably."

Moresby rose to his feet "Well, Mr. Sheringham, I'm much obliged to you, sir. I shall make a report of course to the assistant commissioner of what you've done, and he'll thank you officially on behalf of the department And now I shall have to get busy, because naturally I shall have to check your evidence myself, if only as a matter of form, before I apply for a warrant against Beresford." He scratched his head. "Chance, the Avenger, eh? Yes, it's an interesting notion. But I can tell you one pretty big thing Beresford left to Chance, the Avenger, Mr. Sheringham. Suppose Sir William hadn't handed over the chocolates after all? Supposing he'd kept them, to give to one of his own ladies? That was a nasty risk to take."

Roger positively snorted. He felt a personal pride in Beresford by this time, and it distressed him to hear a great man so maligned.

"Really, Moresby! It wouldn't have had any serious results if Sir William had. Do give my man credit for being what he is. You don't imagine he sent the poisoned ones to Sir William, do you? Of course not! He'd send harmless ones and exchange them for the others on his way home. Dash it all, he wouldn't go right out of his way to present opportunities to Chance.

"If," added Roger, "Chance really is the right word."

Perfect Alibi

"MURDER?" REPEATED SIR Wilfrid reflectively. "No, we're a peaceful county here. I'm sorry, but we haven't had a murder since I became Chief Constable."

"Oh," said Roger Sheringham, disappointed. He helped himself to more port by way of consolation. "Come, Wilfrid," he urged. "Don't tell me you've never had a case in which you *smelt* murder, even if you couldn't prove it."

"I..." His host hesitated. "No!" he added firmly. "It's too absurd."

"You have. Come, on, Wilfrid: out with it We're all alone, so you can be as slanderous as you like." And he insinuated the decanter almost surreptitiously into the other's hand.

"Mind you, there never was any suggestion of murder," Sir Wilfrid said, automatically refilling his glass. "Least of all by myself. The Coroner didn't even refer to the possibility of its being anything but a straightforward accident. You must realise that, Roger, or I shan't say a word. In fact, I only mention the case because it was such a lucky accident, for so many people; for if ever a fellow deserved to be murdered it was Eric Southwood."

"Begin at the beginning," said Roger.

BRIEFLY, THE CHIEF Constable's story was as follows: Before the war, John Allfrey had been the owner of a small estate of about a hundred acres, which meant that he was now, willy-nilly, a farmer; and the house-parties which had once been such a feature of life at Underdale were given now only with a purpose. There had been a very definite purpose in the party which the Allfreys had assembled that September three years ago when Eric Southwood met his death.

The Allfreys had no children of their own. John Allfrey, however, had a ward who lived with them: a charming, pretty girl, unsophisticated for these days, who was by way of being a not inconsiderable heiress. When the affair happened she had just turned twenty-one, and so had come into control of her own affairs. The link between the Allfreys and Eric Southwood was through this girl, Elsa Pennefather.

"FINE LOOKING CHAP he was, too, Eric," reflected Sir Wilfrid. "Six-foot-tall, good athlete, good shot, too: Eton and Oxford, and all that But... I don't know. There was something about him. Men didn't like him much. But women did — too much. And he liked them. In fact he'd got a pretty rotten reputation. You know."

"I don't," said Roger.

"Well, no woman safe with him, and all that sort of thing," said the Chief Constable. "And as it came out at the inquest he was in a deuce of a hole at the time. He'd run through his own money years ago; so he was... what shall I say?"

"Say: 'In the hands of the moneylender,'" Roger suggested.

"Why, that's just what he was," exclaimed the Chief Constable with surprise. "How the deuce did you know?"

"I deduced it. Go on. He was in the hand of the moneylenders, he was making up to Elsa Pennefather, and her fortune; and Mr. and Mrs. Allfrey took a dim view of him. Is that right?"

"You're certainly right that the Allfreys look a dim view. In fact, John Allfrey had been heard to say openly that he'd do any mortal thing to stop the feller getting his hooks into Elsa; and Ethel Allfrey didn't feel any less strongly.

"From their point of view the situation was pretty desperate, too. The silly girl was half-infatuated already and the engagement was expected at any moment. So they gave this house-party, you see."

"And actually invited Southwood? Why?"

"Ah, that was Ethel," said Sir Wilfrid, with the simple man's admiration for feminine cunning.

He explained. "There was a married couple, the de Vesinets: the husband half-French, slight, good-looking, fiery, and as excitable as any Frenchman from the South: the wife ... well even Sir Wilfrid became almost lyrical.

"English all right, though she didn't look it. One of the tall willowy kind that make you feel you've got your collar on back to front, and forgotten to shave. You know."

"Flaming red hair, and the real green eyes. She always reminded me of a tiger somehow: she had that sort of sleepy alertness. De Vesinet absolutely worshipped her, never saw a feller so infatuated with a woman. And his own wife, too," added Sir Wilfrid cynically.

The point was that Eric Southwood had been engaged in a hectic affair with Sylvia de Vesinet when he decided to marry money, and innocence: an affair of course known to the whole county except Paul de Vesinet himself. And Mrs. de Vesinet did not seem the sort of woman who would allow herself to be thrown over without a fight. So...

"So Mrs. Allfrey invited the de Vesinets, in the hope of opening Elsa's blue eyes," Roger commented. "Very ingenious. But it was certainly playing with fire, asking the husband, too. The lady sounds quite incandescent enough by herself."

"She was. It was all hushed up, of course, but I gather there'd been hell to pay already, before the accident."

"I wonder if the scheme would have come off," Roger mused. "A certain type of young girl might have admired her rake-helly lover all the more for such a conquest. We'll never know. Were there any other wheels within this one?"

"Don't think so. Just a couple of make-weights, to make up the party. A friend of Ethel Allfreys; quiet sort of woman, married to a naval officer. And a chap called Merridew. I couldn't stand him," said Sir Wilfrid with candour, "at any price."

"There doesn't seem many of them you could stand, Wilfrid."

"Oh, Ethel and John are two of the best. And the little girl's all right. But this chap Merridew! Last sort of feller you'd ever expect to see in John Allfrey's house. Prim, precise little chap, with pince-nez and a dashed irritating smile. Always putting people to rights. Didn't shoot, didn't fish, didn't hunt — hang it, I believe the feller didn't even drink. Some sort of a writing Johnny, I believe," said Sir Wilfrid with scorn.

"Ah, that's bad," said Roger, who was a writing Johnny himself.

"In fact about the best thing Eric ever did was to throw him into the stream one evening in his dress clothes."

"Did he, though?" said Roger, with interest "By the way, you knew Eric Southwood personally?"

"Oh, yes. He lived mostly in London, but this was his home county. In fact his people had a place not far from here, till Eric sold it and blued the cash. That's what made it all the more queer, him being a countryman. I mean, a countryman doesn't drag a loaded twelve-bore along by the muzzle. He knows better. And through brambles, too."

"Ah, that's how he was shot, was he? In the back?"

"No, not in the back, as it happened. From the front. The

idea was, his gun had caught in something and he turned round to jerk it free: and there just happened to be a bit of bramble across the trigger. Oh, it was all pretty clear. There were footprints. And we even identified the bit of bramble. The thorns had been scraped off it."

"I see. And what ruled the de Vesinets out? At least, I take it they were ruled out."

"Oh, absolutely. Everyone was. Cast-iron alibis. Simply no getting around 'em," said Sir Wilfrid, in a series of jerks. "Let's see now. Ethel was in the house; servant saw her constantly. Merridew was half a mile away, teaching one of John's men his job. The de Vesinets were sunbathing down by the stream, in preparation for Cannes; they confirmed each other's alibis absolutely. Elsa was picking blackberries somewhere —"

"Eh?" said Roger. "No confirmation?"

"Come now, don't be absurd. A child like that. And John Allfrey was actually crossing a field to rescue his man from Merridew, who was stopping him getting on with his work."

"He was, was he? Who confirms that?"

"As it happens, one of my own men," countered the Chief Constable with triumph. "By a stroke of luck the constable for the district was on his way to the farm just at the time, about some agricultural return or other that Allfrey ought to have sent in.

"He was taking the usual shortcuts through the same wood just when it happened. In fact, he found the body. And if you're thinking there's anything fishy about the de Vesinets' alibi, my chap confirmed it; he actually saw them at their back-browning. So deduce what you can from all that you can," Sir Wilfrid concluded, with an impolite grin.

"No signs of a struggle?"

"None. And what's more, an official eye on the body almost from the time it happened. That's rare, you know."

"Ye-es. In fact, quite a lot hangs on this constable, doesn't it? He exonerates the three chief suspects. Would you say he was quite ... incorruptible?"

Sir Wilfrid snorted. "One of the best fellers I ever had. A most conscientious chap. Intelligent, too. Of course, he was incorruptible."

"Sea-green all through, eh? Still, you know. Wilfrid, the case does smell of murder. Positively stinks of it, in fact. I won't say whom I suspect, if anyone: but I would like a word with this incorruptible constable of yours."

"Then I'm afraid you won't get it. The man's dead."

"Dead?" Roger repeated. "The chief witness dead? I don't like the look of that. How was he killed?"

"Killed himself," Sir Wilfrid replied shortly. "No good getting story-book ideas over this, Roger. 'Chief Witness for the Prosecution Bumped Off,' eh? No. It's a sad story, though. He had a daughter — charmingly pretty girl. He brought her up himself after his wife died, and she was..."

"The apple of his eye?"

"That's it, exactly," Sir Wilfrid said gratefully. "The apple of his eye. But it was the old story. I suppose her looks gave her inflated ideas. She ran off to London, and — well, she went to the bed.

"He couldn't get her back, and it broke his heart. Hanged himself on his own kitchen door. I never regretted a chap more. He must actually have been contemplating it at the time of his Southwood business, but I had no idea. No one had.

"And it's no use suggesting that his mind was unhinged, and he was seeing things he didn't see, and people in places where they weren't. He wasn't that sort of chap at all."

"I wasn't going to suggest that," Roger said mildly. "But I do suggest that Eric Southwood's death was murder, not accident. In fact I'm surprised at you, Wilfrid. It's as plain as —"

"The nose on my face?" suggested the Chief Constable.

"Exactly," Roger said, gratefully. "The nose on your face. As plain as that."

"But it's impossible, my dear fellow." Sir Wilfrid stared at him in bewilderment "I keep telling you, everyone had a perfect alibi."

"So they did," Roger agreed. "Including the murderer himself. The most perfect alibi imaginable. Hadn't we better be moving, by the way? Agatha will blame me for this."

"My dear Roger, what do you mean? The most perfect alibi imaginable?"

ROGER ROSE. "Why, a blue tunic, of course. And then, like the conscientious fellow you say he was, he executed on himself the due sentence of the law. Though I'm inclined to think," Roger added judicially, "that there was a little too conscientious. By ridding the world of the man who had betrayed his daughter he did more good than he knew. Wilfrid! Don't sit there gaping at me, like —"

"Like a fish out of water," suggested a rather nice feminine voice from the doorway. "Aren't you two ever coming?"

The Mystery of
Horne's Copse

Chapter I

THE WHOLE THING began on the 29th of May.

It is over two years ago now and I can begin to look at it in its proper perspective; but even still my mind retains some echo of the incredulity, the horror, the dreadful doubts as to my own sanity and the sheer, cold-sweating terror which followed that ill-omened 19th of May.

Curiously enough the talk had turned for a few minutes that evening upon Frank himself. We were sitting in the drawing-room of Bucklands after dinner, Sir Henry and Lady Rigby, Sylvia and I, and I can remember the intensity with which I was trying to find a really convincing excuse to get Sylvia alone with me for half-an-hour before I went home. We had only been engaged a week then and the longing for solitary places with population confined to two was tending to increase rather than diminish.

I think it was Lady Rigby who, taking advantage of a pause in her husband's emphatic monologue on phosphates (phosphates were at the time Sir Henry's chief passion), asked me whether I had heard anything of Frank since he went abroad.

"Yes," I said. "I had a picture postcard from him this morning. An incredibly blue Lake Como in the foreground and an impossibly white mountain at the back, with Cadenabbia sandwiched microscopically in between. Actually, though, he's in Bellagio for a few days."

"Oh," said Sylvia with interest and then looked extremely innocent. Bellagio had been mentioned between us as a possible place for the beginning of our own honeymoon.

The talk passed on to the Italian lakes in general.

"And Frank really does seem quite settled down now,

Hugh, does he?" Lady Rigby asked casually, a few minutes later.

"Quite, I think," I replied guardedly; for Frank had seemed quite settled several times, but had somehow become unsettled again very soon afterwards.

Frank Chappell was my first cousin and incidentally, as I had been an only child and Ravendean was entailed, my heir. Unfortunately he had been, till lately, most unsatisfactory in both capacities. Not that there was anything bad in him, I considered he was merely weak; but weakness, in its results, can be as devastating as any deliberate villainy. It was not really his fault. He derived on his mother's side from a stock which was, to put it frankly, rotten and Frank took after his mother's family. He had not been expelled from Eton, but only by inches; he had been sent down from Oxford and his departure from the Guards had been a still more serious affair. The shock of this last killed my uncle, and Frank had come into the property. It was nothing magnificent, falling far short of the resources attached to Ravendean, but plenty to allow a man to maintain his wife in very tolerable comfort. Frank had run through it in three years.

He had then, quite unexpectedly, married one of his own second cousins and, exchanging extravagance for downright parsimony, settled down with her to make the best of a bad job and put his heavily mortgaged property on its feet once more. In this, I more than suspected, he was directed by his wife. Though his cousin on the distaff side, Joanna showed none of the degeneracy of the Wickhams. Physically a splendid creature, tall and lithe and with a darkness of colouring that hinted at a Spanish ancestor somewhere in the not too remote past, she was no less vigorous mentally; under the charm of her manner one felt at once a well-balanced intelligence and a will of adamant. She was exactly the right wife for Frank and I had been delighted.

It was a disappointment to me that Sylvia did not altogether share my liking for Joanna. The Rigbys' property adjoined mine and Frank's was less than twenty miles away, so that the three families had always been on terms of intimacy. Sylvia did not actually dislike Joanna but it was clear that, if the thing were left to her, they would never become close friends and as Frank had always had a hearty dislike for me, it seemed that relations between Ravendean and Moorefield would be a little distant. I cannot say that the thought worried me. So long as I had Sylvia, nothing else could matter.

Frank had now been married something over two years and, to set the wreath of domestic virtue finally on his head, his wife six months ago had given birth to a son. The recuperation of Moorefield, moreover, had proceeded so satisfactorily that three weeks ago the pair had been able to set out on a long wandering holiday through Europe, leaving the child with his foster-mother. I have had to give Frank's history in this detail, because of its importance in the strange business which followed that homely scene in the drawing-room of Bucklands that evening.

Sylvia and I did get our half-hour together in the end and no doubt we spent it as such half-hours always have been spent. I know it seemed a very short time before I was sitting at the wheel of my car, one of the new six-cylinder Dovers, and pressing the self-starter. It failed to work. On such trivialities do our destinies hang.

"Nothing doing?" said Sylvia. "The wiring's gone, I expect. And you won't be able to swing her, she'll be much too stiff." Sylvia's grasp of the intricacies of a car's interior had always astonished me. "You'd better take Emma." Emma was her own two-seater.

"I think I'll walk," I told her. "Through Horne's Copse it's not much over a mile. It'll calm me down."

She laughed, but it was quite true. I had proposed to Sylvia as a sort of forlorn hope and I had not nearly become accustomed yet to the idea of being actually engaged to her.

It was a lovely night and my thoughts, as I swung along, turned as always then upon the amazing question: what did Sylvia see in me? We had a few tastes in common, but her real interest was cars and mine the study of early civilizations, with particularly kindly feelings towards the Minoan and Mycenean. The only reason I had ever been able to get out of her for her fondness was: "Oh well, you see, Hugh darling, you're rather a lamb, aren't you? And you *are* such a perfect old idiot." It seemed curious, but I knew our post-war generation has the reputation of being unromantic.

My eyes had become accustomed to the moonlight, but inside Horne's Copse everything was pitch black. It was hardly necessary for me to slacken my pace, however, for I knew every turn and twist of the path. The copse was not more than a couple of hundred yards long and I had reached, as I judged, just about the middle when my foot struck against an obstacle right in the middle of the track which nearly sent me flying to the ground.

I recovered my balance with an effort, wondering what the thing could be. It was not hard, like a log of wood, but inertly soft I struck a match and looked at it. I do not think I am a particularly nervous man, but I felt a creeping sensation in the back of my scalp as I stood staring down by the steady light of the match. The thing was a body — the body of a man; and it hardly took the ominous black hole in the centre of his forehead, its edges spangled with red dew, to tell me that he was very dead indeed.

But that was not all. My match went out and I nerved myself to light another and hold it close above the dead face to assure myself that I had been mistaken. But I had not been mistaken. Incredibly, impossibly, the body was that of my cousin, Frank.

Chapter II

I TOOK A GRIP on myself.

This *was* Frank and he was dead — probably murdered. Frank was not in Bellagio. He was here, in Horne's Copse, with a bullet-hole in his forehead. I must not lose my head. I must remember the correct things to do in such a case and then I must do them.

"Satisfy oneself that life is extinct."

From some hidden reserve of consciousness the phrase emerged and, almost mechanically, I proceeded to act on it. But it was really only as a matter of form that I touched the white face, which was quite cold and horribly clammy.

One arm was doubled underneath him, the other lay flung out at his side, the inside of the wrist uppermost I grasped the latter gingerly, raising the limp hand a little off the ground as I felt the pulse, or rather, where the pulse should have been; for needless to say, nothing stirred under the cold, damp skin. Finally, with some half-buried recollection that as long as a flicker of consciousness remains, the pupils of the eyes will react to light, I moved one of my last matches backwards and forwards and close to and away from the staring eyes. The pupils did not contract the hundredth of a millimetre as the match approached them.

I scrambled to my feet.

Then I remembered that I should make a note of the exact time and this I did too. It was precisely eleven minutes and twenty seconds past twelve.

Obviously the next thing to do was to summon the police.

Not a doctor first for the poor fellow was only too plainly beyond any doctor's aid.

I am a magistrate and certain details of routine are familiar to me. I knew, for instance, that it was essential that the body should not be touched until the police had seen it; but as I had no-one with me to leave in charge of it, that must be left to chance; in any case it was not probable that anyone else would be using the right-of-way through Horne's Copse so late. I therefore made my way, as fast as I dared in that pitch darkness, out of the copse and then ran at top speed the remaining half-mile to the house. As always I was in sound condition and I dare swear that nobody has ever covered a half-mile, fully clothed, in much quicker time.

I had told Parker, the butler, not to sit up for me and I therefore had to let myself in with my own latch-key. Still panting, I rang up the police station in Salverton, about three miles away and told them briefly what I had discovered. The constable who answered the telephone of course knew me well and Frank too and was naturally shocked by my news. I cut short his ejaculations, however, and asked him to send someone out to Ravendean at once, to take official charge. He undertook to rouse his sergeant immediately and asked me to wait at the house in order to guide him to the spot. I agreed to do so — and it was a long time before I ceased to regret it. It is easy to blame oneself after the event and easy for others to blame one too; but how could I possibly have foreseen an event so extraordinary?

The interval of waiting I filled up by rousing Parker and ringing up my doctor. The latter had not yet gone to bed and promised to come round at once. He was just the kind of man I wanted, for myself rather than Frank; my nervous system has never been a strong one and it had just received a considerable shock. Gotley was his name and he was a great hulking young man who had been tried for England at rugger while he was still at Guy's and, though just failing to get his cap, had been accounted as a good a forward as any outside the team. For a man of that type he had imagination, too, intelligence and great charm of manner, he was moreover a very capable doctor. He had been living in the village for about four years now and I had struck up quite a friendship with him, contrary to my usual practice, for I do not make friends easily.

His arrival was a relief — and so was the whiskey and soda with which Parker immediately followed his entrance into the library where I was waiting.

"This sounds a bad business, Chappell," he greeted me. "Hullo, man, you look as white as a sheet. You'd better have a drink and a stiff one at that." He manipulated the decanter.

"I'm afraid it has rather upset me," I admitted. Now that there was nothing to do but wait. I did feel decidedly shaky.

With the plain object of taking my mind off the gruesome subject Gotley embarked on a cheerful discussion of England's chances in the forthcoming series of test matches that summer, which he kept going determinedly until the arrival of the police some ten minutes later.

These were Sergeant Afford whom, of course, I knew well and a young constable. The sergeant was by no means of the doltish, obstinate type which the writers of detective fiction invariably portray, as if our country police forces consisted of nothing else; he was a shrewd enough man and at this moment he was a tremendously excited man, too. This fact he was striving nobly to conceal in deference to my feelings for, of course, he knew Frank as well as myself and by repute as well as in-person; but it was obvious that the practical certainty of murder, and in such a circle, had roused every instinct of the bloodhound in him: he was literally quivering to get on the trail. No case of murder had ever come his way before and in such a one as this there was, besides the excitement of the hunt, the certainty that publicity galore, with every chance of promotion, would fall to the lot of Sergeant Afford — if only he could trace the murderer before his Superintendent had time to take the case out of his hands.

As we hurried along the sergeant put such questions as he wished, so that by the time we entered the copse he knew almost as much of the circumstances as I did myself. There was now no need to slacken our pace, for I had a powerful electric torch to guide our steps. As we half ran, half walked along I flashed it continuously from side to side, searching the path ahead for poor Frank's body. Somewhat surprised, I decided that it must lie further than I had thought; though, knowing the copse intimately as I did, I could have sworn that it had been lying on a stretch of straight path, the only one, right in the very middle; but we passed over the length of it and it was not there.

A few moments later we had reached the copse's further limit and came to an irresolute halt.

"Well, sir?" asked the sergeant in a tone studiously expressionless.

But I had no time for nuances. I was too utterly bewildered. "Sergeant," I gasped, "it — it's *gone.*"

Chapter III

THERE WAS NO doubt that Frank's body had gone, because it was no longer there; but that did not explain its remarkable removal.

"I can't understand it, Sergeant. I know within a few yards where he was: on that straight bit in the middle. I wonder if he wasn't quite dead after all and managed to crawl off the path somewhere."

"But I thought you were quite sure he was dead, sir?"

"I was. Utterly sure," I said in perplexity, remembering how icy cold that clammy, clay-like face had been.

The constable, who had not yet uttered a word, continued to preserve his silence. So also did Gotley. After a somewhat awkward pause, the sergeant suggested that we should have a look round.

"Well, I can show you where he was, at any rate," I said. "We can recognise the place from the dead matches I left there."

We turned back again and the sergeant, taking my torch, examined the ground. The straight stretch was not more than a dozen yards long and he went slowly up it one side and back the other. "Well, sir, that's funny; there isn't a match anywhere along here."

"Are you sure?" I asked incredulously. "Let me look."

I took the torch, but it was a waste of time: not a match-stalk could I find.

"Rum go," muttered Gotley.

I will pass briefly over the next hour, which was not one of triumph for myself. Let it be enough to say that search as we might on the path, in the undergrowth and even beyond the confines of the copse, not a trace could we discover of a body, a match-stalk, or anything to indicate that these things had ever been there.

As the power of my electric torch waned so did the sergeant's suspicions of my good faith obviously increase. More than once he dropped a hint that I must have been pulling his leg and wasn't it about time I brought a good joke to an end.

"But I did see it, Sergeant," I said desperately, when at last we were compelled to give the job up as a bad one and turn homewards. "The only way I can account for it is that some man came along after I'd gone, thought life might not be extinct and carried my cousin bodily off with him."

"And your burnt matches as well, sir, I suppose," observed the sergeant woodenly.

Gotley and I parted with him and his constable outside the house; he would not come in, even for a drink. It was clear that he was now convinced that I had been playing a joke on him and was not by any means pleased about it. I had to let him carry the delusion away with him.

When they had gone I looked enquiringly at Gotley, but he shook his head. "My goodness, no, I'm not going. I want to go into this a little deeper. I'm coming in with you, whether you like it or not."

As a matter of fact I did. It was nearly half-past one, but sleep was out of the question. I wanted to talk the thing out with Gotley and decide what ought to be done.

We went into the library and Gotley mixed us each another drink. I certainly needed the one he handed to me.

"Nerves still a bit rocky?" Gotley remarked, looking at me with a professional eye.

"A bit," I admitted. I may add in extenuation that I was supposed to have been badly shell-shocked during the war. Certainly my nervous system had never been the same since. "I'm glad you don't want to go. I want your opinion on this extraordinary business. I noticed you didn't say much up there."

"No, I thought better not."

"Well, it'll be light in just over an hour. I want to get back and examine that copse by daylight, before anyone else gets there. I simply can't believe that there aren't some indications that I was telling the truth."

"My dear chap, I never doubted for one moment that you were telling what you sincerely thought was the truth."

"No?" This sounded to me rather oddly put, but I didn't question it for the moment "Well, the sergeant did. Look here, are you game to stay here and come up with me?"

"Like a shot. If any message comes for me, they know at

home where I am. In the meantime, let's try to get some sort
of a line on the thing. I thought your cousin was abroad?"

"So did I," I replied helplessly. "In fact I had a card from
him only this morning from Bellagio."

"Did he give the name of his hotel?"

"Yes, I think so. Yes, I'm sure he mentioned it."

"Then I should wire there directly the post office opens
and ask if he's still there."

"But he isn't," I argued stupidly. "How can he be?"

Gotley contemplated his tumbler. "Still, you know," he
said airily — rather too airily, "still, I should wire."

The hour passed more quickly than I could have expected.
I knew now that Gotley did not consider that I had been
deliberately romancing, he suspected me merely of seeing
visions; but he did not give himself away again and discussed
the thing with me as gravely as if he had been as sure as I
was that what I had seen was fact and not figment. As soon
as the dawn began to show we made our way to the copse;
for no message had arrived from the police station to throw
any light on the affair.

Our journey, let me say briefly, was a complete failure.
Not a single thing did we find to bear out my story — not
a burnt match, a drop of blood, nor even a suspicious foot-
print on the hard ground.

I could not with decency retain Gotley any longer, especially as he was having more and more difficulty in concealing
from me his real opinion. I made no comment or protestation.
His own suggestion of the telegram to Bellagio could be left
to do that; for I had now determined to adopt it in sheer self-
defense, to prove that there was at least the fact of Frank's
absence to support me. If he had been in Horne's Copse he
could not be in Bellagio and, conversely, if he had suddenly
left Bellagio, he could have appeared in Horne's Copse.

I did not go to bed till past eight o'clock, at which hour I
telephoned my telegram.

The rest of the day dragged. Sylvia telephoned after lunch
to say that the chauffeur had now put my car right, but I
put her off with a non-committal answer. The truth was
that nothing would induce me to leave the house until the
answer to my telegram had arrived.

Just after six o'clock it came.

I tore open the flimsy envelope with eager fingers. "Why

the excitement?" it ran. "Here till tomorrow, then Grand Hotel, Milan. Frank."

So Gotley had been right. I *had* been seeing visions.

Chapter IV

I SANK INTO a chair, the telegram between my fingers.

But I had *not* been imagining the whole thing. It was out of the question. The details had been too vivid, too palpable. No, Gotley was wrong. I had seen someone — it might not have been Frank.

I hurried to the telephone and rang up Sergeant Afford. Had he heard anything more about last night's affair? I might possibly have been mistaken in thinking the dead man my cousin. Had any other disappearance been reported? The sergeant was short with me. Nothing further had developed. He had been himself to the scene of the alleged death that morning and found nothing. He advised me, not too kindly, to think no more about the affair.

I began to feel annoyed. Now that it was proved that the body could not possibly have been Frank's, my feeling towards it was almost resentment. Only by the chance of a defective wire on my car had I stumbled across it and the contact had resulted in suspicion on the part of the police of an uncommonly callous practical joke and the conviction on the part of my doctor that I was mentally unbalanced. The more I thought about it the more determined I was that the mystery must be unveiled. I resolved to tell Sylvia the whole story that very evening.

Unlike Gotley, Sylvia asked plenty of questions; still more unlike him she accepted what I said as a statement of fact. "Rot Hugh," she said bluntly, when I told her of that young man's suspicions. "If you say you saw it you did see it. And anyhow, how could you possibly imagine such a thing? Hugh, this is terribly exciting. What are we going to do about it?" She took her own part in any subsequent action for granted.

I looked at her pretty gray eyes sparkling with excitement and, in spite of the gravity of the affair, I could not help smiling. "What do you suggest, dear?" I asked.

"Oh, we must get to the bottom of it, of course. We'll

make enquiries in the neighbourhood and go round all the hospitals, oh and everything." As I had often noticed before, Sylvia had been able to translate into realities ideas which to me had remained a trifle nebulous.

So for the next few days we played at being detectives enquiring into a mysterious murder and traveled all over the country in pursuit of our ridiculous but delightful theories. We enjoyed ourselves tremendously; but if real detectives got no further in their cases than we did, the number of undetected murders would see a remarkable increase; for we discovered exactly nothing at all. No man resembling Frank had been seen in the vicinity; there was not the vaguest report of a man with a bullet wound in his forehead.

All we really did determine was that the man must have been dead (for that he had been dead I was absolutely convinced) for about four to six hours because, though the body was cold, the wrist I had held was still limp, which meant that *rigor mortis* had not set in. This information came from Gotley who gave it with a perfectly grave face and then quite spoilt the effect by advising us to waste no more time on the business. Sylvia was most indignant with him.

Perhaps it is not true to say that we discovered nothing at all, for one rather curious fact did come to light. Although we knew now that the man must have been dead at least four hours, must have died, that is, not later than eight o'clock, we found no less than three persons who had passed over the path between that hour and midnight; and at none of those times had he been there.

"There's a gang in it," Sylvia pronounced with enjoyment. "He was shot miles away, brought to the copse and then carried off again, all by the gang."

"But why?" I asked, wondering at these peripatetic activities.

"Heaven only knows," Sylvia returned helplessly.

And there, in the end, we had to leave it.

At least a month passed and my mysterious adventure gradually became just a curious memory. Gotley ceased to look at me thoughtfully and when I met him at the local flower show even Sergeant Afford showed by his magnanimous bearing that he had forgiven me.

At first, I must confess, I had tended to avoid Horne's Copse at night, although it was much the shortest route between Bucklands and Ravendean. Then, as the memory faded, reason reasserted itself. By the third of July I had shed the last of my qualms.

That third of July!

There is a saying that history repeats itself. It did that night with a vengeance. Once again I had been dining at Bucklands. Before leaving home my chauffeur had found a puncture in one of the back tyres of the Dover and had put the spare wheel on. I risked the short journey without a spare, only to find, when it was time to go home, that another puncture had developed. Once again Sylvia offered me her own car: once again I refused, saying that I should enjoy the walk. Once again I set out with my mind busy with the dear girl I had just left and the happiness in store for me. That very evening we had fixed our wedding provisionally for the middle of September.

Indeed, so intent was I upon these delightful reflections, that I had got a third of the way through Horne's Copse before I even called to mind the sinister connection which the place now held for me. It was not quite such a dark night as that other one, but inside the copse the blackness was as dense as before as I turned the last twist before the stretch of straight path in the centre.

"It was just about six yards from here," I reflected idly as I walked along, "that my foot struck, with that unpleasant thud, against —" I stopped dead, retaining my balance this time with ease, as if I had subconsciously been actually anticipating the encounter. For my foot had struck, with just such another unpleasant thud, against an inert mass in the middle of the path.

With a horrible creeping sensation at the back of my scalp, I struck a match and forced myself to look at the thing in my way, though I knew well enough before I did so what I should see. And I was right. Lying across the path, with unnaturally disposed limbs and, this time, a small dagger protruding from his chest, was my cousin Frank.

Chapter V

THE MATCH FLICKERED and went out and still I stood, rigid and gasping, striving desperately to conquer the panic which was threatening to swamp my reason.

Gradually, in the darkness, I forced my will to control my trembling limbs. Gradually I succeeded in restoring my brain to its natural functions. Here, I told myself deliberately, was the real thing. As for the other — vision, pre-knowledge, clairvoyance, or whatever it might have been, I had at the moment no time to find explanations; here I was in the presence of the real thing and I must act accordingly.

I suppose it can really have been scarcely more than a couple minutes before, restored to the normal, I felt myself not merely calm but positively eager to investigate. With fingers that no longer quivered I struck another match and bent over my unfortunate cousin. It did not even repel me this time to touch the cold, clammy face, glistening in the match-light with unnatural moisture, as I made sure that he really was dead.

It was with an odd sense of familiarity that I made my swift examination. Except for the dagger in his chest and the bloodstained clothes around it instead of the bullet wound in his forehead, everything was exactly the same as before and my own actions followed more or less their previous course. There was the same outflung arm, cold wrist uppermost, whose motionless pulse I could conveniently feel for; there were the staring eyes, unresponsive to the movements of my match; there was the damp, chilled skin of his face. It was only too plain that he was dead, without it being necessary for me to disarrange his clothing to feel his heart and I was again unwilling to do this, knowing how much the police dislike a body to be tampered with before they have examined it themselves.

But one thing further I did this time. I made sure that the body was, beyond all possibility of dispute, that of Frank himself. Frank had a scar on his left temple, just at the edge of the hair. I looked for the scar and I found it. Then I hurried home at the best speed I could, to ring up Sergeant Afford and Gotley. I was conscious as I did so of a rather ignoble feeling of triumph. But after all, self-vindication *is* a pleasant feeling.

Sergeant Alford himself was not at the police station, but

to Gotley I spoke directly. "Right-ho," he said with enthusiasm. "Really has happened this time, has it?"

"Yes," I replied. "There's no doubt this time. I shall want to go into that other affair with you sometime. It must have been a vision of some kind, I suppose."

"Yes, extraordinary business. And apparently not quite an accurate one. What about getting the Psychical Research Society on to it?"

"We might. In the meantime, I'm going back to the copse now. Meet me there. I'm taking no risks this time."

Gotley promised to do so and we rang off.

As I passed out of the front door I looked at my watch. The time was three minutes to twelve. It had been twenty-one minutes to the hour within a few seconds, when I left the body. I walked back at a good pace and the journey took me about twelve minutes. In all, then, I was absent from the centre of Horne's Copse for about half-an-hour. The importance of these figures will be apparent later.

I am not sure what motive prompted my return alone to the spot where I had left the body. I think I wanted, in some vague way, to keep guard over it, almost as if it might run away if left to itself. Anyhow I certainly had the feeling, as I had mentioned to Gotley, that this time I would take no chances.

I had my torch with me now and I turned it on as I reached the copse. It threw a powerful beam and as I turned the corner on to the straight I directed the light along to the further end. The whole dozen yards of straight path was thus illuminated, the undergrowth at the sides and the dense green foliage beyond the twist at the end. But that was all. Of Frank's body there was no sign.

Incredulously I hurried forward, thinking that I must have been mistaken in my bearings; the body must have lain round the further corner. But neither round the corner was there any sign of it, nor anywhere along the path right to the further edge of the copse. Filled with horror, I retraced my steps, sweeping the surface of the ground with my beam. It was as I feared. Again there was not even a litter of spent matches to show where I had knelt by Frank's remains.

In the middle of the path I halted, dazed with nameless alarm. Was my reason going? The thing was fantastic, inexplicable. If I had had my suspicions about the reality of my former experience, I had none concerning this one. I *knew* there had been a body; I *knew* I had handled it, physically and materially; I *knew it* was Frank's — Frank who was supposed to be that moment in Rome. I knew all these things as well as I knew my own name, but... But the alternative simply did not bear thinking about

But for all that, hallucinations...

And yet I felt as sane as ever I had been in my life. There *must* be some ordinary, simple, logical explanation...

I was still trying to find it when the police and Gotley arrived together.

I turned to meet them. "It's gone!" I shouted. "Would you believe it but the damned thing's gone again. I saw him as plainly as I see you, with the dagger in his chest and the blood all round the wound — I touched him! And now there isn't a sign that he was ever there at all. Damn it the very matches have disappeared too." I laughed, for really if you looked at it one way, the thing was just absurd.

Sergeant Afford eyed me austerely. "Is that so, sir?" he said, in his most wooden voice.

He was going to say more, but Gotley brushed him aside and took me by the arm.

"That's all right, Chappell, old man," he said, very soothingly. "Don't you worry about it anymore tonight I'm going to take you home and fill you up with bromide and tomorrow we'll go into it properly."

Gotley thought I was mad, of course. After all it was only to be expected.

Chapter VI

"OUGHT I TO marry, then?" I asked drearily. I had been trying for some minutes to summon up the courage to put this question.

It was the next evening and Gotley and I had been talking for over an hour. He had succeeded in convincing me. I had seen nothing, felt nothing, imagined everything. To pacify me he had telegraphed that morning to Frank in Rome; the answer, facetiously couched, had left no room for doubt.

Gotley had been perfectly open with me during the last hour. It was better, he said, to face this sort of thing frankly. The thing was not serious; I must have been overworking, or suffering from nervous strain of some kind. If I took things easily for a bit these hallucinations would disappear and probably never return. Above all, I must not brood over them.

"Ought I to marry, then, Gotley?" I repeated.

"Oh dear, yes. In time. No need to hurry about it."

"You mean, not in September?"

"Well, perhaps not quite so soon. But later, oh, yes."

"Is it fair? I mean, if there are children."

"My dear chap," Gotley said with great cheerfulness, "it's nothing as bad as that. Nothing but a temporary phase."

"I shall tell Sylvia."

"Ye-es," he agreed, though a little doubtfully. "Yes, you could tell Miss Rigby, but let me have a word with her too. And look here, why not go away somewhere with her and her mother for a bit of a holiday? That's what you want. Drugs can't do anything for you, but a holiday, with the right companionship, might do everything."

And so, the next day, it was arranged.

I told Sylvia everything. She, of course, was her own loyal self and at first refused to believe a word of Gotley's diagnosis. If I thought I had seen a body, then a body I had seen, and felt and examined. Even Frank's facetious telegram did not shake her. But her private talk with Gotley did, a little. She was not convinced, but she went so far as to say that there might be something in it, conceivably. In any case there was no reason why I should not have a holiday with herself and her mother, if that was what everyone seemed to want; but neither Sir Henry nor Lady Rigby were to be told a word about anything else. To this, though somewhat reluctantly, I agreed.

Nevertheless, rumours of course arose. Not that Gotley said a word, but I cannot think that Sergeant Afford was so discreet. When we got back, in August from Norway, I was not long in gathering, from the curious looks which everywhere greeted me, that some at any rate of the cat had escaped from its bag.

I saw Gotley at once and he expressed his satisfaction with my condition. "You'll be all right now," he predicted confidently. "I shouldn't go to that place at night for a bit yet, but you'd be all right now really, in any case."

A couple of days later I had a letter from Frank. It was in answer to one I had written him from Norway, asking him, just as a matter of curiosity, exactly what he had been doing just before midnight on the 3rd of July, as I had had rather a strange dream about him just at that time. He apologised for not having answered earlier, but the hotel in Rome had been slow in forwarding my letter, which had only just now caught him up in Vienna, from which town his own letter was written. So far as he could remember, he was just coming out of a theatre in Rome at the time I mentioned: was that what I wanted? My recovery had been so far complete that I could smile at a couple of very typical spelling mistakes and then dismiss the matter from my mind.

That was on the 9th August. The next morning was a blazing day, the sort of shimmering, cloudless day that one always associates with the month of August and, about once in three years, really gets. I made a leisurely breakfast, read the newspaper for a little, and then set off to keep an appointment with a farmer, a tenant of mine, concerning the re-tooling of his barn. The farm adjoined the Bucklands estate and lay about three miles away by road, but little over a mile if one cut through Horne's Copse. It was a little hot for walking and I had intended to take the Dover, but a message reached me from the garage that something had gone mysteriously wrong with the carburetor and a new float would have to be obtained before I could take her out. Rather welcoming the necessity for exercise, I set off on foot.

As I approached Horne's Copse I reflected how complete my recovery must be, for instead of feeling the slightest reluctance to pass through it I positively welcomed its prospect of cool green shade. Strolling along, my thoughts on the coming interview and as far as they well could be from the unhappy memories that the place held for me, I turned the last corner which hid from me the little length of straight path which had played so sinister a part in those memories — even, I think, whistling a little tune.

Then the tune froze abruptly on my lips and the warmth of the day was lost in the icy sweat of sheer terror which broke out all over me. For there at my feet, incredibly, impossibly, lay the body of Frank, the blood slowly oozing round the dagger that projected from his heart.

This time I stayed to make no examination. In utter panic I took to my heels and ran. Whither, or with what idea, I had no notion. My one feeling was to get away from the place and as soon and as quickly as possible.

Actually, I came to my senses in a train, bound for London, with a first-class ticket clutched in my hand. How I had got there I had no conception but the vaguest. It had been a blind flight.

Fortunately, the compartment was an empty one and I was able to take measures to control the trembling of my limbs before trying to take stock of the situation. I was not cured, then. Far from it. What was I to do?

One thing I determined. I would stay a few days in London now that I was already on the way there and, when I felt sufficiently recovered to tell my story coherently, consult some experienced alienist. Obviously, I was no longer a case for Gotley.

It was no doubt (as I reflected in a strangely detached way), a part of my mania that I did not go to my usual hotel, where I was known, but sought out the most obscure one I could find. In an effort to shake off my obsession and complete the process of calming myself I turned after the meal into a dingy little cinema and tried to concentrate for three hours on the inanities displayed on the screen.

"Shocking murder in a wood!" screamed a newsboy almost in my ear, as I stood blinking in the sunlight outside again. Mechanically I felt for a copper and gave it to him. It was in a wood that I had seen...

And it was an account of the finding of Frank's body that I read there and then, on the steps of that dingy cinema — Frank who had been found that morning in Horne's Copse with a dagger in his heart.

"The police," concluded the brief account, "state that they would be grateful if the dead man's cousin, Mr. Hugh Chappell, who was last seen boarding the 11.19 train to London, would put himself in touch with them as soon as possible."

Chapter VII

I TURNED AND began to walk quickly, but quite aimlessly, along the pavement. The one idea in my mind at the moment was that nobody should guess, from any anxiety I might display, that I was the notorious Hugh Chappell with whom the police wished to get in touch as soon as possible. It never occurred to me to doubt that I was notorious, that my name was already on everyone's lips and that not merely every policeman but even every private citizen was eagerly looking for me. Such is the effect of seeing one's name, for the first time, in a public news sheet.

By and by my mind recovered from this temporary obsession and I began to think once more. So this time my hallucination had not been a hallucination at all. Frank *had* been killed — murdered, almost certainly: it *was* his body I had seen that morning. But what, then, of the two previous times I had seen that same body and even handled it? Or so I had fancied at the time. Obviously they were not the meaningless delusions that Gotley and, finally, I myself, had believed them to be; they really were definite pre-visions of the real event. It was most extraordinary.

In any case, be that as it might, my own immediate action was clear. I must return at once to Ravendean and offer Sergeant Afford any help in my power.

It did not take me much over half-an-hour to ring up my hotel, cancel my room and make my way to Paddington. There I found that a train was luckily due to start in ten minutes and, having taken my ticket, I strolled to the bookstall to see if any later edition with fuller details was yet on sale. As I approached the stall I noticed a figure standing in front of it which looked familiar to me. The man turned his head and I recognised him at once as a fellow who had been on my staircase at Oxford, though I had never known him well: his name was Sheringham and I had heard of him during the last few years as a successful novelist with an increasing reputation, Roger Sheringham.

I had not the least wish, at the present juncture, to waste time renewing old acquaintances, but as the man was now staring straight at me I could hardly do less than nod, with what pleasantness I could muster and greet him by name.

His response surprised me enormously. "Hullo, Hugo!" he said warmly, indeed with a familiarity I resented considering that we had never been on terms of anything but surnames before. "Come and have a drink." And he actually took me by the arm.

"I'm sorry," I said, a little stiffly, "I have a train to catch." And I endeavoured to release myself.

"Nonsense!" he said loudly. "Plenty of time for a quick one." I was going to reply somewhat peremptorily when, to my astonishment, he added in a hissing sort of whisper without moving his lips: "Come *on*, you damned fool."

I allowed him to lead my away from the bookstall, completely bewildered.

"Phew!" he muttered, when we had gone about thirty yards. "That was a close shave. Don't look round. That man in the grey suit who was just coming up on the left is a Scotland Yard man."

"Indeed?" I said, interested but perplexed. "Looking for someone, you mean?"

"Yes," Sheringham said shortly. "You. One of a dozen in this very station at this very minute. Let's get out — if we can!"

I was surprised to hear that so many detectives were actually looking for me. Evidently the police considered my evidence of the first importance. I wondered how Sheringham knew and asked him.

"Oh, I'm in touch with those people," he said carelessly. "Lord," he added, more to himself than to me, "I wish I knew what to do with you now I've got you."

"Well," I smiled, "I'm afraid you can't do anything at the moment. If you're in touch with Scotland Yard, you'll have heard about my poor cousin?" He nodded and I explained my intentions.

"I thought so," he nodded, "seeing you here. Well, that confirms my own opinion."

"What opinion?"

"Oh, nothing. Now look here, Chappell, I don't want you to take this train. There's another a couple of hours later which will do you just as well; there's no particular urgency so far as you're concerned. In the interval, I want you to come back with me to my rooms at the Albany."

"But why?"

"Because I want to talk to you — or rather, hear you talk. And I may say I was about to travel down to your place by that same train for just that purpose."

This was the most surprising news I had yet received. I demurred, however, at missing the train, but Sheringham was so insistent that at last I agreed to accompany him.

"We'd better get a taxi, then," I remarked with, I fear, no very good grace.

"No," Sheringham retorted. "We'll go by tube."

And by tube we went.

Sheringham took me into a very comfortable paneled sitting-room and we sat down in two huge leather armchairs.

"Now," he said, "don't think me impertinent Chappell, or mysterious, and remember that I'm not only in touch with Scotland Yard but I have on occasions even worked with them. I want you to tell me, from beginning to end, in as much detail as you can, your story of this extraordinary business of your cousin's death. And believe me, it's entirely in your own interests that I ask you to do so, though for the present you must take that on trust."

The request seemed to me highly irregular, but Sheringham appeared to attach such importance to it that I did, in fact, comply. I told him the whole thing.

"I see," he said. "Thank you. And you proposed to go down and give the police what help you could. Very proper. Now I'll tell you something, Chappell. What do you think they want you for? Your help? Not a bit of it They want you in order to arrest you, for killing your cousin."

"What?" I could only gasp.

"I have it from their own lips. Shall I tell you what the police theory is? That your two false alarms were the results of hallucinations, which left you with the delusion that you had a divine mission to kill your cousin and that meeting him accidentally in the flesh in that same place you, under the influence of this mania, actually did kill him."

Chapter VIII

IN A MINUTE OR two Sheringham's revelation of this hideous suggestion left me quite speechless with horror. I was beginning to stammer out a refutation when he waved me into silence.

"My dear chap, it's all right; I don't believe anything of the sort I never did and now I've seen and talked to you I do still less. You're not mad. No, I'm convinced the business isn't so simple as all that In fact, I think there's something pretty devilish behind it. That's why I was on my way down to try to find you before the police did and ask you if I could look into things for you."

"Good heavens," I could only mutter, "I'd be only too grateful if you would. I've no wish to end my days in a madhouse. This is really terrible. Have you any ideas at all?"

"Only that those first two occasions were no more delusions than the last. You did see something that you were meant to see — either your cousin or somebody made up to resemble him. And the plot which I'm quite certain exists is evidently aimed against you as well as against your cousin. For some reason a certain person or persons do want you locked up in an asylum. At least, that seems the only possible explanation, with the result that the police are thinking exactly what they have been meant to think. Now, can you tell me of anyone who would benefit if you were locked up in a madhouse?"

"No one," I said in bewilderment "But Sheringham, how can it possibly be a deliberate plot? It was only by the merest chance on all those three occasions that I went through Horne's Copse at all. Nobody could possibly have foreseen it."

"Are you sure? On each occasion, you remember, you had to pass from one point to another, with Horne's Copse as the nearest route, provided you were on foot. And on each occasion, you also remember, your car just happened to be out of action. You think that's coincidence? I don't."

"You mean — you think my car had been tampered with?"

"I intend to have a word or two with your chauffeur, but I'm ready to bet a thousand pounds here and now what the implications of his answers will be — though doubtless he won't realise it himself. What sort of a man is he, by the way? Sound?"

"Very. A first-rate mechanic and an excellent fellow. In fact, he has rather a sad story. Not that he's ever told me a word himself; actually I had it from Frank who sent him along to me, not being able to find a job for him himself. He's a public school and University man whose people lost all their money while he was up at Cambridge, where Frank knew him slightly. So, having a bent for engineering, he buckled down to it, worked his way through the shops and turned himself into a most efficient chauffeur."

"Stout fellow," Sheringham commented. "We may find him very useful. Now look here, Chappell, you're absolutely convinced that the man you saw each time in Horne's Copse was your cousin? You're sure it wasn't somebody disguised as him?"

"I'm practically certain," I replied.

"Yes; well, we must check up on that; which means that someone must go abroad and cover the ground."

"But you forget the telegrams I had from Frank."

"Indeed I don't," Sheringham retorted. "A telegram's no evidence at all."

"But who is to go?"

"There you have me," he admitted. "I simply can't spare

the time myself if I'm to go into things properly at this end, and we've got none of it to lose. I want to get the case cleared up before the police find you and we don't know when that may be."

"Oh! I'm to go into hiding, then?"

"Well, of course. Once arrested it's the dickens of a job to get free again. We must put it off as long as we possibly can."

"But where am I to hide?"

"Why, I thought here. Meadows, my man, is perfectly safe. Any objection?"

"None, indeed. This is extraordinarily good of you, Sheringham. I needn't say how very grateful I am."

"That's all right, that's all right. Now then, if I'm to do any good down in your neighbourhood I must put a few questions before I leave you. I'm going to catch that train."

Sheringham hurriedly put his queries, some concerning my own affairs and Frank's and some upon local conditions and personages and rushed off to catch his train. Before he went I obtained his promise to see Sylvia and secretly inform her of my plans and whereabouts, together with his own hopes of getting me out of this trouble, which I urged him to put as high as possible to save the poor girl anxiety. This he undertook to do and I was left alone.

It need not be said that my reflections were not pleasant ones; but rack my brains as I might, I could see no possible solution of the mystery of my cousin's death, nor even discover the least bit of evidence to support Sheringham's theory that some person or persons unknown, having murdered Frank, were now trying to get me confined as a homicidal lunatic. Who was there who could possibly benefit by this double crime?

To all practical purposes I was a prisoner in the Albany for an indefinite period. Outside the shelter of Sheringham's rooms I did not dare to put my nose. And for all the company that the silent-footed, respectfully taciturn Meadows proved himself, I might just as well have been completely alone. The time hung heavily on my hands, in spite of the numbers of newspapers I examined, Meadows silently bringing me each fresh edition as it appeared. There was, however, little fresh to be found in the reports so far as real information went, though columns of balderdash were printed concerning myself, Frank and everything relevant and irrelevant to the case. The only piece of complete news was that the dagger with which Frank had been stabbed had been identified as my own dagger, from the wall in my library, a fact which lent superficial support to the police theory but, to me, more to Sheringham's.

The latter had not been able to say how long he would be absent. Actually it was nearly forty-eight hours before he returned, looking considerably graver than when he departed.

I had jumped up eagerly to question him as to his success and his reply was anything but reassuring.

"I've found out a little, but not much. And the police have found out a good deal more. They've got evidence now which has made them change their theory completely. You'd better prepare for a shock, Chappell. They think now that you feigned the first two hallucinations in order to create the impression that you were mad and then, having established that, killed your cousin in extremely sane cold blood in accordance with a careful plan of murder, knowing that as a homicidal maniac you couldn't be executed but would get off with a year or so in Broadmoor before proving that you'd recovered your sanity. That's what we're up against now."

Chapter IX

I HAD STILL found no words to answer Sheringham's appalling news when the door behind him opened and Sylvia herself appeared.

"Oh, Hugh!" she said, with a little cry and ran to me.

"She would come," Sheringham said gloomily. "I couldn't stop her. Well, I'll go and unpack." He left us alone together.

"Hugh dear," Sylvia said, when our first disjointed greetings were over, "what does this terrible business all mean? Frank dead and you suspected of killing him! I knew all the time there was something dreadful behind those 'hallucinations' of yours, as that idiot of a Dr. Gotley would call them."

"I can tell you one thing it must mean, darling," I said sadly, "and that is that our engagement must be broken off. It wouldn't be fair to you. Though when I'm cleared I shall —"

"Hugh!" she interrupted me indignantly. "How dare you say such a thing to me! What kind of a girl do you imagine I am? Engagement broken off indeed. Do you know *why* I've come up with Mr. Sheringham?"

"Well, no," I had to admit.

But I was not destined to learn just then exactly why

Sylvia had come up to London, for Sheringham himself followed his own discreet tap on the door into the room.

We settled down into a council of war.

"There's no disguising the fact," Sheringham said gravely, "that the position's uncommonly serious, Chappell. The hunt for you is up, with a vengeance."

"Look here," I returned, "in that case I must leave your rooms. You could get into serious trouble for harbouring a wanted man, you know."

"Oh, that," Sheringham said scornfully. "Yes, you can go all right, but you'll have to knock me out first I'll hold you here if necessary by main force."

Sylvia's face, which had become highly apprehensive at my remark, lightened again and she shot a grateful smile at our host

"Then you really don't think I should surrender to the police and let them hold me while you're working?" I asked anxiously, for, magistrate as I was, the way in which I was evading arrest seemed to me just then almost more reprehensible than the ridiculous charge which was out against me.

"I do not," Sheringham replied bluntly. "That is, not unless you want to turn a short story into a long one. Give me just a few days and I'll clear the mystery up — granted one thing only."

"And what's that?"

"Why, that the agent we send abroad is able to establish the fact that your cousin was *not* at his hotel abroad on those first two occasions; because unless you're completely mistaken in your identification, there can't be any doubt about that, as a fact."

"But wait a minute!" Sylvia cried. "Mr. Sheringham, that would mean that — that his wife is in it too."

"Oh, yes," Sheringham agreed carelessly. "Naturally."

"Joanna!" I exclaimed. "Oh, that's impossible."

"I wouldn't put it past her," said Sylvia. "But why 'naturally,' Mr. Sheringham? Have you got a theory that brings her in?"

"Yes. My idea is that so far as your cousin and his wife were concerned, Chappell, the thing was a joke, just to give you a fright. Rather a gruesome joke, perhaps, but nothing more. He was home on business for a day or two and, with the help of somebody else, rigged himself up as a sham corpse. *Then* that unknown third person turned the joke against him most effectively by really killing him the third time. All we've got to do, therefore, is to find this mysterious person (which, with your cousin's wife's help, shouldn't be difficult), and we've got the murderer."

"Joanna's on her way home now, of course," Sylvia told me. "They expect her to arrive tonight or tomorrow. Mr. Sheringham's going down again to see her."

"I understand," I said slowly, though I was not altogether sure that I did. "And supposing that she says that Frank was with her all the time and our agent confirms that?"

"Well, in that case there's only one possible explanation: your identification was mistaken."

"I'm sure it wasn't," I said. "And what's more I'm equally sure that Frank was dead the first time of all — quite dead. I tell you, his face was icy cold and his heart wasn't beating; I felt his pulse most carefully. It's impossible that I could have been mistaken."

"That does make things a little more difficult," Sheringham murmured.

There was a gloomy little pause, which I broke to ask Sheringham what this fresh evidence was which the police imagined they had discovered against me. Apparently it amounted to the facts that, according to Jefferson, my chauffeur, the car had on each occasion shown every sign of having been deliberately tampered with (which Sheringham had expected), and by myself (which he had not); that the police had obtained my finger-prints from articles in the house and the finger-prints on the dagger corresponded with them; and that I had been heard to use threatening language as regards Frank — which so far as his escapades before marriage were concerned, was possibly in some degree true, though I could not in any way account for the finger-prints.

"Whom are you going to send abroad for us, Mr. Sheringham?" Sylvia asked suddenly, when our discussion on these points was over.

"Well, I've been thinking about that. It must be someone who knew the dead man and all the circumstances. In my opinion the very best thing would be for Hugh to go and act as his own detective. We can easily lay a trail to make the police think he's still in London, so the foreign forces won't be warned."

"Hugh!" Sylvia echoed in surprise. "Well, really, that

mightn't be at all a bad idea. Though as to detecting... Still, I can do that part of it."

"You?" we exclaimed in unison.

"Oh, yes," said Sylvia serenely. "I shall go with him, of course."

"But, darling," I was beginning to expostulate.

"Which brings me back to my real reason for coming up to London, Hugh," Sylvia went on with the utmost calmness. "It was so that we can get married at once, of course. Or at any rate, within the usual three days. It will have to be in false names, I'm afraid, owing to this fuss, but it's just as legal and we can go through a ceremony again in our own names if you like after it's all over. I've applied for the special license already, in the name of —" She began to giggle and dived into her handbag, from which she extracted a crumpled piece of paper. "Yes, Miss Arabella Whiffen. And you, darling, are Mr. Penstowe Stibb."

Chapter X

AND SO, IN SPITE of my misgivings, Sylvia and I actually were married three days later. In my own defence I may say that when Sylvia has really made her mind up to a thing...

How we got safely out of the country, while the police were feverishly chasing clues ingeniously laid by Sheringham to show that I was still in London, I do not propose to say. In the public interest such things are better kept quiet.

It was a strange honeymoon upon which we embarked, with its object of finding out whether or not Frank really had been abroad at the time when I had seen him (as I was now more convinced than ever that I had), lying dead in Horne's Copse. Nor was there any time to lose. With only one night to break the journey in Dale on the way, we went straight through to the Italian lakes. We did not, however, stay in Bellagio, where Frank had been (or said he had been), but at Cadenabbia opposite. For all we knew, we might encounter an English detective in Bellagio and we did not intend to remain in the danger zone longer than necessary.

We arrived at Cadenabbia late at night. The next morning, before crossing the lake to Bellagio, I received a letter from Sheringham, addressed to me in the assumed name in which we were traveling. Its contents were most disturbing:

DEAR STIBB,

I am keeping in close touch with S.Y. and they still have no doubt that London is the place. Meanwhile here is news.

Both the police and I have seen J. and she tells the same story to both of us: that her husband never came back to England at all, until the day before his death, when he had to return for a few hours to see in person to some business connected with the estate and left saying that he was going straight to you to ask you to put him up. That is bad enough, but this is worse. The police now think they have found a definite motive for you. They say you were in love with J. (Your late marriage, of course, would be put down to an act of panic.)

Now this information can have come from one person only, J. herself, so I tackled her about it. She was very reluctant to tell me anything but finally, while admitting the possibility that she might have been totally mistaken, did hint that in her opinion your attentions to her since her marriage have been a good deal more marked than one might have expected in the case of a man engaged to another girl. I need not tell you my own opinion that J. is a vain hussy and all this is pure moonshine due to her inordinate conceit; but I must admit that it would not sound at all a pretty story in court.

I am more than ever certain that everything now hinges on your being able to establish that F. was not where he pretended to be. So do your level best.

Yours, R.S.

P.S. J. is very bitter against you. She seems to have no doubt in her empty head that you did the deed.

"Well, I am blessed!" I exclaimed and showed the letter to Sylvia. "Really, I can't imagine how Joanna can have got such an extraordinary idea into her head. I'm quite certain I never gave her the least grounds for it."

Sylvia read the letter through carefully. "I never did like Joanna," was all she said.

It can be imagined that, after this news, we were more anxious than ever to succeed in the object of our journey. It was, therefore, with a full realisation of the fateful issues involved that we approached the Grand Hotel in Bellagio, which Frank had given as his address there.

While Sylvia engaged the reception clerk in a discussion regarding terms for a mythical stay next year I, as if idly, examined the register. My heart sank. There was the entry for the date in question. "Mr. and Mrs. Francis Chappell," unmistakably in Joanna's handwriting. Apparently they had only stayed for two nights.

Concealing my disappointment, I turned to the clerk. "I believe some friends of ours were staying here last May. English, of course. I don't suppose you remember them. The lady was very dark, with quite black hair and her husband was just about my build and not at all unlike me in face, except that he had a scar just here." I touched my right temple.

"Was he a gentleman of fast temper — no, quick temper, your friend?" asked the clerk, who spoke excellent English, with a slight smile.

"Yes," I agreed. "Occasionally perhaps he is. Why?"

"Oh, nothing. It was nothing at all," said the clerk hastily. Too hastily, for it was evidently something. "Just something that displeased the gentleman. Quite natural. Yes, signor, I remember your friends very well. Their name is Chappell, is it not? And they went on from here to Milan. I remember he told me he got the scar playing cricket when a boy. Is it not so?"

"It is," I said gloomily.

"You have a very good memory," remarked Sylvia.

"It is my business," beamed the clerk, evidently pleased with the compliment.

Disconsolately we made our way back across the lake to our hotel, where Sylvia vanished indoors to write a letter.

Rather to my surprise, considering how urgent our business was, Sylvia refused to go on to Rome the next day, nor even the day after that. She had always wanted to see the Italian lakes, she said and now she was here she was going to see them all. And see them all we did, Lugano, Maggiore and the rest at the cost of a day apiece. It was almost a week later before at last we found ourselves in Rome.

And there it seemed that our enquiries were to meet with

just the same fate. The conversation with the hotel clerk was
repeated almost word for word. Did he remember my friend?
Certainly he did and again by name as well as behaviour
(Frank seemed from the hints we had had to have traveled
across Europe blazing a trail of fiery temper). There was no
doubt at all about his having been there. Even the scar was
once more in evidence.

Sylvia drew something out of her bag and pushed it across
the counter. I saw what it was as she did so. It was a small
but excellent photograph of Frank himself.

"Is that anything like Mr. Chappell?" she asked, almost
carelessly.

The clerk took the photograph up and looked at it carefully. "It is like him, just a little. But it is not Mr. Chappell
himself, as the Signora well knows. Oh, no."

Sylvia glanced at me. "I knew you'd need someone with
you to do the real detecting," she said calmly, though her
eyes were dancing.

Chapter XI

BUT THAT WAS not the end of my surprises.

Sylvia was contemplating the clerk thoughtfully. "Are
you ever able to get away from here for the weekend?" she
asked. "A long weekend?"

The man shook his head regretfully. "No, never. We do
not have the English weekend in Italy."

"Oh!" said Sylvia.

"Only a week's holiday in a year we have. My holiday
begins in three days' time. I shall not be sorry."

Sylvia brightened. "Look here, how would you like to go
to England for your week's holiday, all expenses paid?"

The man's voluble answer left no doubt of his liking for the
idea. Sylvia arranged the details with him there and then.

"My darling," I said, when at last we were seated in a
cafe a few streets away and could talk properly, "what on
earth is it you're doing and how did you know the man with
Joanna wasn't Frank at all?"

She gave me a superior smile. "It didn't strike you as
curious, Hugh, that both those men remembered Frank so
well, what with his temper and his scar, about which he
was so confidential, and the rest? It didn't occur to you to
wonder whether they remembered all the visitors at their
hotels quite so thoroughly? It didn't strike you as though

Frank had almost gone out of his way to be remembered at those two places so clearly?"

"Go on. Rub it in. No, it didn't."

"Poor lamb! Well, why should it have? You haven't got such a suspicious mind as I have. But all those things struck me. Also the fact that it was Joanna who signed the register. Very fishy, I thought. So I wrote off to Mr. Sheringham to get hold somehow of a photograph of Frank and send it to me *poste restante* at Rome. That's why I insisted on staying so long on the lakes, to give it time to arrive."

"Well, well," I said. "I'm quite glad I married you. So what is our programme now?"

"I must write to Mr. Sheringham at once and tell him what we've discovered and that we're bringing the witness back with us in two or three days' time."

"But why are we doing that?"

"I'm not going to let him go off on his holiday where we can't get hold of him," Sylvia retorted. "Besides, aren't there things called affidavits that he'll have to swear? Something like that. Anyhow, Mr. Sheringham will know, so to Mr. Sheringham he's going."

And to Mr. Sheringham, three days later, the man went .I think I have already hinted in this chronicle that when Sylvia makes up her mind to a thing...

Sheringham seemed scarcely less pleased to see him than us. He handed him over to Meadows with as much care as if he had been made of glass and might fall into pieces at any moment.

As soon as he had gone and Sylvia had received Sheringham's congratulations on her perspicacity, I asked eagerly whether anything further had come to light at this end of the affair.

Sheringham smiled, as if not ill-pleased with himself. "I think I've made some progress, but I'd rather not say anything just at the moment. I've arrived at one decision, though, Chappell, and that is that you must now come out in the open."

"Stop skulking?" I said. "I shall be only too pleased. I've nothing to hide and I dislike this hole and corner atmosphere I've been living in."

"But is it safe?" Sylvia asked anxiously.

"On that we've got to take a chance," Sheringham told her. "Personally, I think it will be. In any case, since getting your letter I've arranged a conference here this evening. I'm

going to do my best to bring everyone into the open and with
any luck developments may result."

"Who's coming?" I asked, a little uneasily. I was not sure
that I cared for the sound of the word "conference."

"Well, Mrs. Chappell, for one."

"Joanna? Really, Sheringham, do you think it advisable
—"

"And her brother, for another," he interrupted me. "You
know him, I expect?"

"Well, very slightly. I met him at the wedding. That's all.
I've heard of him, of course. Rather a — a —"

"Bad egg?"

"Exactly."

"Well, bad egg or not he's coming to support his sister
in my omelet."

"Yes, but what have you found out, Mr. Sheringham?"
Sylvia insisted. "What have you been doing these last ten
days?"

"What have I found out?" Sheringham repeated whim-
sically. "Well, where to buy ice in your neighbourhood, for
one thing. Very useful, in this hot weather."

Sylvia's eyes dilated. "Mr. Sheringham, you don't mean
that Frank was killed right back in May and — and —"

"And kept on ice till August?" Sheringham laughed. "No,
I certainly don't. The doctor was quite definite that he hadn't
been dead for more than a couple of hours at the outside when
he was found. And now don't ask me any more questions,
because I'm determined not to spoil my conference for you."

It was by then nearly dinner time and Sheringham, refus-
ing to satisfy our curiosity any further, insisted on our going
off to dress. We had to take what heart we could from the
fact that he certainly seemed remarkably confident.

Joanna and her brother, Cedric Wickham, were to arrive
at nine o'clock. Actually they were a minute or two early.

The meeting, I need hardly say, was constrained in the
extreme. From the expression of acute surprise on their faces
it was clear that the other two had had no idea that we were
to be present a fact which Sheringham must have purposely
concealed from us. Recovering themselves, Joanna greeted
us with the faintest nod, her brother, a tall, good-looking fellow, with a scowl. As if noticing nothing in the least amiss,
Sheringham produced drinks.

Not more than three minutes later there was a ring at the

front doorbell. The next moment the door of the room was opened, a large, burly man was framed in the doorway and Meadows announced: "Detective Chief Inspector Moresby."

Expecting as I did to be arrested on the spot, I put as good a face on the encounter as I could, though I had a task to appear altogether normal as the C.I.D. man, after a positively benevolent nod to the others, advanced straight towards me. But all he did was to put out a huge hand and say: "Good evening, Mr. Chappell. And how are you, sir? I've been wanting to meet you for some time." His blue eyes twinkled genially.

I returned his smile as we shook hands — a proceeding which Joanna and her brother watched decidedly askance. They too, I think, had been expecting to see me led off, so to speak, in chains.

"Now," said Sheringham briskly, "I'm glad to say I've got news for you. A new witness. No credit to me, I'm afraid. Mrs. Hugh Chappell is responsible. We'll have him in straight away, shall we, and hear what he's got to say." He pressed the bell.

The Chief Inspector, as it were casually, strolled over to a position nearer the door.

I think our little Italian thoroughly enjoyed his great moment, though his English suffered a little under the strain. He stood for a moment in the doorway, beaming at us and then marched straight up to Cedric Wickham.

"Ah, it is a pleasure to meet antique faces again, *non e vero?* Good evening, Mr. Frank Chappell!"

Chapter XII

JOANNA, HER BROTHER and Chief Inspector Moresby had gone.

Almost immediately, as it seemed, after the little Italian clerk's identification of Cedric Wickham as the impersonator of Frank at Bellagio and Rome, the room had appeared to fill with burly men, before whom the Chief Inspector had arrested Joanna and Cedric, the latter as the actual perpetrator of the murder and the former as accessory to it both before and after the fact. My own chauffeur, whose real name I now learned was Harvey, not that under which I had engaged him on poor Frank's recommendation, was already under arrest as a further accessory.

It was a terrible story that Sheringham told Sylvia and myself later that evening.

"There were two plots in existence," he said when we were settled in our chairs and the excitement of the treble arrest had begun to calm down. "The first was invented by your cousin himself, who called in his wife, his brother-in-law and Harvey to help him carry it out. The second was an adaptation by these three aimed against the originator of the first. Both, of course, were aimed against you, too.

"This was the first plot I'm not quite clear myself yet on some of its details, but—"

At this point the telephone bell in the hall rang and Sheringham went out to answer it.

He was away a considerable time and when he returned it was with a graver face even than before.

"Mrs. Chappell has confessed," he said briefly. "She puts all the blame on the other two. I have every doubt of that and so have the police, but I can give you her whole story now. It fills up the gaps in my knowledge of the case." He sat down again in his chair.

"The first plot then," he resumed, "was aimed against you, Chappell, by your cousin. It did not involve murder, although it was designed to put your possessions in his hands. To put it shortly, Frank had worked hard for two years and he didn't like it. What is more, he did not intend to work any longer. He determined to anticipate his inheritance from you. But rotter though he was, he drew the line at murder. To get you shut up in a lunatic asylum for the rest of your life, with the result that he as your heir and next-of-kin would have the administering of your estate, was quite enough for his purpose.

"To achieve this result he hit on the idea of causing you several times to come across his apparently dead body, knowing that you would give the alarm and then, when the searchers and the police came, have nobody to show for it. When this had happened three or four times, the suspicion that you were mad would become a certainty and the rest would follow. I think it only too likely that if the plan had been left at that it would almost certainly have succeeded."

The devil!" Sylvia burst out indignantly.

"I'm quite sure it would," I agreed soberly. "The police were taken in and Gotley too and, upon my word, I was ready to wonder myself whether I wasn't mad. But what I can't understand is how he copied death so well. I hadn't the slightest suspicion that he wasn't dead. He not only looked dead, he *felt* dead."

"Yes — in the parts you did feel, which were the ones you were meant to feel. If you'd slipped your hand inside his shirt and felt his actual heart, instead of only the pulse in his wrist, you'd have felt it beating at once.

"Anyhow, the way he and Harvey went about it was this. About an hour before you were expected, Frank gave himself a stiff injection of morphia. They couldn't use chloroform, because of the smell. Harvey meantime was watching for you to start, having, of course, already put the car out of action so as to ensure your walking and through Horne's Copse at that. As soon as you set out or looked like doing so, Harvey ran on ahead at top speed for the copse, which he would reach about ten minutes before you.

"Ready waiting for him there was a tourniquet, a bottle of atropine drops and a block of ice fashioned roughly to the shape of a mask and wrapped in a blanket. He clapped the ice over your cousin's face and another bit over his right hand and wrist and fastened it there, put the tourniquet on his right arm above the elbow and slipped off the ice mask for a moment when his hand was steadier, to put a few of the atropine drops into Frank's eyes to render the pupils insensible to light. Then he arranged the limbs with the dead pulse invitingly upwards and so on, waited till he could actually hear you coming, and then whipped off the ice blocks and retreated down the path. After you'd gone to give the alarm, of course, he cleared the ground of your traces, match sticks and so on and carried Frank out of the way, coming back to smooth out any footprints he might have made in so doing.

"In the meantime, Joanna's brother was impersonating Frank abroad, just in the unlikely event of your making any enquiries over there, though as your wife very shrewdly spotted, he overdid his attempts to impress the memory of himself on the hotel staff. And, of course, she answered your telegrams. By the way, as an example of their thoroughness I've just heard that your cousin engaged two single rooms instead of one double one through the whole tour, so that the fact of it being done at Bellagio and Rome, where it was necessary, wouldn't appear odd afterward. Well, that's the first plot and, as I say, it very nearly came off.

"The second was, in my own opinion, most probably instigated by Joanna herself, or Joanna and Harvey. Frank didn't know, when he brought into his own scheme a man who would help because he was in love with Frank's wife, that Frank's wife was in love with him. You told me yourself that the Wickhams are rotten stock, though you didn't think that Joanna was tainted. She was, worse than any of them (except perhaps her own brother), but morally, not physically. To take advantage of Frank's plot by having him actually killed in the hope that you (if the evidence was rigged a little on the spot, which Harvey was in a position to do) would be hanged for his murder, was nothing to her."

"Is that what was really intended?" Sylvia asked, rather white. Sheringham nodded. "That was the hope, in which event of course her infant son would inherit and she would more or less administer things for him till he came of age, marrying Harvey at her leisure and with a nice fat slice of the proceeds earmarked for brother Cedric. If things didn't go so well as that, there was always Frank's original scheme to fall back on, which would give almost as good a result, though with that there was always the danger of your being declared sane again."

"And the police," I exclaimed, "were for a time actually bamboozled!"

"No," Sheringham laughed. "We must give Scotland Yard its due. I learned today that, though puzzled, they never seriously suspected you, and what's more, they knew where you were the whole time and actually helped you to get abroad, hoping you'd help them to clear up their case for them, and in fact you did."

"How silly of them," Sylvia pronounced. "When we were out of the country they lost track of us."

"Yes?" said Sheringham. "By the way, did you make any friends on the trip?"

"No. At least, only one. There was quite a nice man staying at Cadenabbia who was actually going on to Rome the same day as we did. He was very helpful about trains and so on. We took quite a fancy to him, didn't we, Hugh?"

"He is a nice fellow, isn't he?" Sheringham smiled.

"Oh, do you know him? No, of course you can't; you don't even know who I mean."

"Indeed I do," Sheringham retorted. "You mean Detective Inspector Peters of the C.I.D., though I don't think you knew that yourself, Mrs. Chappell."

Unsound Mind

Part I

THE TELEPHONE-BELL at Chief Inspector Moresby's elbow tinkled. "Hullo, sir? There's a man on the line says he wants to speak to one of the chief officers. Will you take the call, sir?"

"Switch him through," said Moresby.

"Who is that, please?" asked a different and fainter voice.

"Chief Inspector Moresby speaking."

"Chief Inspector, eh? Well, that should do. Listen, Chief Inspector. I'm ringing up to save you bother. I just want to let you know that I'm committing suicide in a minute or two. Prussic acid. The name is Carruthers. I've left a note, of course; this is just to confirm it. Good-bye." The line went dead.

Moresby joggled the receiver-rest. "Trace that call! It's urgent."

The information came through in under two minutes. "Hampstead 15066: Dr. James Carruthers, 42 Hill Walk, Hampstead."

Within a few seconds, Moresby was speaking to the Detective Inspector of the Hampstead Division. "Go round at once to 42 Hill Walk, Dr. James Carruthers. Don't waste a second. He's threatening suicide. Leave word for one of your men to ring up your surgeon, to follow you. I'll meet you there, and bring a doctor too, in case. Hurry, man."

He had been pressing a buzzer on his desk as he spoke.

Three minutes later he was entering a police car in the yard. With him were a doctor, carrying a bag that contained among other things antidotes for prussic acid poisoning, a detective sergeant, and a fingerprint expert. To look at Chief Inspector Moresby, with his burly, bulky frame and his walrus moustache, you would have thought him a deliberate man, slow off the mark. But when the mark is so often that of sudden or threatened death, it is necessary to be able to move off it swiftly. Moresby was no exception to the rule of Scotland Yard.

A constable met them at the door of the house. An open and broken window in the room next to it told a graphic story of unceremonious entrance.

"Inspector Willis inside?" panted Moresby, running up the steps.

"Yes, sir. With the doctor. Carruthers. Our Dr. Peters hasn't got here yet."

Moresby did not waste time asking if Carruthers was still alive. He hurried into the house. "Willis!"

A voice answered from down a passage. Moresby followed the sound, the other two on his heels, and found himself in a surgery. On the floor a man was lying, bent horribly like a bow, his body supported on head and heels. A scream came from the distorted mouth.

"Prussic acid!" muttered the Scotland Yard doctor. "That isn't prussic acid. It's strychnine. Where does he keep his chloroform? Oh, here." He snatched up a jar that was standing open on the surgery counter and sniffed at it.

Moresby drew the divisional detective inspector into the passage. Neither of them could do anything now; the case was in the doctor's hands.

"I got here within nine minutes after you telephoned, sir," murmured Willis.

"I wonder why the deuce he said prussic acid," murmured Moresby.

The body on the floor had relaxed from its dreadful arch and subsided limply. The two detectives watched from the passage as the doctor bent over it.

He rose to his feet, dusting the knees of his trousers. "He's gone," he said briefly. "That was the last convulsion."

Moresby clicked. It could not by any stretch of responsibility be called his fault, and yet he felt as if he had let the man's life slip through his fingers.

"Very rapid," the doctor was muttering. "How long is it since he was speaking to you on the telephone?"

Moresby glanced at his watch. "Twenty-six minutes."

"I'd been here about twelve minutes before you came," confirmed Willis, with a nod.

"H'm!" The doctor rubbed his chin. "Did he speak to you, inspector?"

"Yes," said Willis. "He was pretty bad, but he spoke once

between the convulsions. He said: 'Changed my mind. Took strychnine'."

"Ah! He said that."

"Yes; and that's all. I tried to get out of him what the right antidote was, but he wouldn't say. The convulsions were coming on pretty quickly." Willis shuddered. "It's an awful way to die."

"Horrible," muttered Moresby. "Wonder why he changed his mind. Poor devil! I'll bet he was sorry he did. There's no one else in the house?"

"No. We had to break a window to get in. Taking a chance, if it was a spoof call; but we risked it. Lucky we did, too."

Moresby was staring down at the body. "No doubt at all about the cause of death, doctor, I suppose?"

"Good heavens, no; there's no mistaking strychnine poisoning. Except for tetanus, of course; and there's no sign of — hullo, though, what's this?" He picked up one of the dead man's hands. On the ball of the thumb was a piece of sticking-plaster. The doctor peeled it off, and revealed a nasty little wound. "Five or six days old, by the look of it, too."

"Could that have given him tetanus?"

"Certainly it could."

A new voice spoke from the doorway. "Dead, is he? Poor chap, poor chap. Tetanus did set in, then?" It was the divisional surgeon, who had just arrived.

"Why do you say that, doctor?" Moresby asked quickly, before the other surgeon could speak.

The doctor looked slightly surprised. "He's been afraid of it for some days, from that wound on his thumb. He didn't get it cleaned up quickly enough, and thought he might have got something in it."

"You knew Dr. Carruthers, then?"

"Very well indeed. Poor fellow. I should have liked to be with him at the end. It must have been remarkably quick, for tetanus?"

"Yes, far too quick," put in the headquarters surgeon. "Anyhow, we know it wasn't tetanus. It was strychnine." The newcomer was put in possession of the facts.

While the doctors talked, Moresby and the divisional man moved into the consulting-room which adjoined the surgery.

"He'd sent everyone out of the house, you see," remarked the latter.

Moresby nodded absently. "Yes. He's married, I suppose?

Your doctor had better take on the job of breaking it to her. What sort of a woman is she?"

ᴹI don't know her, only by sight. Fine-looking lady. It'll be a shock to her. They'd got a reputation round this for being pretty well wrapped up in each other. What he wanted to do it for beats me. He'd got a good practice, and a fine wife. If you'd asked me, I should have named him yesterday as the happiest man in Hampstead."

Moresby shrugged his shoulders. "Why do they do it? But we can't say for certain he did yet, not till after the p.m.; though the doctor didn't seem to have much doubt. Funny that, thought about the tetanus. But he said strychnine to you himself; that's conclusive enough. I supposed this is the note."

Propped against the inkstand on the consulting-room table was an envelope, addressed: "To the coroner."

"It's not sealed," said Moresby, and drew out the sheet of paper inside.

> To the Coroner,
> Dear sir: For reasons which concern no one but myself, I am taking my life.
> James Carruthers.

"Well, that's to the point, anyhow. I'm not needed here any longer, Willis. You'd better have a look round and see if you can find any of those reasons that concern no one but himself. The coroner will want them, of course. Mrs. Carruthers may be able to help you. I'll be getting along."

"Seems he had another shot at that letter, sir," said Willis from the fireplace. "Look at this."

Lying in the empty hearth was a sheet of charred paper. The ink had turned white in the heat, and by a close scrutiny the words could be made out with fair ease.

> I am sick and tired of this uncertainty, and I can't stand it any longer. What I propose to do may be drastic, but it is better than this wretched existence.
> J.C.

"Humph! Toned it down a bit in the second draft. Wait a minute, though! That wasn't meant for the coroner. See the envelope, sir? 'Leila'. That's his wife. Wonder why he burnt it."

"And why did he write on a single sheet of notepaper to her, and a double one to the coroner?" said Moresby. "He seems to have changed his mind a good many times, what with the prussic acid and so on. I don't think I will go just yet, after all. I'd like to see the case just tidied up first. We haven't seen the vessel that he took the stuff in yet, have we? I'll put Afford on to that, while you go through his papers."

He went out to the hall, where the sergeant he had brought with him was still waiting, and, having given his instructions, passed on to the surgery.

"Well, there's nothing to keep you, gentlemen. If you could show me his bedroom, doctor, I'll have him moved up there."

"You wouldn't like me to wait and break the news to his wife? It will be a terrible blow to her. They were wrapped up in each other. Poor girl!"

"Thank you, sir, but I don't think there's any need. I'll be staying on a bit myself, and I'll see to it."

"I'll be getting along, then, Chief Inspector," said the headquarters surgeon, and went.

As the two were coming downstairs again, after Moresby had been given a brief idea of the layout of the bedrooms, he turned to the other and said suddenly: "I suppose, doctor, that if he had taken prussic acid, as he said, you wouldn't look during the p.m. for signs of any other poison?"

"Not if the cause of death were obviously prussic acid," returned the other, in some surprise, "and that's quite unmistakable; no, we shouldn't."

"And the analyst would test for prussic acid only?"

"He'd test for prussic acid first, of course; and if he found it I'm quite sure he wouldn't test for anything else. Why?"

"Oh, only something I happened to think of," said Moresby, almost apologetically.

To the constable at the door, when he had seen the doctor out, he said: "Don't let anyone in without reference to me, not either of the maids, nor even Mrs. Carruthers herself."

Then he called Sergeant Alford off his job for a moment to help him get the body upstairs.

Chief Inspector Moresby's actions after that were rather curious. He called the finger-print man upstairs to him, took him into the Carruthers' joint bedroom (the body had been put in the doctor's dressing-room), and said: "I want you to test the handles of all the drawers in this room, and of the cupboards, for the dead man's own prints. Take a record of them first, and then see if you can find 'em where I said."

He left the man at work, and went down again to the consulting-room.

"Nothing here that I can find," said Inspector Willis, looking up from the desk. "Everything's perfectly in order, hardly any bills; plenty of patients; can't be money trouble."

"I wish that his wife would come back," grumbled Moresby. "She may be able to save us any amount of trouble." He thrust his hands into his pockets and stood staring down at the burnt papers in the hearth. "Wonder who was the last person to see him alive," he muttered.

"It'd save us a whole heap of trouble, too," lamented Willis, "if coroners didn't want to go so deep into their cases. If I was a coroner, that note would be good enough for me; I wouldn't worry about the reasons. Why shouldn't the poor chaps keep 'em secret, if they want to?"

"Coroners always had long noses, and always will," Moresby opined. He walked across to a bookshelf, stood for a moment examining the titles, and then took down Taylor's *Medical Jurisprudence.*

"It says here," he remarked a few minutes later, "that in strychnine poisoning death usually occurs in about two hours after swallowing the stuff. That looks as if he must have taken it pretty well immediately after his lunch. Those maids ought to know something." He put the book back on its shelf and strolled again into the surgery.

On a top shelf stood a jar labeled: Liq. Strych. It was about one-third full.

Moresby was still looking at it when Sergeant Afford came in to report

"Can't find anything that might have been used as the vessel, sir, except a clean glass in the scullery. Have you been in the dining-room? There's the remains of a meal for one on the table, and a half-full bottle of beer, but no glass. I suggest he took the stuff in beer, and then washed the glass out."

"I wonder why he should do that." Moresby mused.

He looked into the dining-room and then followed Afford to the scullery. On the draining-board stood a single tumbler, globules of water still adhering to its sides. Moresby contemplated it with a puzzled expression. Then he looked searchingly round the room.

The only thing that seemed to hold his attention was an empty beer-bottle, standing on the floor under the sink. While the Sergeant looked in on surprise, Moresby plumped down on his knees and put his nose to the mouth of the bottle, which was unstopped. As he rose he said, in answer to Alford's glance: "That seems to have been washed out, too; at least, there's no smell of beer. Now, why do you think he bothered to do that?"

"Perhaps he didn't, sir, it may have been there for some time. Or perhaps he put the strychnine in the bottle and shook it well up before he poured it out 'Shake well before taking,' " quoted Afford humorously.

Moresby shook his head. "This is the most deliberate suicide I ever struck. Don't touch that bottle and glass."

He marched out of the scullery and lumbered up the stairs into the bedroom.

"How are you getting on, Patterson?"

"Nearly finished, sir. Only this cupboard-knob to do. There's the doctor's prints on three of the dressing-table drawers, but not on any of the cupboards."

"I see," said Moresby; and watched the finger-print man test the last knob, which proved also to be negative. "There are three articles I want you to try next, Patterson." He described the jar in the surgery, and the bottle and glass in the scullery. "Test all of them for prints of any sort."

The man nodded, and went out of the room.

Moresby waited till he had gone and then sat down at the dressing-table drawers, a grotesquely incongruous figure before the usual array of aids to feminine beauty. The finger-print man's voice floated up to him from the hall: "What's the Chief want to bother himself with a suicide for? Waste of time, I call it." Moresby smiled his disagreement; some suicides are remarkably interesting.

With experienced fingers he made a swift examination of the contents of each drawer, paying particular attention to the only one on which the doctor's prints had not been found. His large hands rummaged lightly among stockings and handkerchiefs, old bills, powder-puffs, gloves, discarded bags, scribbled notes, the ordinary paraphernalia of a woman's dressing-table drawers. Only to the notes and bills did he pay any attention. When he got up, however, it was with empty hands; everything he had examined had been replaced exactly as he found it.

He turned his back on the dressing-table and looked slowly round the room, his eyes ranging over every piece of furniture with slow deliberation.

When the divisional inspector came upstairs a little later, Moresby had in his hands a small packet of letters tied up with blue ribbon, and was glancing through one of them with complete shamelessness. In reply to the other's questioning look, he said briefly: "Found 'em in a bit of space behind a drawer in her wardrobe; good hiding-place."

"Well, you've found more than I have," grumbled Willis; and then, more eagerly: "Any use to us?"

The chief inspector handed over the letter he had been reading. "Take a look for yourself."

The other glanced through it, a typical love-letter. Phrases here and there caught his eye. "I miss you more than I can find words to write."

"Your sweetness and gentleness..."

"The only woman in the world for me, and always will be."

"... longing to get back and be with you again."

"This is the goods," said Willis coarsely. "Well, we've found the reason all right." Then he turned to the signature, and his expression changed to one of acute disappointment The letter was signed: "Your own adoring Jim."

"Too bad," he said, as he gave the letter back. "I thought you'd get hold of something good. My sakes, I wonder how long they'd been married, for him to write to her like that. Over six years, to my knowledge." A married man himself, Willis managed to look both scornful and envious at the same moment "Ah," said Moresby, who was not married.

The constable poked his head in at the door. "Mrs. Carruthers has come, sir," he mouthed. "She's in the hall with the sergeant."

"All, right," nodded Moresby; and thrust the packet of letters mechanically into his pocket.

As he ran downstairs he glanced at his watch. The time was twenty minutes to six. He had been in the house for over two hours already.

In the hall a tall woman was standing, her back towards him as he came down the stairs. "But what bad news?" she was saying, in an anxious voice. "I don't understand. Why are you trying to stop me from coming into my own house?

Why are the police here at all? If the house has been burgled, why can't you say so?"

Sergeant Afford looked at Moresby with relief.

"It's worse than burglary, I'm afraid, madam," said the chief inspector gently. "You must prepare yourself for very bad news. Won't you come into the drawing-room with me?" He held the door open for her.

"Not — my husband?" Mrs. Carruthers faltered, one gloved hand to her throat "You don't mean...? He's had an accident? The car...?"

As kindly as he could Moresby told her of the telephone message he had received, and its sequel. Before he had spoken half a dozen words Mrs. Carruthers had swayed, recovered herself, and tottered over to a couch as if her legs could no longer support her. She did not utter a word as Moresby told his story; just sat there and looked at him with her violet eyes painfully wide and an expression in them of almost unbearable horror. Even when he had finished she still sat motionless, as though the very power of movement had left her. Moresby ostensibly turned away to give her time, but kept a wary eye on her in the mirror over the fireplace; he felt extremely uneasy about the possibility of her having a stroke through sheer shock.

At last she managed to force out huskily: "You say... a note? For me?"

"No, madam. It was addressed to the coroner."

"Nothing... for me, at all?"

"I'm afraid not."

She relapsed into her stone-like pose. Moresby fiddled with the ornaments on the mantelpiece. He had thought Mrs. Carruthers a handsome woman when he first saw her; now her face was almost ugly in its strained intensity. From a possible twenty-eight she had changed suddenly to a charitable forty.

"He didn't even — say anything... about me? For you to tell me?" The words seemed forced out of her by a subconscious urge that had taken possession of her impotent consciousness.

"No. He said nothing, except that he had taken strychnine, and not prussic acid. He didn't utter another word."

"Oh." Her unnatural rigidity dissolved. She buried her face in her hands.

Moresby waited patiently.

When her paroxysm was over, he asked her if she felt up to answering a few questions, and proceeded to put them before she could reply, thinking he saw his justification in the quite visible effort with which she pulled herself together and controlled her trembling limbs. He did not ask her at first whether she could throw any light on her husband's action, confining his questions to impersonal matters of fact. Obviously better but still shaken, Mrs. Carruthers answered him in a voice that slowly became steadier, though every now and then a look of utter bewilderment appeared in her fine eyes, as if the realization of what had happened had struck her once more with ever-fresh incredulity.

The story Moresby obtained from her was simple enough. Her husband had been alone in the house at lunch-time. The two servants, who were sisters, had been promised a day's holiday to attend their parents' silver-wedding festivities, and had left the house soon after eleven o'clock, after setting the table with cold food for the doctor's lunch. She herself had been lunching at the flat of a friend in Kensington, whose name and address she gave; after lunch she and her friend had gone to the West End to do some shopping and had had tea at one of the big stores, whence she had come straight home. When had she left the house in the morning? At about a quarter past twelve, and her husband was still out on his rounds; he rarely got in to lunch before half-past one.

Moresby approached the delicate subject of Dr. Carruthers' reasons for his action, but Mrs. Carruthers could offer no help at all; she simply could not understand it. They had been so happy together. Nor could she understand how her husband could have done such a thing without leaving any word for herself at all, and pressed Moresby again and again on the point; she seemed to think that he must have found something and be concealing it from her. At last Moresby told her of the charred paper in the hearth; could she suggest what the "uncertainty" might be to which he referred?

"Oh!" Mrs. Carruthers cried. "Oh, I see now. Oh, why didn't you tell me before? Poor, poor James."

"What do you see, madam?" Moresby asked patiently.

"He was so terribly afraid of getting tetanus from a bad place he had on his thumb. It — it was really a morbid fear. He was convinced that he would get it and die. I tried to joke him out of it, but for the last week he has been getting more and more depressed. Oh, how terrible — how terrible!

He might never have had it at all. Inspector, haven't you learned everything you want now? I can't answer any more questions. I simply can't. Oh, please leave me alone now."

As, in fact, he had now learned everything he wanted, Moresby did leave her, with a few clumsy words of sympathy.

In the hall he collected his men and glanced enquiringly at Patterson, who told him in a low voice that he had found the doctor's finger-prints on all three articles. Alford and Patterson were then packed into the police-car and sent back to Scotland Yard, and Moresby offered to stroll back to the district station with Willis, "to help get out of the report."

"Phew!" said Willis, as they got underway. "Nasty business that. Made me miss my tea, too. What do you say to a glass of beer before we go to the station, Mr. Moresby? This is a very good house we're just coming to."

"Yes," said Moresby.

They turned into the private bar, empty but for themselves. "Surprised to see you taking so much trouble over a suicide, sir," remarked Willis, when the barman had served them and gone. The room was cut off from the other bars, and their voices could not be overheard.

Moresby looked at him quizzically. "So you think the doctor committed suicide, Willis, do you?"

"Don't you, Mr. Moresby?" asked Willis, in astonishment

"I do not," Moresby replied with energy. "I know he was murdered; but I'm bothered if I know how to prove it."

Part 2

"HOW DO YOU make out that it was murder, sir?" asked Willis.

"I'll tell you," said Moresby. "There were a number of curious little facts, you remember, that you wouldn't expect in a suicide case. The doctor ringing up, the washed glass, still more the washed bottle, the burnt note to his wife, the open chloroform jar on the surgery counter as if he'd been trying to give himself the proper antidote to his own poison; the whole place reeked of chloroform. But what put me on to the idea that things mightn't be so simple as they looked was his changing his mind from prussic acid to strychnine. Why on earth should he change his mind from a quick, not too painful poison to the most painful of the whole lot? The only reason I could see was that he had the strychnine in him already, knew his case was hopeless, and intended to finish himself off less painfully; but the strychnine convulsions caught him and stopped him getting at the prussic acid at all."

"Coo!" said Detective-Inspector Willis unprofessionally.

"Somebody wanted Dr. Carruthers out of the way, Willis — someone who knew that there was quite a possibility of him getting tetanus, and knew, too, that the symptoms of strychnine poisoning are pretty well the same as those of tetanus. I haven't the least doubt that the doctor's death was intended to be put down to tetanus; and with his own fears so widely expressed, it wasn't anticipated that there'd be any trouble about the death certificate. But just to make things certain, that letter addressed to his wife was left somewhere handy, to be found if it was wanted and not if it wasn't."

"But — wasn't it a genuine letter?"

"Genuine so far as the doctor had written it but not genuine so far as its meaning went. It was the back page torn off a longer letter, if I'm right and it referred to something quite different and I shouldn't be at all surprised if it wasn't the possession of that letter, and the realization of what those words could be made to imply, that was responsible for the doctor's death."

"But the letter to the coroner, sir, and him ringing you up. Oh, I see. You mean it wasn't him on the telephone at all?"

"Oh, yes it was. I'll tell you what happened. The doctor came in, had his lunch, poured himself out a glass of beer, and drank it off. It wasn't till he'd got it down that he realized how bitter it was. 'That's funny,' he thinks. 'Tastes almost as if there's something in it And yet it's a new bottle. Well, well.' And he takes something to get rid of the bitter taste — a bit of cheese, perhaps. Then he thinks: 'Now's my chance. Servants out. Leila's out I'll have a scout round.' Upstairs he runs, and starts going through his wife's dressing-table drawers."

"Why ever did he do that, sir?"

"Because he was her husband, and desperately in love with her, and therefore jealous; and therefore suspicious; and he's got a pretty good idea, and perhaps more than an idea, that she isn't as true to him as he'd like. Well, he goes through two drawers, and in the third he finds that bit torn off his letter, in an envelope on which he himself had once written 'Leila.' And at about the same time, I should imagine, the first convulsion comes along. He knows all right then; he's been poisoned, with strychnine. He runs down to the surgery as soon as he can move, and sees there's a good deal less in the strychnine jar than there should be; that makes him certain. He gets down the chloroform jar, and starts trying to dope himself. He daren't call another doctor in, because that would give away the fact that he's been poisoned; and his one idea now is to shield the person who poisoned him, even at the risk of his own life. Perhaps he doesn't care much for life now in any case, knowing what he knows at last.

"So between the spasms, instead of going on doping himself, he carries that beer-bottle out to the scullery, empties it and rinses it out, and the glass, too, and writes that note to the coroner. By that time he knew it was hopeless; he couldn't save himself now even if he wanted to, and the convulsions are coming on quicker and quicker; he can hardly drag himself about between them. So he rings us up at Scotland Yard, and then crawls back to the surgery to get the prussic acid. But he's left it too late. He can't even stand up. He has to stick it out. That's all."

"You mean... Mrs. Carruthers?"

"His wife put the strychnine in the beer-bottle before she left home. She murdered him all right, Willis. But we'll never get her. He's covered her traces too well. My goodness, he must have loved her."

"But — why did she, sir? Where's the motive?"

"In my pocket man. Those letters. You made a bad mistake there, Willis. Jimmy isn't such an uncommon name, you know. Besides, she called him 'James.' Those letters weren't in the same handwriting as the note to the coroner."

"Oh! But you've got them, Mr. Moresby. Surely...?"

"No, we can't do a thing, that I can see. It'll give her a nasty jar when she finds they're gone; but the evidence of suicide is too strong for us. And, of course, I may be wrong from beginning to end; there's always that possibility. But, mark my words: if, not too long ahead, Mrs. Carruthers marries a man whose Christian name is James, that will prove me right."

Eleven months later Detective-Inspector Willis received a cutting from *The Morning Post*. There was no letter with it, but the paper in which it was folded bore the address of Scotland Yard.

The cutting ran as follows:

"Grey — Carruthers. On November 19, at St. Agatha's, N.W., James Roland Grey, second son of Robert Grey, of Wellington, Dorset, lo Leila Joan Carruthers, only daughter of Mr. and Mrs. Herbert Thomas, of The Mount, Bishop's Stratford; very quietly, owing to mourning in bride's family."

White Butterfly

ROGER SHERINGHAM FROWNED at the paper in his hand.

"Well, Mr. Sheringham?" asked his guest, in tones of resignation.

"This is most disturbing, Moresby," said Roger. He had been amusing himself for the last half-hour by testing the word reactions of Detective Chief Inspector Moresby. The results indubitably proved the chief inspector to be an introvert, a potential murderer, and a trafficker in illicit drugs.

"Most disturbing," he repeated, eyeing the burly form of his guest with a new interest. "Have some more beer."

"Well, thank you, Mr. Sheringham. I don't mind if I do."

As he replenished the tankards Roger acquainted Moresby with the discoveries he had just made.

"Ah, well," said Moresby comfortably, "it's a wonderful science, this psychology, I expect. Why don't you apply it to this affair at Clearmouth?"

Roger pricked up his ears. "What affair at Clearmouth?"

"What you haven't heard of it, Mr. Sheringham?" grinned Moresby maliciously. "Well, there. But it hasn't got into the papers, so perhaps you wouldn't."

"Tell me," Roger demanded.

Moresby took a deep pull at his tankard, wiped his walrus moustache with some care, and told him.

The county authorities (said Moresby) had been perturbed by the rumours concerning the disappearance of a certain Mrs. Warrington from her home in the small seaside town of Clearmouth. Mrs. Warrington, a pretty and charming but somewhat volatile woman, had not been seen for about six weeks. Her husband, who was a man of some consequence in Clearmouth, being the little town's only solicitor, had confided to a couple of close friends, under the strictest promises of secrecy, that she had left him to go to her lover and that he had no expectation of ever seeing her again; nor indeed would he take her back should she try to return.

There had been a scene during the evening she left when Warrington had first discovered the intrigue. According to his account she had flung in his face the information that it had been in progress for two years, that she had never cared for him, and had married him only for his position, which at the time of their marriage had certainly been a great deal better than hers.

He had upbraided her, and she had retorted by taunting him with having been deceived so successfully and so long. Repeated questions failed to bring out the name of her lover, and Warrington could only gather that he was a married man, that the plans discussed by the two for over a year were now ready, that the man was going to get a divorce from his wife in order to marry Mrs. Warrington as soon as her own divorce was through, and that evidence enabling Warrington to file his petition for this would shortly be offered him.

Mrs. Warrington appeared to feel no shame, and Warrington was thunderstruck by the revelation of her real character, hitherto quite unsuspected by him.

That this scene, or something like it, had certainly taken place was confirmed by the servants, who had heard the raised and angry voices.

In the end Warrington had given his wife a week in which to leave the house. She had thanked him ironically, and cut down the period to half an hour. Her lover was staying in the neighbourhood, she told him, and she would simply take a small case to hold her jewels and a few necessaries and leave at once; the rest of her clothes could be sent on later, when she was able to furnish an address, or maybe she would never send for them at all as she wished to take into her new life nothing that would remind her of the distasteful old one.

She had then flounced up to her bedroom, and shortly afterward had left the house on foot. The servants did not hear her leave, for the time of her departure, according to Mr. Warrington, was after half-past eleven and by then they were in bed.

Since then, Mr. Warrington informed his close friends, he had not heard from her, nor expected to do so; and once the first shock had worn off, considered that he was well rid of her. As to the identity of her lover, he had not the least idea; and a search of her room and belongings since she went had revealed nothing.

The close friends then went out and, overlooking their promises, spread the good news far and wide.

So much for Mr. Warrington's story. Subsequent gossip, on the other hand, was quite different.

Boiled down, and with the toothsome details steamed out of it, this amounted in substance to the conviction that Mr. Warrington had killed his wife that evening, taken the body out to sea in his convenient little motor-launch and there buried it, without benefit of clergy. The circumstantial story which he subsequently told, so the gossips affirmed, had been carefully thought out and divulged to the close friends under pledges of secrecy because Mr. Warrington knew that this was the surest way of broadcasting it without embarrassment to himself, and he had chosen the friends in question with a canny eye to their fallibility in the matter of solemn pledges. So if Mr. Warrington himself was harshly treated by the gossip, the friends, too, did not altogether escape.

"And the authorities believe there's something in the rumours?" Roger asked, when Moresby had finished.

"There's no evidence for or against the man's story, Mr. Sheringham. Not a jot. But if he is lying — well, it wouldn't be the first case where the police were put on the track by local gossip, would it?"

"No. But usually there's a body to exhume, and that makes the real point of departure for the case. Here, I take it, there's nothing. What have the police done?"

"Oh, they've questioned Warrington, of course, and searched the house. But he sticks to his story, and, of course, he's up to every trick of the law; and as for the house, there was nothing incriminating at all. I happen to know about it because the super down there's a friend of mine, and he consulted me unofficially. He told me that when Warrington was away they even probed the flower-beds with iron rods, and any other place in the garden that looked as if it had been disturbed lately, but they couldn't find a thing. No, it looks as if he'd got away with it all right."

"They really do think he killed his wife, then?"

"They're not satisfied that he didn't," corrected Moresby, with official caution.

Roger smiled. "And what do you want me to do about it, Moresby?"

"I wouldn't want you to do anything, Mr. Sheringham. But it did occur to me, since they can't very well send for us just on the strength of a bit of local gossip, that if you did happen to be taking a bit of a holiday soon in the neighbourhood of Clearmouth, I could give you a note to the super there and I wouldn't say that he mightn't mind having a bit of a chat with you."

"Oh, you wouldn't?" Roger laughed. "Very well, Moresby. I'm due for a bit of a holiday in any case. I'll go down to Clearmouth tomorrow. You can write that note here and now."

ROGER PRESENTED HIS note at the headquarters of the County Police two days later. Superintendent Fisher, a bulky, red-faced, friendly man, made no bones about being pleased to see him.

"We're in a difficult position, you see, Mr. Sheringham," he told Roger as they sat together in his office. "Between you and me, there's a grave suspicion that the man's made away with his wife. But we've nothing to go on. Nothing at all. His story holds water and unless we can find the body we can't do a thing. And since that's probably at the bottom of the sea a couple of miles out, we don't stand much chance of finding it."

"You think he buried her at sea, then?"

"It'd be his best move, wouldn't it? We can't get any evidence about his launch being out that night, but if he killed her, that's about what he did."

"I wonder," said Roger.

The superintendent looked at him sharply. "You don't agree?"

"Oh, I don't say that. In any case it's impossible to say what he might or might not do till I've had a look at him. I'll call on him this afternoon. I shall be a wealthy manufacturer of electric belts and I want to make my will. I'm staying at Clearmouth for a holiday, and I understand the bathing's dangerous. I'm consulting a strange solicitor because I don't want to let my own solicitor know of a change I'm making in the disposition of my fortune after death."

The superintendent laughed heartily. "Very well, Mr. Sheringham. And perhaps after you've made your will you'll come and tell me what your impressions were."

"Certainly I will. And, of course, the first thing I've got to try to decide is whether the man seems capable of murder at all. Very few people are. If he isn't, he's probably telling the truth about that last evening with his wife. We mustn't after all lose sight of that possibility."

"Oh, of course, it's quite on the cards that the lady's alive and well with her gentleman-friend, and all our trouble's for nothing," agreed the superintendent. It was, however, clear from his tone that he considered the possibility a remote one.

Roger went out to catch his bus.

Clearmouth proved to be a charming little old-fashioned town. Lying a mile or two up an estuary, it had escaped the appalling fate which has overtaken most charming towns on the South Coast during the last couple of decades. It contained no banana-stalls, no charabancs, and scarcely any horrid little bungalows; but it did contain a quantity of scandalmongers.

The house in the cobble-pavemented main street in which Mr. Warrington had his offices was in keeping with the rest: a mellow little Queen Anne affair with the tint of a ripe peach. Its bay-windows and carved door-frames almost reconciled Roger to the half-hour's delay before he was admitted to the presence. Mr. Warrington, he gathered in casual chat from the clerk in charge, was a very busy man.

Then a rubicund face, almost exactly matching the ripe colour of the brick outside, was poked abruptly round one of the carved doorframes, a rich, fruity voice that harmonised excellently with the face inquired for Mr. Merribrook, and a plump little hand waved a simultaneous welcome and invitation into the adjoining room. The interview had begun.

Sitting in a comfortable armchair, Roger studied his quarry. If Mr. Warrington, plump, red-faced and jolly, really was a murderer, he was as unlike the popular idea of one as he was unlike the popular idea of a solicitor. To Roger he appeared more like a modern edition of the Cheeryble brothers, with his fruity little chuckle that punctuated almost every other sentence, whether called for or not. Was it possible, Roger wondered as the interview progressed, that such a chuckle could get on a wife's nerves until she could bear it no longer and took to a lover as a kind of relief?

Mr. Warrington might look like a combination of a Cheeryble brother and a hunting squire, but he was a shrewd man. Roger realised that soon enough, to his own discomfort, for the solicitor's questions concerning his alleged electric-belt business were so searching, and, as time went on, even so artful, that Roger had difficulty in keeping the discussion on the topic of his mythical family. He began to regret his semi-humorous choice of so impossible a profession; the more as he thought he detected an increasing twinkle in the other's blue eye.

The disposal of the electric-belt manufacturer's wealth went on. Legacies were made to imaginary aunts, nephews, nieces and even cousins, till Roger was hard put to it to invent their names; and still he could not make up his mind whether the man sitting on the opposite side of the table was a potential murderer or not. He tried to imagine Mr. Warrington in a rage.

Undoubtedly he might possess a violent temper. But was he not shrewd enough to control it? Or was he capable of carrying out a murder planned in advance? What were the secret springs under that hearty, squire-like exterior? For the life of him Roger could not decide. Was there even a haunted expression at the back of the man's blue eyes, a hint of tragedy, remorse, fear, anything you like? If there was, Roger could not discern it.

His imagination began to flag. He mumbled something about having forgotten his notes. Might he come in again tomorrow? Mr. Warrington agreed that he might and made a note of the appointment. His mission still unfulfilled, Roger rose to go, not too well pleased with himself. Hearty Mr. Warrington, now heartier than ever, rose too, his eyes twinkling.

"Well till tomorrow, then, Mr. Sheringham."

"Yes," nodded Roger, and then jumped. "Eh?"

"Oh, I recognised you at once. You know, you didn't carry that electric-belt business off very well," chuckled Mr. Warrington. "Why electric-belts, after all? In fact, why this interview at all?"

Roger had succeeded in getting control of himself. He decided in a sudden inspiration to try shock tactics.

"Because," he said deliberately, "I want to size you up, Mr. Warrington, in view of all these rumours about you."

"I'm honoured." Mr. Warrington did not seem in the least put-out. On the contrary, he appeared much amused. "You wanted to find out whether I'm a potential murderer, I suppose. Well, well, I knew the police were interested in this absurd gossip; after all, it's their duty to be so; but I didn't know I'd attracted the amateurs. Dear me, if this kind of thing goes on I shall have to offer a large reward to Marian to make herself known. If I've learned anything about her now, that should do the trick.

"As it is, I can't even have the divorce papers served on

her. Seriously, Mr. Sheringham, instead of trying to make me out a murderer, which I'm not, why don't you try to trace Marian for me? That would be much more useful work, and I'd be quite ready to offer you a substantial fee in the event of success." He smiled inquiringly.

"I intend to trace your wife, Mr. Warrington," Roger said significantly, "And there'll be no question of fee."

"Oh, just as you like. Still, let me give you a pointer. Try an interview with our local philanderer, Major Cresswell, out at Filleys — about a mile along the Axminster road. I don't say he can help you, but if anyone round here can he's the most likely person."

Somewhat stiffly Roger took his leave. He did not usually mind having his leg pulled, but there were occasions when it seemed to him out of place.

Pondering, he walked absently through the sunny little town and took the first road that offered on the other side. He felt he needed exercise, to help in sorting out the impressions of this ambiguous interview. Not even the last exchange had been able to make up his mind about Warrington. Glancing at a signpost, he saw that he was on the Axminster road. Glancing, twenty minutes later, at a name on a gate, he saw that he was abreast of Filleys. He turned in at the drive a little defiantly. Chance and no set purpose had brought him here. Very well. He would see what chance had to offer.

Filleys was one of those box-like Georgian houses, and Roger estimated that its grounds, and a field or two which obviously belonged to it, covered about six acres. The people living here would be comfortably off though not wealthy.

This time, discarding subterfuge, he sent in his own name and asked for Major Cresswell. The message came back that Major Cresswell was in the garden, and would Mr. Sheringham join him there. Led by a neat parlourmaid through a long, high-ceilinged drawing room, Roger took the path indicated to him through the wide-open French windows to the rose garden, where the major was pottering.

If Major Cresswell was Clearmouth's local philanderer, he certainly did not look the part. A tall man with a clipped moustache and the typical soldier's small, round head, he advanced briskly, his face questioning. Roger realised that, this time, his name conveyed nothing.

"Good morning," he began, with a briskness to match the

other's. "I'm sorry to interrupt you, Major, but I'm making a few inquiries concerning the disappearance of Mrs. Warrington, and I understand that you can help me."

The major first looked astonished. Then he frowned. "Did Warrington tell you that?"

"Yes," Roger replied deliberately.

The major's frown deepened. "Did he tell you why?"

"No."

"Then I will. Warrington suspected me of having an affair with his wife. The idea's absurd, of course, but the man was insanely jealous. I suppose this is a piece of petty spite."

"Then you can't tell me anything?"

"No more than anyone else can around here, and no doubt you know that. I suppose you're from county headquarters?"

"I came over from there this morning," Roger agreed, realising that the other had mistaken him for a plain-clothes man.

"Well, I'm afraid I've nothing to tell you. Wish I had." The major began to thaw. "How are you fellows getting on, eh? Got any clues?"

"Not much yet, I'm afraid."

"No. Nasty business. Gives the neighbourhood a bad name."

"That's a lovely Mme Jules Bouche," Roger said suddenly. It was one of the few roses he could name, and he seized the opportunity eagerly. There is nothing like meeting a man on his own hobby to gain his confidence.

The major's eye lightened at once. "You a rose-grower? Yes, by Jove —" He was off.

Chatting amiably, the two men circled the rose garden. As they walked a butterfly, an ordinary cabbage white, fluttered down and settled in a friendly way on the major's sleeve. Still chatting, the mayor swooped down on it with cupped hand, held it by one wing, and tore it in two like a scrap of white paper. "Don't often get a chance like that," he said. "Too many of those about this year. They've hardly left me a single lettuce."

At that moment a tall lady appeared in the drawing-room window and called commandingly. The major's face took on the expression of a small boy who has not washed behind the ears.

"By Jove, yes, that reminds me. I promised — yes, well,

I'm sorry, inspector, or whatever you are, but I can't help you. Er — you'll excuse me if —"

"Of course," said Roger, and turned towards the drive. His way took him close enough to the house to afford a good view of a massive lady with a large nose and several determined chins, who appeared capable of dealing adequately with any number of small boys who had omitted to wash behind the ears.

As Roger turned out of the drive into the road again a white butterfly was circling aimlessly above the gate.

"You'd better not go in there, Miss Butterfly," Roger told it. "There's a murderer of your sort about, at all events."

But seated again in the superintendent's little office a couple of hours later, Roger had to confess that his interview with the possible other kind of murderer had been mainly negative. He recounted its progress and admitted the debacle in the end, while the superintendent shook a sympathetic head.

"He advised me to go and see a Major Cresswell, and I did; but, of course, with no results. The local philanderer, Warrington called him. I gather he was jealous. Well, it's all very difficult, Superintendent. I hardly know what to say."

"Difficult it is, sir, and that's a fact," agreed the superintendent heartily.

Roger stared at his shoes. It was not often that he found himself unable to make up his mind about a man, but Warrington certainly had him flummoxed. On the surface so genial, so humorous, yet underneath — what? In any case, there was so little to go on. What were Warrington's hobbies? According to his own account, the man seemed horrified by his wife's infidelity, but what about himself? Was there even another woman?

"Tell me, Superintendent," Roger said suddenly, "what's your opinion of the man? Your own private, personal opinion?"

The superintendent, who had been ruminating too, roused himself with a jerk. "Eh? What's that, sir? Oh well, I've always found him a very pleasant gentleman, speaking personally, but it's true he has got a bit of a reputation for chasing the ladies. Can't leave them alone, they say. But I dare say that's all gossip, too. We get a lot of gossip round here."

"He has, has he?" Roger sat up. "If true, that's important." He considered. "You've never heard whether there's supposed to be a special one, have you?"

"Well, I believe there's been a goodish bit of talk lately about him and Mrs. Colbrook. At any rate, they say his car's been seen standing more than once outside her house. Mrs. Colbrook's a widow — pretty, she is, too — and lives in a little house, well, not much more than a cottage it is, out Lampton way, about eight miles from Clearmouth. Right in the country, she is, hardly another house in sight. Very convenient, people said."

"That's most interesting, Superintendent."

"But it doesn't help us much with Mrs. Warrington."

"Doesn't it? I'm not so sure." Roger spoke energetically. "Look here, let's try to reconstruct what might have happened, just from our very slight knowledge of the man: assuming, of course, that murder was committed. He's got a corpse on his hands, that's the position. Never mind for the moment how he came to kill her. Well, what's he going to do with it?

"There's the sea, of course. But somehow I'm not so sure. I don't think I should like to trust the sea myself. Weights can break away. Clothes tear, ropes rot, chains rust. There are plenty of cases in criminal history where the sea has given up its murdered dead too quickly for convenience, and he'd know all about that. No, the sea may have a fifty-fifty chance, but no more. In any case, for our argument we'll eliminate the sea.

"So what else? Did he burn the body piecemeal? Did he try to dissolve it in acid? There'd be some kind of evidence for anything like that. No, he must have hidden it. And that amounts to hiding it in the ground — burying it. Well, where did he bury it?"

"Sounds like a tall order, to work that out."

"It does. But we can get a few pointers at least. We're dealing with a clever man, obviously, in spite of his appearance, and sometimes cleverness itself offers its own clues. We can be sure, for instance, that he didn't bury it in his own garden, or on any piece of ground that could be traced to him. On the other hand —" Roger paused. "On the other hand, the ground must have been familiar to him. We can take it for granted that he did the work at night. Well, he wouldn't go off into the darkness and just take any piece of land he came to. It would have to be a piece of land where he could be reasonably sure that the body would remain undiscovered."

"We're fairly close to Dartmoor here," put in the super-intendent.

"Fairly, but not close enough," Roger countered. "He got the job done quickly. It must have been between midnight and four or five a.m. That allows no time to get to Dartmoor and back, and dig a grave. And knowing our man, we can assume that he dug a real grave, not a shallow hole. How long would that take? Not less than three hours. Probably four. That only leaves an hour or so for the journey. I'd wager Mrs. Warrington's body, if it was buried at all, is within fifteen miles of Clearmouth."

"Maybe," said the superintendent "Maybe."

"And what else can we deduce?" Roger went on, with growing enthusiasm. "Why, one thing, surely. Our murderer has all his wits about him. He's not going to dig in hard, stony round. He's going to choose some place where the digging's easy. He lives in the country; he knows land; and he knows that easy digging doesn't necessarily follow from a soft surface, or grass or marshy stuff and so on. It means land that's been worked.

"Well, what have we got to date? That the burial spot is a piece of cultivated ground within fifteen miles of Clearmouth familiar to the murderer. And, we can add, where a standing car would be hidden or would arouse no comment from the rustic beholder. Well!" exclaimed Roger, jumping to his feet, "we know of a place that answers all those requirements, don't we? It all depends on one thing. Are the fields surrounding Mrs. Colbrook's cottage put down to pasture this year or are they in com or roots?"

The superintendent stared. "Mrs. Colbrook's?" he repeated, in a voice of complete bewilderment.

"Certainly," Roger replied briskly. "It's worth a trial, at any rate. Come along, Superintendent. Get a couple of constables, with spades. We can be there in your car in under an hour."

"But what's Mrs. Colbrook got to do with —"

"Come on, man!" cried Roger dancing with impatience. "I tell you, I've got a hunch. Don t waste time."

Roger had a way with him. In less than an hour a still bewildered and openly skeptical superintendent, accompanied by two equally puzzled constables, was surveying with Roger the fields surrounding a solitary cottage that lay a couple of miles off the main road. As the superintendent had said, not another house was in sight.

"Well, perhaps you'll tell me where we're to begin digging, Mr. Sheringham," said the officer heavily.

Roger, who had not the least idea either, was still convinced that he was on the right track. He threw his eyes over an orderly field of roots lying to their left.

"It's a good farmer who owns this land," he murmured. "Those swedes are planted as straight as an arrow-flight. Except — except," Roger said loudly, "for that patch near the centre. Of course! That's what he did. He lifted the roots, put them to one side, and replanted them afterward. Oh, the cunning fellow! But being pressed for time, and rather raided, and working in the faint dawn, he didn't get the rows quite straight. Come along, men. That's our place."

"We must get permission first, Mr. Sheringham," panted the superintendent in Roger's rear.

"Permission nothing," Roger said over his shoulders. "I'll take responsibility. I'll put the first spade in."

Ten minutes later the grins had disappeared from the faces of the two constables. One of them looked up from the work and said: "This ground's been dug over recently, and that's a fact."

Forty minutes later, the mystery of Mrs. Warrington's whereabouts had been solved, very definitely.

The superintendent did not stint his praises before he left to obtain a warrant for the arrest. "Though how you hit on Major Cresswell instead of Mr. Warrington, sir, still beats me."

Roger looked at him dumbly. "Major Cresswell?" he just managed to repeat.

"Yes. I wondered at the time why you should want to know my opinion of him, and seem so interested in the talk about him and Mrs. Colbrook. It was real smart of you, Mr. Sheringham."

Roger said nothing. He had the wit to realise that there had been a misunderstanding: the superintendent had thought he was still asking about the major when his mind had progressed to Warrington. In any case, the reasoning had been correct from the data supplied.

"Oh, Major Cresswell, yes," he said rapidly. "You see, I saw his wife. A very determined lady. And the major very much under her thumb. Just imagine the situation: Mrs.

Warrington arrived at midnight, hysterical, demanding to be taken in and this and that. He lost his head, no doubt, when he found he couldn't quieten her. Terrified of his wife hearing. Yes, it's quite easy to reconstruct what happened."

A sudden thought struck him. The case was by no means solved yet. The finding of Mrs. Warrington's body, even in the vicinity of a house occupied by Major Cresswell's mistress, did not necessarily mean that he was the murderer. There was no real evidence to connect him with the crime. Warrington was a clever man. Suppose he had an insane grudge against the major, and had buried the body here himself to throw suspicion on the man whom he suspected of seducing his wife — there were all sorts of possibilities.

"Wait a minute, superintendent," he said. "I don't think I should apply for that warrant yet You see, we've no real evidence that —" He broke off. His eye had caught a white object lying on the ground a few yards away.

He went over and examined it. There were two tiny white scraps, one wedged against a stalk on the ground, the other caught up in the leaves of a plant Roger picked them up carefully and gave them to the superintendent.

"You'd better take these. Murderers don't seem able to keep well away, do they?"

The superintendent looked at the two broken scraps lying in his big palm. "What's this, Mr. Sheringham? A white butterfly?"

"The two halves of one. And," said Roger soberly, "they're going to hang a man."

The Wrong Jar

"EH?" SAID ROGER SHERINGHAM sharply. "What's that, Moresby? — "Have some more beer," he added perfunctorily.

"Well, thank you, Mr. Sheringham. I don't mind if I do. — That Marston poisoning case, I was saying," resumed the chief inspector, when his tankard had been satisfactorily refilled. "You've read about it, I suppose. Well, can you see that man Bracey poisoning his wife? I'm not sure that I can. Smashing her over the head with a hammer, yes; that's his type. But putting arsenic in her medicine? No, I shouldn't be surprised to hear that the local police have made a bit of a bloomer there. Not a bit I wouldn't, though that's strictly between ourselves. Anyhow, they didn't call us in so it's none of my business. But if I were you—"

"Yes?" said Roger eagerly.

"You like poking about in that sort of thing, don't you? Well, if you were to go down to Marston and get in touch with this man's solicitors, and offer to do a bit of unofficial nosing around, I shouldn't wonder if you mightn't find something to interest you."

"Look here, give me the facts. I've hardly looked at a paper for the last fortnight. I thought the coroner's jury brought in a verdict of accidental death?"

"They did. But now the local people have arrested the husband. So far as I can make out, it's like this."

A certain Mrs. Bracey (said Moresby), living in the small market-town of Marston, in Buckinghamshire, found herself suffering from some gastric trouble, and called in her doctor. It was apparently a straightforward case, and the doctor treated her on normal lines. The treatment undoubtedly did her good, but she was still confined to her bed.

The Braceys were people of some consequence in Marston. Bracey himself was a builder. He had been trained as an engineer, but finding no opening in that line had bought up a local building firm soon after the war and set out to specialise in steel-concrete work. He had done very well, and the two had become as comfortably off as anyone in the neighbourhood. So far as could be made out from the newspaper reports Bracey was very popular, a big, hearty, jovial man, with a greeting for everyone, whose workmen never went on strike. Mrs. Bracey had been a cut or two above him socially; her father was a regular army officer who had risen to the rank of major-general during the war, but she had never appeared to think that she had married beneath her. She was a particularly charming woman, and her husband, as everyone thought, worshipped her, while she was hardly less in love with him. A phenomenally happy couple, was the opinion of Marston. There were two children.

Mrs. Bracey's illness had seemed to be running its normal course, when one evening her doctor had received an urgent telephone call from Bracey to come at once to Silverdene (as the house was called) as his wife had suddenly been taken very much worse. The doctor, whose name was Reid, was surprised, as he had anticipated no development of such a nature. He found Bracey apparently in a state of great agitation, and Mrs. Bracey very bad indeed. He did what he could, but she died in the small hours of the next morning.

Dr. Reid was no fool. A less conscientious man might have said: "Ah, well; gastro-enteritis; never quite know where you are with it." Not so Dr. Reid. He refused a certificate. The coroner ordered a postmortem, and the cause of death at once became plain. Dr. Reid had been justified. Mrs. Bracey's body contained at least three grains of arsenic. A great deal more must of course have been administered.

The local police at once took the matter in hand with energy. The only possible vehicle of administration which could be discovered was a bottle of medicine, which on analysis was found to be liberally laced with arsenic. By exhaustive enquiry the police were able to account for every minute of the bottle's existence.

It was a new one. Dr. Reid had made it up himself after his morning surgery, an ordinary sedative composed of sod. bicarb., bismuth oxycarb., mag. carb. pond., with aqua menth. pip., or in other words peppermint water. With his own hands he had corked it, wrapped it, sealing the wrapping, and given it to the boy to take round. When it arrived at Silverdene ten minutes later the seal was still intact. There was no possibility of the bottle having been tampered with on the way.

The bottle arrived at Silverdene at twenty-five minutes past ten. Bracey had gone to his office an hour before. The seal was broken and the bottle opened by the professional nurse whom Bracey had insisted upon engaging for his wife, although in such a mild case her services were hardly necessary. The directions on the label stated that a tablespoonful was to be administered every four hours. The nurse at once gave her patient a dose, and subsequent doses were given punctually at half-past two that afternoon and at half-past six. The bottle remained in the sick room all day, and under the nurse's eye the whole time except for one hour in the afternoon when she was off duty from three to four. During that time, it was established, Mrs. Bracey had been asleep and no one had gone into the room.

At about twelve o'clock Mrs. Bracey had complained of a feeling of nausea and just before her lunch she had been sick, which seemed to relieve her. This was such an ordinary symptom of her illness that the nurse had taken it for granted; and as Mrs. Bracey retained her lunch and seemed better for it, the nurse had felt no scruples about taking her usual hour off duty in the afternoon. Mrs. Bracey was just waking up when she came back, and complained again of nausea, accompanied by a burning pain in her stomach. She took her tea, but was unable to retain it. This too had been a common symptom with her during her illness, and the nurse had no cause to attach particular importance to this manifestation of it.

Bracey got home about five o'clock, and at once went in to see his wife, who was again feeling better but still had some pain, though she concealed the fact from her husband. The nurse left them alone together, and Bracey stayed in the bedroom for about an hour, at the end of which he went down to the garden to get some exercise by mowing the tennis-court. He stayed out till dinnertime.

It was not until after the third dose of medicine, at half-past six, that Mrs. Bracey became appreciably worse. She and the nurse both attributed it to a normal development of her illness, and Mrs. Bracey insisted that her husband should not be informed as it would only make him worry unnecessarily. When he went up to see his wife before dinner he was kept out of the sickroom therefore by the pretext that Mrs. Bracey was asleep. By nine o'clock, however, her condition had become so pronounced that the nurse was alarmed, sent for Bracey, and asked him to telephone for the doctor.

No more of the medicine was administered after the dose at half-past six.

At the inquest, of course, the main question was how the arsenic could have found its way into the medicine. A number of facts, already discovered by the police, were brought out by the coroner from Dr. Reid. Contrary to the usual practice, he kept white arsenic in his surgery, in a jar, on the shelves, not in a poison-cupboard. Why? Because he occasionally carried out chemical experiments, and as he and his partner did all their own dispensing he had not considered the habit a dangerous one; as for poison-cupboards, nobody used them outside the hospitals. And there was no question of outside interference here because he had made up the medicine with his own hands and was ready to take full responsibility. Was the arsenic jar kept on the top shelf in the surgery, almost exactly above the jar containing the carbonate of magnesia? Certainly it was, why not? Dr. Reid, a middle-aged man, showed signs of approaching irascibility. Somewhat curtly the coroner told him to stand down.

The surgery used by both partners was a ground-floor room in the house occupied by the other, a younger man of the name of Berry. Dr. Berry confirmed Dr. Reid's evidence. No, he had never considered it a dangerous thing to keep white arsenic in the surgery, in the circumstances. Yes, they did all their own dispensing. Yes, his sister was learning to dispense, but she had not yet taken it over. No, she had never made up a bottle of medicine for a patient. Yes, Dr. Berry had seen her in the surgery that morning.

Miss Berry, rather frightened, was called. She was a fluttery woman, several years older than her brother. Yes, she was learning to dispense. Yes, she had been in the surgery that morning. But not when that particular bottle was being made up. She was helping the house-maid make the beds at about that time.

Dr. Reid was recalled. Yes, Miss Berry had looked into the surgery that morning. No, she had not been there when he was making up this particular medicine. No, there was no possibility that she had inadvertently handed him the wrong jar, because she had handed him no jars at all, because she was not there; he had taken down the jars he needed himself. No, there was no possibility of a muddle in the prescription. The prescription register showed that that had been the only bottle of medicine to be made up that morning.

Was there a chance that he himself had taken down the wrong jar? There was not Dr. Reid had been in practice long enough not to make fool mistakes like that. Besides, all this talk about the jars was beside the point. Evidence had already been given by the official analyst that the medicine did in fact contain all the ingredients which Dr. Reid had put into it if it were a case of accidental substitution of arsenic for one of them, that one would be missing. Did Dr. Reid then stake his professional reputation on the fact that when that bottle of medicine left his surgery it contained no arsenic? With a full realisation of what his answer must imply, Dr. Reid agreed that he did.

The jury however did not agree with Dr. Reid. They found that Mrs. Bracey had died through an overdose of arsenic contained in the medicine made up by Dr. Reid owing to his having taken down the wrong jar from the shelf.

This verdict, imputing to the doctor what amounted to culpable negligence, was tantamount to a verdict of manslaughter against him; but the police made no arrest. It was felt that Dr. Reid's point could not be gainsaid. If arsenic had been accidentally substituted for another ingredient, that ingredient would be lacking; and it was not. The verdict was ignored. Dr. Reid was held to be right in his assertion that when the bottle of medicine left his surgery it contained no arsenic.

The next step in the case was the arrest of Bracey. The reasons for this had not yet been made public, but Moresby had information that it had followed immediately on the acquisition by the local authorities of the information that at the time of his wife's death Bracey had arsenic in his possession. His own explanation was that he had bought it months earlier, in quantity through the ordinary trade channels for use in some experiments he was making in wood-preservation. In support of this, there was clear evidence both that Bracey had been making such experiments and that he had recently obtained excellent results with certain arsenic compounds. Nevertheless it was equally indisputable that arsenic was in his possession.

As for opportunity, he had been alone with his wife and the medicine bottle for an hour. Only on the question of motive were the police at a loss. If they had been French they would have shrugged their shoulders and said: "Cherchez la femme." Not being French they shrugged their shoulders only, but the shrug carried the cynical implication that marriage itself is a motive for murder.

"I see," Roger nodded, when the chief inspector had finished. "After all, they've got logic behind them. We can certainly eliminate an accident on the doctor's part; and so far as opportunity goes, and if nobody else really did enter the bedroom, that narrows it down to Bracey and the nurse. And why the nurse? Anyhow, we must see what we can see. But one thing remains clear enough — it was done from the inside."

"An inside job," Moresby amended, more professionally.

"I think I'll look into it," said Roger.

There was no difficulty with Bracey's solicitors. Their welcome was almost eager, and they undertook to put every possible resource at the disposal of their new ally. In a discussion on the case, however, they were unable to offer any helpful ideas or even to bring forward any new facts of the least importance, though agreeing that the case was narrowed down to those having access to the bedroom between the times of the opening of the bottle and Mrs. Bracey's first serious symptoms at about seven o'clock.

"But of course we mustn't overlook the possibility of some kind of accident on the doctor's part," said Roger thoughtfully, "even if not the particular one suggested at the inquest. Mrs. Bracey was bad earlier in the day I understand."

That was so, but only in the same way as she had been on previous days. It was impossible to say that those two slight attacks were due to the action of the arsenic; not until seven o'clock could arsenic be definitely diagnosed. And there was no possibility of previous administrations; the postmortem had proved conclusively that the poisoning was acute, and not chronic. Owing to the eliminations it was not possible to state with any accuracy the size of the dose, though the analyst estimated it at about five grains. A test of the medicine showed nine grains of arsenic to the fluid ounce. The dose having been one tablespoon, or half a fluid ounce, this agreed quite well with the theory of a single fatal dose.

"Very well indeed," nodded Roger. "Well, now, what about the inmates of the house? The nurse for instance. Nurses have been known to murder their patients just for the fun of the thing. Marie Jeanneret, for instance."

"No doubt, no doubt," agreed the other. "But there is not the slightest evidence of that here. Naturally we have gone closely into her history. She has the reputation of a very respectable woman with a good record; there are no curious incidents connected with her at all."

"A pity," Roger murmured. "It would have been so simple. Well, the servants?"

The servants similarly had been the subjects of close investigation. Not one of them had been in the house for less than five years; they all bore excellent characters; from the butler downwards they were all exceedingly upset at the death of a much-loved mistress, and hardly less so at the predicament of a very popular master; not one of them but was ready to stake everything on the fact of Bracey's innocence.

It was clear too that the solicitor held the same opinion, which Roger thought an excellent sign.

"Well," he said at last, "all I can do is look round. I think I'd like to see Bracey first of all. That can be arranged, I suppose?"

It could be and it was, on the spot. Within half an hour Roger found himself facing the engineer across a table in the county gaol.

Bracey was a large man, with one of those simple red faces which delight publicans and prospective wives. At present his blue eyes wore an expression of pathetic bewilderment, like a dog that has been punished for something it did not do.

"Of course I'll help you all I can, Mr. Sheringham," he said, when he had read the note from the solicitor that Roger had brought with him. "And remarkably good it is of you to lend us a hand. I only hope you won't be wasting your time."

"It won't be a waste of my time if I can get you out of here."

"That's what I meant. They can't keep me here long in any case. They only arrested me because they didn't know what to do. I mean, it's too ridiculous. Me poison Cynthia? Why — why —?"

He was so obviously on the point of breaking down that Roger hurriedly interposed with a question. "What is your own opinion, Mr. Bracey, then?"

"Why, it was an accident. Must have been. Who'd have poisoned her deliberately? She hadn't an enemy in the world. Everyone loved her. It was that fool of a doctor. Made some ghastly mistake, and now he's trying to save his face. Oh, I know they say there couldn't be any mistake, because everything was in the medicine that should have been; but how else can it have happened?"

"We must examine every possibility, nevertheless," Roger said, and went on to ask about the servants.

Bracey was stout in their defence. It was utterly out of the question that any of them could have done such a thing.

Nor was there any other person with a conceivable motive for murder. "I believe the police are nosing round, trying to find out if I haven't been mixed up with some other woman," Bracey said scornfully. "I could have saved them the trouble if they asked me. I haven't even looked at another woman since I first met Cynthia."

"No." Roger stroked his chin. This did not seem to be leading anywhere. "Look here, who was your wife's best friend in Marston?" A wife's best friend knows far more about her than a husband.

"Well, I don't know. She wasn't particularly intimate with anyone. Plenty of friends, but few intimates. I should think she knew Angela Berry as well as anyone."

"That's Dr. Berry's sister, who was called at the inquest?"

"Yes. She used to help Cynthia with the children when they were smaller, before we could afford a nurse. Wouldn't take a penny for it, either. Said she wanted something to do. She and Cynthia got very thick. They haven't seen so much of each other lately perhaps, not since Angela took up helping with the practice, but yes, I should think you might say she was Cynthia's closest friend in Marston."

"I see." Roger mentally noted Angela Berry as a person to whom he could put certain questions about the dead woman which he could not very well put to her husband.

That interview however would turn upon motive; opportunity was the more urgent matter for investigation. On leaving the prison Roger headed his car for Marston again with the intention of making direct for Silverdene.

The trained nurse was still in residence at the house, in case the police wished to question her further, and Roger, having handed the buffer a note from Bracey, asked to see her.

She proved to be a pleasant-faced woman, with greying hair and the usual air of competent assurance of the trained nurse.

She answered Roger's questions readily, with a marked Scottish accent. There were only two periods during which the bottle had been out of her observation: during her hour off duty in the afternoon, when she had gone for a short walk, and while Bracey was with his wife. "As if anyone would think o' that poor man daeing any such thing. A fine mess the pollis have made."

"They seem to think he may have been carrying on with some other woman," suggested Roger.

"Blether! I ken his kind. It's one woman and one only for that sort. Ay, it's grand husbands they make."

"Then what do you think, nurse?"

There, the nurse admitted, he had her. She did not know what to think. It was a mystery to her. She seemed doubtful about the idea of an accident in the surgery; Mrs. Bracey's symptoms, she pointed out, would surely have been much more pronounced had arsenic been present in the medicine from the beginning.

"Then you do think it was murder," Roger persisted.

"Ay," replied the nurse gloomily. "I fear it must have been. Though who could have wanted to murder that poor lamb?"

"And if it is murder, and Mr. Bracey didn't do it, the whole thing boils down to the time while you were out for your walk. Someone must have got into the room then, while Mrs. Bracey presumably was asleep, and put the arsenic in the medicine-bottle. I must see the servants."

Roger saw the servants, but they could not help him. The butler had been on duty all the afternoon, and had let not a single person into the house. There had been two callers, a Mrs. Ayres and a Miss Jamieson, to ask after Mrs. Bracey, but neither of them had come in. Was there any other way into the house? Well, there were the French windows in the drawing-room opening on to the garden. It was just possible, the butler admitted, that someone might have reached them unseen, got inside the house that way, and crept up unobserved to Mrs. Bracey's room.

"Having already watched the nurse leave," Roger added. "But it would have been a great risk."

"A very great risk, sir. The person would have to cross the hall and go up the stairs, which as you see are under observation from here right up to the landing, and I was in and out of the hall all the afternoon."

"And yet I don't see how else it would have been done," Roger said. He had already dismissed the idea that the crime had been committed by someone of the household; apart from any motive, he was satisfied that not one of them was capable of such a thing; it was an outside, not an inside, job. "Well, I suppose I'd better have a word with Mrs. Ayres and

Miss Jamieson. They might have seen someone. Can you give me their addresses?"

He set off for the interviews.

Mrs. Ayres, an elderly lady with a very precise manner, was anxious to help but unable to do so. She had seen no one, she had noticed nothing unusual, she had just left her flowers and gone.

Without very much hope Roger set out to interview Miss Jamieson. He finally ran her to earth at the local tennis club, and had to wait till she finished a set She was a large, well-muscled lady and hit a shrewd ball, and Roger was not unthankful to sit in a deck chair for ten minutes and watch her.

On hearing his name and business she exclaimed loudly that precisely the same idea had occurred to herself, as it would have to the police if they had not all been congenital idiots from the chief constable downwards. But alas, there was no evidence that she could produce to support the theory.

"But it was a woman, Mr. Sheringham," she boomed, mopping her red forehead. "Take it from me. The idea of Tom Bracey's so absurd we needn't even consider it. No, it was some woman who fancied she had a grudge against poor Cynthia."

"Arsenic's certainly a woman's weapon," agreed Roger, who had already reached the same conclusion.

"What I say exactly," Miss Jamieson said, nodding violently. "But it's no use asking me who it could have been, because I've racked my brains and racked 'em, and I can't think."

"I thought of asking Miss Berry if she could suggest anyone who might have had a grudge against Mrs. Bracey."

"Yes, I should do that. Angela would know if anyone did."

"By the way," said Roger, "what time was it that you called at Silverdene?"

"I couldn't say to the minute, but not later than ten past three, because I was playing here by a quarter past I know."

Roger had an idea. "Could you possibly remember who among Mrs. Bracey's friends was here when you arrived, Miss Jamieson? You must have reached Silverdene only just after the nurse went out, you see, so that anyone who was here before you, and who remained here till four, has a complete alibi for that hour."

Miss Jamieson screwed up her eyes and managed to produce five names, of which only Angela Berry was known to Roger. He wrote them down carefully, feeling that he had established something at last however negative. Angela Berry, too, had stayed at the tennis club till nearly dinnertime, so she at all events was cleared.

Roger's next call was on Dr. Reid, whom he was lucky to find at home. The doctor was indignant over the verdict at the inquest and entirely in agreement with Roger's theories. Mrs. Bracey's death was plain murder; the nurse was out of the question; someone must have got into the house at that fateful hour, but he could not even suggest whom.

"Yes, a nice mess those fools of jurymen have got me into," were his last words. "I've had the police round at the surgery half a dozen times, weighing my stock of arsenic, and comparing it with my poison-book."

"I suppose it tallies?" Roger asked perfunctorily.

"No, it doesn't," the doctor chuckled. "I've actually got more arsenic than my records show, which seems to worry them."

"But how could that happen?"

"Well, obviously I must have bought an ounce once and forgotten to enter it up. As I told them, it's at least eight years since I gave up making my own pills, and I can't profess to remember what happened eight years ago."

"And the jar hasn't been touched since?"

"It hasn't."

As he left Dr. Reid's house and walked down Marston High Street in search of that of Dr. and Miss Berry, Roger found himself more at sea than ever. That he was on the right track, he felt sure; but it seemed a track impossible to retrace. Still, one could only go on trying.

Dr. Berry was out and the maid seemed very doubtful whether it was possible to see Miss Berry.

Roger produced a card and scribbled a line on it "Take her this," he said, "and tell her it's very urgent."

The maid returned with the information that Miss Berry would see him.

Angela Berry must have been a plain woman at the best of times; at present her eyes were red-rimmed with crying, and her face ravaged. Her voice was uncertain as she asked her visitor to be seated.

Roger came to the point at once. "I'm sorry to worry you, Miss Berry, but it is literally a case of life and death." He explained briefly his position and ideas, and asked her whether she could name anyone who might have had a grudge against Mrs. Bracey.

Miss Berry hesitated. "N-no. No, I can't."

"Quite sure?"

"Quite," she said, more firmly.

"That's a pity. Well, can you suggest anyone with some other motive for eliminating her? You think Bracey is speaking the truth when he says there was no other woman? He's not shielding anyone? Forgive me; I must speak plainly."

"Certainly not," Miss Berry answered, with a touch of indignation that seemed a little out of place. "Mr. Bracey never — there is no question of such a thing. Mr. Bracey is a very honourable man.'

"I see. Then you can suggest nothing at all? Not even a line along which I might make enquiries? I understand you were Mrs. Bracey's closest friend. Is there nothing at all you can tell me that might help? It's no time for secrets, you know."

"No, nothing at all, I'm afraid," said Miss Berry. She looked at Roger with eyes that slowly widened. "Mr. Sheringham, he's not in — in *danger is* he?"

Roger returned her look. He was not satisfied. The woman's manner struck him as just a little evasive. I believe she does know something, he thought, or imagines she does; something discreditable to the wife, I fancy; there was a touch of reserve; but she won't bring it out unless she's frightened. I must frighten her.

"Yes," he said slowly. "Mr. Bracey is undoubtedly in the gravest danger."

"Oh!" It was a little cry. She clasped her hands on her breast. "Mr. Sheringham, I *know he* didn't do it. He couldn't do such a thing. He's the most upright of men. It's terrible. I — isn't there anything I can do? Shall I go to the police and tell them it *was* an accident — that I was handing the jars to Dr Reid, and must have given him that jar as well as the others? I will if you think it would do any good. I'd do anything. It's too terrible."

"But Dr. Reid has sworn you weren't in the surgery."

"No, I wasn't. But I might be able to persuade him to say that he said that to shield me."

"That might lay you open to a charge of manslaughter," Roger said slowly.

She brushed it aside with scorn. "What does that matter? Anything's better than that Tom — Mr. Bracey should be punished for something he didn't do." She buried her face in her hands. "He — they were my best friends. My only real friends in Marston."

Roger leaned forward. "Miss Berry," he said distinctly, "who did put that arsenic in the medicine-bottle?"

She dropped her hands abruptly, staring at him. "Wh-what did you say?" she asked shakily.

"You think you know, don't you? Please tell me. It's a better way surely of clearing Mr. Bracey by finding the real criminal than by your accusing yourself of all sorts of things you didn't do. Whom have you got in mind?"

She shook her head. "You're mistaken, Mr. Sheringham. I haven't anyone in mind. I — I only wish I had."

Roger stared at her, puzzled. It was true that she was on the verge of hysterics, but even that could not account for the contradictory impression she gave. In spite of the firmness with which she uttered them Roger felt sure that her last words were a lie; she did suspect someone. Then if she were so anxious to clear Bracey, why not give the name?

Hurriedly Roger tried to find a set of circumstances to account for this reluctance. Was it possible that she had been lying all through — lying when she said that Bracey was an honourable man and there was no other woman? Was it possible that there *was* another woman, and that Mrs. Bracey had confided as much to her friend, that Miss Berry knew who this woman was and suspected her, but that she would not name her, thinking that this should be Bracey's decision and he must be the judge of whether he was to shoulder the responsibility or not? Such a theory postulated a guilty knowledge on the part of Bracey, but that was not impossible.

In any case Roger himself was bound by no such considerations, though acting as he was on behalf of Bracey it was not easy to know quite what to do. However, this was only theory. The first thing was to find out the truth; one could decide after that what to do with it.

"Miss Berry," he said meaningly, "are you sure you've told me all you wish to tell me?"

She started, and seemed to hesitate for a moment "Yes," she answered, but in a not very certain voice. "Yes."

"I'd like to remind you that Mr. Bracey is in grave danger."

"He can't be!" she cried, with sudden passion. "It's too preposterous. The police themselves will see that in a day or two. They'll release him. Of course they will. I mean, they *must.* "

She believes it too, Roger thought, marking the conviction in her voice. No, I can't frighten her; she's one of the ostrich type; she believes what she wants to believe, and that's all there is to it. "May I see the surgery?" he asked.

Miss Berry took him through the hall and down a dark passage.

Roger inspected the businesslike little surgery with care. At his request Miss Berry pointed out to him the arsenic jar. It was on the top shelf and certainly above the jar of magnesium carbonate, but it was smaller and by no means so directly above the other as the evidence at the inquest had suggested. Even without the presence of magnesia in the medicine, it would have been an almost inconceivable mistake that one jar should have been taken down for the other. On asking, he learned that the relative positions of the jars had not been changed. Any lingering doubts about the possibility of an accident were dispelled.

Roger assured Miss Berry that he could see himself out

The front door leading on to the small front garden was already ajar. As Roger pushed it wider he jumped for his life, for a loud explosion right in his ear nearly blew the hat off his head.

In the garden outside a small boy mocked him ecstatically.

"You jumped! I saw you. I made you jump. Sux!"

Roger regarded the revolting child coldly. The urchin appeared to be about ten years old, and he was excessively dirty even for that.

"Did you make that bang?" he asked.

"It was a booby-trap," replied the small boy with pride. "I knew you'd have to come out when you'd finished with Aunt Angela, so I put up a booby-trap for you. When you opened the door it went off. And you jumped like anything. Sux!"

"I have a way of dealing with unpleasant children who set booby-traps," said Roger, and grasped the infant by the shoulder. "Is there a nice thick stick anywhere around?"

"What for?"

"Because I'm going to beat you."

"You're not," asserted the child with confidence. "No one beats me, not ever. Mummy doesn't let them. Uncle Robert

wanted to beat me when I stayed here last year, but Aunt
Angela wouldn't let him. When I go to school I'm going to
one of those where they don't punish you. Mummy says so.
She says it's bad for children to be punished. But I shall
punish my children when I'm grown up. I shall punish them
like billy-o."

At that moment an agitated housemaid arrived round
the corner of the house and relieved Roger of his charge.
She was apologetic.

"Did he set a trap for you, sir? I'm ever so sorry. He's
always doing it. Regular little demon, he is. Seems to like
making people jump just for the fun of it."

"I don't!" said the child indignantly. "I do it because I'm
going to be a doctor like Uncle Robert, and I have to begin
studying their reactions."

"A lot you know about such things, I'm sure,"

"I do. I know everything. If you jump far enough when
a bang goes off, it's a reaction, and you have to be cut open
for it. You don't know anything, Effie."

"It's thankful we'll all be when he's gone, sir," confided
the maid to Roger. "He's a handful. Why, only this morning
I caught him in the surgery again. He'd got ever so many
bottles down and was pretending to make up the medicines.
What the doctor would say, I don't know."

"I wasn't pretending," shouted the outraged urchin. "I
was making up real medicine. Doctors have to know about
medicines, don't they? And I can go in the surgery whenever
I like. Aunt Angela said I can. So sux."

"Well, my prescription," said Roger to the housemaid, who
really was a charmingly pretty girl, "is six across the hinder
parts with the whippiest switch you can find. Good-bye."

He went on his way.

As he walked down the road, busy with his thoughts, he
became aware that someone was asking him respectfully if
he was Mr. Sheringham. He admitted as much.

"Been looking everywhere for you, sir. Mr. Dane, him as
is butler at Silverdene, said for me to come and find you."

"Yes?"

"I'm the gardener, sir, and Mr. Dane was talking to me
after you'd gone, and I told him I was working all that afternoon when the mistress died, bedding out the asters. He
thought you'd be interested to know."

"It sounds most interesting; though I can't say asters have ever been favourites of mine. Is that all?"

"Well, Mr. Dane thought you'd like to know, seeing you'd spoken to him about the drawing-room windows."

"Oh!" Roger's expression changed. "Where were you working then?"

"Why, in the bed up against the house there, just outside the drawing-room."

"Were you there from three to four?"

"I was there from two till five, sir. I had to clear it a bit before I could get the plants in."

"Hell!" said Roger.

The whole basis of all his theorising had gone at a blow.

He turned on his tracks and made for the High Street again and the office of the solicitor, his mind working furiously. As he reached the threshold he shrugged his shoulders and said aloud: "Well, that must be the truth, then."

He asked to see the head of the firm again.

The little elderly solicitor looked up with a wry smile. "Well, Mr. Sheringham? Have you solved our mystery yet?"

"Yes," said Roger, and dropped into a chair.

"What's that? You have, eh? Bless my soul!" He adjusted his gold-rimmed glasses and peered at Roger dubiously.

Roger crossed his legs and gazed with Apparently absorbed interest at the toe of his swinging feet "I have, yes. I must have, because it's the only possible explanation. But I've had to readjust my ideas considerably." He recounted the gist of his interviews, and the theory he had based upon them.

"Assuming murder, you see, and taking for granted that the bottle, which had not passed out of Dr. Reid's hands from the time it was filled until it was given to the boy to deliver, was uncontaminated when it reached the sickroom, and relying on my own judgment that none of the inmates of the house was guilty, I was left with only one possible inference — that the arsenic was inserted during the nurse's absence from three till four by someone from outside entering the house through the French windows in the drawing-room, the only apparently unguarded way in. But now we have the gardener's evidence that no one could have entered that way, and so we have to start again from the beginning."

"Yes, yes," nodded the other. "I quite see that."

"So having already proved that only during that period and in that way could the arsenic have been put into the bottle after it arrived at the house, we are obviously forced to the conclusion that it was *not* put in after it arrived at the house. In other words, it was already there."

"God bless my soul! Then Dr. Reid *did—*"

"On the other hand we have Dr. Reid's positive assurance that he didn't, and couldn't have: which I accept. Therefore it was introduced not by Dr. Reid, but by somebody else."

"But I understand that the police are convinced the arsenic must have been inserted after the medicine reached the house, because the first two doses produced no symptoms of poisoning."

"I think we can explain that. No, the real point of the case seems to me the fact that the medicine contained all the proper ingredients, plus the arsenic. You may say that this proves that the arsenic must have been inserted later, but does it?"

"You don't mean — that arsenic was already in the bottle before Dr. Reid made the medicine up at all?"

Roger smiled. "Well, isn't that feasible?"

"It's — just possible, I suppose," hesitated the solicitor. "But hardly feasible, is it?"

"That depends upon who might have left the arsenic there."

"But surely," the solicitor objected, "no one would be so criminally careless."

"That again depends." Roger thought for a moment "As to the first two doses not producing symptoms, a very simple explanation would be that the nurse didn't shake the bottle. Arsenic isn't readily soluble in water, and there couldn't have been a great deal in the medicine. It's a heavy powder, and it sank to the bottom leaving only enough at the top of the bottle to produce mild discomfort. For the third dose the nurse obviously did shake the bottle."

"Yes, yes," approved the little solicitor. "That is a sound point without doubt. Perhaps the nurse may remember."

"She may, but I doubt it."

"But who put the arsenic in the bottle? That is our real puzzle after all."

"1 think," said Roger, choosing his words, "that I know who caused the arsenic to be put into the bottle. And how it was done. But I can't prove it. At this stage the responsible person would certainly deny it I think — yes, I think I'll take a chance. May I borrow your telephone?" He ruffled the pages of the local directory, and called a number. "Marston 693? I want to speak to Miss Berry, please. It's urgent . Please tell her it's Mr. Sheringham." He waited.

"But what are you going to do?" asked the solicitor.

"Prove my case," said Roger shortly. "It's the only possible way — Hullo! Yes? Is that Miss Berry? Listen, Miss Berry, please. You remember telling me that you'd do anything to clear Mr. Bracey? Well, I'm ringing up to advise you what you can do. Just write out the truth, the whole truth, and nothing but the truth, and post it to the police. Yes, I think you understand. I mean, how the arsenic got into the medicine. No, I know exactly; and in two hours' time I'm going to give my knowledge to the police. Not for two hours, I undertake. Let me show you that I really do know by telling you this: the mag. carb. pond, jar was washed out and refilled from the stock cupboard, to make sure that no traces remained. Isn't that so? I'm sure you understand. Put it all in your letter to the police, every detail. Otherwise Bracey will hang. Good-bye."

He hung up the receiver.

"What is all this, Mr. Sheringham? What is all this?"

Roger looked at him. "Did you know that Miss Berry is hopelessly in love with Bracey?" he said abruptly. "She is. And just the sort of person who can believe just what she would like to believe. In this case she found no difficulty in believing that if Bracey hadn't a wife already, he would marry her. So that's why she took advantage of Mrs. Bracey's gastro-enteritis to slip a couple of pinches of arsenic into the top of the mag. carb. pond. jar. The powders are much alike, you see, and so are the symptoms. She saw from the prescription book that there was no other medicine that morning requiring mag. carb. pond.; so if she emptied the jar as soon as Dr. Reid had gone out, washed it clean, and refilled it, she would run no risk of poisoning anyone else. Ingenious, wasn't it?"

"Well, upon my word — but what did she say? What did she say?"

"Nothing. But I think she'll do it."

"But you shouldn't have warned her," squeaked the little solicitor. "It was most improper. You should have laid the theory before the proper authorities. I don't know what to do at all."

"Why, let her have her chance. If she doesn't take it, that's her affair. But let her have it. Though she's not really a very nice person. She had a second line of defence all prepared in the shape of a loathly nephew, whom she's obviously been encouraging to go into the surgery and play with the drugs. Very cunning. Too cunning. But let her have her chance."

"Her chance? I don't understand. What chance?"

"I notice," said Roger drily, "that contrary to all the rules. Dr. Reid doesn't keep his poisons under lock and key."

Double Bluff

"A GRAIN OF CIRCUMSTANTIAL evidence is worth a ton of direct almost every time, Alec," pronounced Roger Sheringham. "Almost every time," he repeated loudly.

The large bulk of Alec Grierson shifted slightly and his eyes jerked back from his book to his host "Is it really? A ton?"

"Well, say a couple of pounds. Counsel for the defence profess to sneer at circumstantial evidence. Naturally. 'Ah, yes', they say, 'but who actually saw Mr. A trousering Miss B's pearls? Then we'd know where we are.'"

"Seems reasonable," opined his audience wistfully.

"Stuff!" Roger was shaping an article for *The Daily Courier,* but his guest did not know that "What about the human factor? How many women identified Adolf Beck as the man who had robbed them — positively swore to him?"

"Haven't the foggiest. How many?"

"That's beside the point," Roger said quickly. "The thing is, they were wrong. The real culprit wasn't even much like Beck. Well, circumstantial evidence eliminates the human factor. A complete chain of circumstantial evidence is the only logical, irrefutable — oh, come in!"

"A Miss Meadows, sir. She says, can she see you?"

Roger stared at Alec. "Meadows? Surely she can't have anything to do with that Monckton Regis case?"

"Couldn't say. Shall I go?"

"No, stay. All right: show her in, Barker."

A minute later a tall, squarely-built young woman in a blue stockinette suit and a small blue leather hat entered the room with an air of complete self-possession. She was not so much pretty as good-looking, with dark hair and a firm mouth, and she gave an impression of health and energy.

"I know you," said Roger, shaking hands. "You're Claire Meadows, the tennis player."

The girl smiled faintly. "At present I'm more notorious as James Meadows' sister. That's why I'm here. I won't beat about the bush, Mr. Sheringham. I know Jimmy's innocent. He couldn't kill a fly. Will you help us?"

Roger nodded. He introduced Alec, and then said: "Sit down, Miss Meadows. We'll talk over the case."

Already he knew the main details. There are few shooting cases among the British upper middle classes, and the newspapers had made the most of this one.

Briefly, the newspaper stories as amplified by the sister of the accused man amounted to the following relevant facts. James and Claire Meadows were orphans, he twenty-four years old, she twenty-six; they were comfortably off and lived in the small Dorset village of Monckton Regis. In nature they were utterly unlike; James was a quiet, rather frail young man with ambitions towards poetry, Claire held the Ladies Tennis Championship of her county and had played for England.

Living also near Monckton Regis was a wealthy couple named Greyling: a big, red-haired man of about forty-five, known for his kindness to his tenantry and popular but credited with a violent temper, and his wife, ten years his junior and equally well-liked but something of a harmless snob. There was one child, a girl named Sheila, a few years younger than Claire Meadows, and the two were close friends.

"As a matter of fact, it was Sheila who suggested I should come and see you," Claire explained. "Or rather, Jack Frensham — Sheila's boyfriend."

There had been some hope that one day Sheila and James Meadows might make a match of it, but so far James had shown more interest in the older woman than in her daughter. For Mrs. Greyling, seeing herself perhaps in the role of inspiration to a budding poet, had adopted James, in a perfectly harmless way, and the two had formed the habit of making long and solitary expeditions together to discuss Life and other fascinating abstractions. That had been quite enough for an English village, and Mr. Greyling had had to ask James not to be seen in public with Mrs. Greyling quite so much.

"James agreed, of course. There had never been anything more than a rather high-falutin friendship between him and Mrs. Greyling. But though he told me Mr. Greyling spoke quite nicely about it," Claire said doubtfully, "he wasn't sure that there hadn't been rather an acid undertone; enough at any rate to make Jimmy wonder whether Mr. Greyling could possibly have been a bit jealous. It hadn't occurred to him before. It wouldn't, of course. Jimmy's like that."

In any case, the two cut down their expeditions; but they did begin to meet instead at a little dell in some woods near the Greyling estate called Tommy Deaton's Hole. It was a silly but quite harmless piece of romanticism, especially as Mrs. Greyling told Jimmy she said nothing to her husband about it, just in case of misunderstandings.

Then, on the fatal Tuesday just over a week ago, Mrs. Greyling had written to young Meadows to meet her at the spiritual trysting-place at half-past three, and bring a practical picnic tea. Claire, who although it was mid-July happened to be at home that week, got the tea ready herself, and James set out in his car. Mrs. Greyling usually walked through their own park, but on this occasion, though James waited for at least two hours, she never reached the dell.

"He did wait there?" Roger asked impassively.

"He did, Mr. Sheringham. He told me so himself."

In any case, whether James Meadows was in Tommy Deaton's Hole or not during those two hours, at about a quarter-past four that same afternoon Mrs. Greyling was shot dead in the main road just outside the village, in full view of a dozen witnesses, by a man leaning out of a blue Morris Oxford saloon car exactly like that driven by James Meadows and bearing the same number-plates, whom all the witnesses had unhesitatingly identified as James Meadows himself, shock of black hair, light brown tweed coat, horn-rimmed spectacles and all.

After the shooting the car had driven rapidly away, leaving Mrs. Greyling dead in the road, with three bullets in her head. James Meadows' arrest had followed as a matter of course.

"Direct evidence, eh?" nodded Alec.

Roger frowned at him. "It's an awkward situation, Miss Meadows," he could only say helplessly.

"Don't I realise it?" retorted the girl with spirit "But I'm going to light it. Will you help me? Of course your fee —"

"Fee?" repeated Roger, pained. "Don't be absurd, my dear girl. Of course I'll help you — if I can. I'll bring Alec too: he's useful in a scrap. We'll pack at once."

"My car's outside," the girl said eagerly.

But when he was alone with Alec while Barker packed their things he looked rueful. "I don t know what we can do for the poor girl. If ever there was a clear case —"

"Direct evidence, eh?" Alec observed, not without malice.

Roger winced. "Yes, my remarks were a little ill-timed. In fact there's only one point that strikes me." He thought for a moment "Why all the shouting? It seems that when

Meadows stopped his car he began to shout at Mrs. Greyling at the top of his voice. Upbraiding her, apparently. That's what attracted the witnesses' attention."

"Brainstorm," Alec supplied. "Poet, isn't he. Sure to be a bit hysterical."

Roger stared at him. "Alec, I believe I have an idea."

Ten minutes later they were on the road.

The journey was quick. Claire drove well, and fast; and the two were able to install themselves at the local inn just in time for a belated supper. To keep his purpose secret Roger gave out that he was going to write up the case in one of his articles in *The Daily Courier* and Alec was a freelance Press photographer. The little village was already alive with the gentlemen of the Press, so this announcement was received as a matter of course.

For the rest of the evening Roger discussed the case with Alec, trying to find some angle from which an inductive theory of young Meadows' innocence might be drawn; but nothing presented itself. Roger decided that the only thing to do was to begin with the usual interviews, and hope that something might emerge from them.

"And as the important thing is to hear what Meadows himself has to say about it all," he told Alec, "I shall start on him. Miss Meadows must take me over to their solicitor first thing tomorrow."

The introduction was duly effected the next morning; the solicitor, a hearty fox-hunter of the name of Andrews, had heard of Roger and welcomed his help; and the two of them set out by car for the county gaol. Within a surprisingly short time Roger found himself confronting a white-faced boy with a shock of black hair and frightened eyes peering through horn-rimmed spectacles.

Roger explained his mission, and a momentary hope lightened the pale, almost girlish face; but of help Roger could get none. The boy could only repeat over and over again that he had been in Tommy Deaton's Hole all the afternoon and knew nothing at all about anything.

"With your car?" Roger asked desperately.

"With my car," the other affirmed.

"The note, then, supposed to have been sent by Mrs. Greyling. She couldn't have sent it, of course. Did you notice anything odd about it?"

"I don't think so. It was just a scrawl —3.30, T.D.H. Bring

tea.' — and her initials. Something like that I just looked at it and threw it away. It must have got burnt later. Of course the police think there never was a note."

Roger groaned. "When did you get it?"

"I found it in the letter-box, with the morning's post."

"That means it could have been delivered any time during the night. Didn't that seem odd to you?"

"I didn't think about it."

Roger stayed half an hour, but could get no more.

"Went berserk, or whatever they call it," pronounced the police station Superintendent not unkindly, as he saw them after the interview. "Ran amuck. You know, Mr. Sheringham. If I can't have her, no one else shall. That sort of thing. Pity. Nice young feller, too. But highly-strung, Mr. Sheringham. That's his trouble. Not a shadow of doubt he did it if that's what you've been hoping. Why, we've got a dozen witnesses and more who saw him. Can't get round that you know."

"And yet do you know, Superintendent," Roger said, "I don't believe he did it."

The other stared. "Oh, come now, sir, how in the world can you make that out?"

"I can't," Roger regretted. "That's the trouble."

But back in the inn again he repeated his opinion to Alec more forcibly.

"Alec, that boy's telling the truth. I'm sure he is. He's not the sort that commits murder, not in his wildest moments. Tommy Deaton's Hole, eh? Well, we'd better have a look at the place."

"After lunch," said Alec.

They were to lunch with Claire Meadows, who had undertaken to collect Sheila Greyling and her boy-friend; when Roger and Alec arrived Miss Greyling was already there, a wistful young person in a black frock with a kind of helpless prettiness. With her was a young man with very black hair and very white teeth and eyebrows which met across the bridge of his nose and a manner of supreme self-confidence, who shook hands with Roger as if he himself were responsible for the latter's entire existence, and had made rather a good job of it

He was in any case responsible for Roger's presence in Monckton Regis, and Roger duly expressed his gratification at the fact

"The police here are just plain fools," pronounced young

Mr. Frensham. "They can't see through a glass window, let alone a brick wall. Of course I suggested calling in you."

"Very good of you," murmured Roger, and turned back to his hostess. The question in her eyes was obvious.

She drew him aside. "You've seen Jimmy?"

"Yes. I got nothing fresh from him, I'm afraid; but I'm glad I saw him. Because I agree now with you completely; it's out of the question that he could have done it."

The girl drew a breath of relief and gave his hand a sudden grip which made Roger wince.

"Sheila's just as sure about Jimmy as I am. Jack? Oh, no; he's not local. He lives in Bridport. He's got an estate agent's business there, one of those old family businesses that run themselves; he seems to be able to leave it whenever he wants to. Which is lucky for Sheila. I told you Mrs. G was a bit of a snob, poor woman. The idea of Sheila throwing herself away on an estate agent would have given her a fit. Sheila had to keep Jack dark."

"I see. Did Mr. Greyling share this somewhat antiquated outlook?"

"Not exactly." Claire hesitated. "But there was a terrific row once over something quite different. Some land that Mr. Greyling sold, or something. He put the deal through Jack, and then practically accused him afterward of twisting him — acting for the purchaser on the quiet while he pretended to act for Mr. Greyling. I can't remember the details."

"Very forgiving of Frensham to come courting his daughter then," Roger commented. "Was there any truth in the accusation, do you think?"

"N-no, I shouldn't think so. Though I believe Jack hasn't an awfully good name for — well, you know: he likes making money, and doesn't much care how. But of course Mr. Greyling won't have him in the house now. Still, Jimmy quite likes him and he likes Jimmy, though he rags him rather a lot. In any case he's been a brick over helping to get you down here and everything — All right, Finch," she nodded, as a discreet butler intimated that lunch was ready.

At lunch Frensham told Roger what to do. "You'd better have a look at Tommy Deaton's Hole this afternoon. Try and find some evidence that Jimmy really was there. Ask at the farms on the way if anyone saw him going or coming."

"That," said Roger a little coldly, "was my intention."

Frensham seemed to him altogether too free with his

orders. He issued them even to Sheila Greyling, and with a careless confidence in the result which annoyed Roger. Not to put it too delicately, Roger found himself thoroughly disliking this assertive young man.

He began to toy with the idea that Frensham himself might be the murderer. After all he had a grudge against both the Greyling parents; he was as dark as Jimmy Meadows himself; even if his hair was cut particularly short while Jimmy's was much too long; he... Regretfully Roger dismissed the idea. If Frensham had committed the murder and then gone out of his way to ensure its detection by summoning Roger himself, he could only be a driveling imbecile. And Frensham, offensive as he might be, was no driveling imbecile.

Lunch over, Frensham insisted on driving them himself to the Hole. The little dell was deserted when they reached it, and Roger set out to examine it thoroughly. Assisted by the others, he left not a square inch unsearched; but two hours later the results were absolutely negative. There were cigarette ends, a few mouldering crumbs from earlier picnic meals, car tracks on the soft ground; but nothing at all to show that anyone had occupied the place on that particular afternoon beyond any other. Regretfully Roger had to call the search off and set off, once more under the pilotage of Frensham, on a round of the farms.

Here again a blank was drawn. Not a single person could be found who saw either Jimmy Meadows or his car that day.

Roger looked at his watch. It was long past tea-time.

"I'd like to have a look at the scene of the murder," he said to Frensham. "Can you take me there?"

"Surest thing, you know," Frensham returned. "Hop in."

Roger hopped.

The murder had taken place in the main road, unusually wide at this point, not fifty yards beyond the edge of the village. Any person in the village street at the time could have had a first-class view, and many did. Roger turned his attention to some of these. Their descriptions added little to Roger's knowledge, but he learned with interest from two witnesses who had been nearest that they had distinctly heard Mrs. Greyling say, as if in protest to the upbraiding, "Jimmy!"

To Frensham he refused all comment, or even speculation, but to Alec when they were alone in their quarters once more he gave a hint of what was in his mind.

"The important thing still is: why was she shot there, in full view of anyone who cared to have a look? Why go out of his way to advertise himself? Had he a definite reason? Or did he simply lose his head and not know what he was doing?"

"Who?" Alec asked acutely. "Young Meadows?"

"Upon my soul," Roger had to admit, "I'm beginning to wonder. After all she seemed to recognise him. She called him by name — I want some aspirin. Let's go out."

They made their way down the street, Alec with the camera of his adopted profession dutifully slung over his shoulder. Just outside the shop they ran into Claire Meadows. She was beginning to ask eagerly for their news, when suddenly Roger saw her face flush up.

"I'm sorry," she said, "but that's Mr. Greyling across the street. I — don't want to meet him just now."

"Of course." Roger looked with interest at the tall, upright figure striding along the opposite pavement, the sunburnt, out-of-door face which in its brick-red colour seemed almost to match the hair that framed it "He's — taken it hard?"

"Very. He was devoted to his wife; she was the only person who would put up with his temper. And now — well, the impression I get is that the only joy he has left is to hear that Jimmy will be — will be —"

"He believes your brother guilty?"

"He must. He was positively hounding the police after him, on that dreadful Tuesday."

"I think," Roger said unexpectedly, "that we'll have a photograph of the gentleman. Ready, Alec?"

He hurried across the road, followed by Alec, and planting himself in Greyling's path, said in a loud voice: "Excuse me, sir. Press!"

Greyling stopped, and Alec hurriedly snapped the shutter.

Greyling's face contorted with rage. He lunged forward and aimed a smashing blow at the camera with his stick. Alec was able to step back just in time.

Greyling glared at them. "If you publish that photograph in your beastly rag," he said loudly, "I'll knock both your heads in." He strode on.

"Well, well," said Roger mildly.

They rejoined the girl.

"I think," said Roger, "that to even things up we'll have

photographs of everyone connected with the case, beginning with Miss Meadows here. Alec, that's your job. There's still enough light. Get busy."

"You really want them?" Alec asked in surprise.

"By tonight," Roger affirmed.

An exciting shouting made them turn round quickly. Jack Frensham was leaning out of his magnificent Sports Bentley as he drove along the street towards them. The car came to a halt beside them.

"Sheringham! I believe I've found something."

"What?"

"The number-plates — the faked number-plates of the car Jimmy was supposed to be driving," Frensham explained impatiently.

"Oh!" Roger came awake. "Where?"

"I'll show you. I haven't touched 'em. Hop in."

Once more Roger hopped. His last glance showed him Alec automatically snapping his camera.

Frensham drove with his usual speed a couple of miles out of the village and turned up a side road. He pulled up at a gap in a rather derelict fence which bounded the road on one side, shutting off a private wood.

"This is near Tommy Deaton's Hole, isn't it?" Roger asked.

"Yes, about five hundred yards. Through here." Frensham led the way through the gap, and turned to the left. By a big rhododendron bush he stopped. "Look!"

Roger looked. Tucked away under the bush was the unmistakable corner of a number-plate; the rest was covered with leaves. Roger went down on his knees, crawled in, and very gently removed the leaves.

"XLOP 47," he read out "Is that right?"

"That's the number of Jimmy's car," Frensham confirmed.

Roger crawled out again. "We must tell the police at once. I won't disturb them; there may be finger-prints. How the devil did you find them?"

Frensham lit a cigarette with a casual air, as if the finding of clues was all in the day's work to him.

"Not so difficult," he said complacently. "In fact I wonder you didn't get on to them yourself. I reasoned it out that the chap would have come this way. Perhaps he wanted to make sure that Jimmy was still safe in the Hole. He'd be wanting to get rid of the plates, so he'd probably stop at the first gap in the fence and shove them in the woods. This is the first gap."

"I see," said Roger, eyeing his cocksure companion with distaste. "I suppose you realise that this tells against Meadows just as much as for him? The police will reason that it was he who put them there, on his way to establish his alibi in the Hole."

The other looked genuinely surprised. "Well, no, now you mention it, I hadn't thought of that."

"Perhaps you can see the answer to it?"

"Well—"

"Meadows never did establish his alibi," Roger said shortly. "Now let's go back."

Frensham drove into the village again, and Roger duly reported the discovery of the number-plates to a not very intelligent sergeant of police. He took malicious pleasure in handing Mr. Frensham over to lead the sergeant to the spot — but was glad later that he stayed long enough to hear one remark from the sergeant.

"About a quarter-mile before you get to Tommy Deaton's Hole?" said the sergeant absorbing laboriously. "On the left? Well, that'll be on Mr. Greyling's land, then?"

"I believe it is. But what about it?"

"Nothing, sir, nothing," said the sergeant.

Roger escaped.

That evening Alec handed over to Roger one spool of films, undeveloped. Roger received them with gratitude and announced he was going to ring up Frensham and invite him to a conference.

"Yes, he's an exasperating piece of crust but he's clever, Alec. And frankly I want to pick his brains."

Frensham had no objection to running over; in fact he intimated that perhaps it would be just as well.

But when they were settled in the little stuffy parlour, it was Roger who took charge. Before Frensham could air any views of his own, he said: "Now, the way I look at it is this. We have a dozen witnesses that Jimmy Meadows shot Mrs. Greyling. Mrs. Greyling herself seemed to think it was Jimmy Meadows who shot her. But that's direct evidence, and direct evidence is notoriously fallible; there's not one single item of circumstantial evidence to support the case against Meadows.

"If therefore we take an inductive line and begin with the

assumption that the man seen was not Meadows, obviously the first conclusion we get is that it was someone impersonating Meadows — black hair, horn spectacles and all."

"I've got black hair," Frensham smiled.

"I know. But it's short. So I particularly enquired if the murderer's hair was long or short. All the witnesses," said Roger with scarcely disguised regret, "were agreed that it was unmistakably long. It couldn't have been your hair."

"Thanks," said Frensham.

"So black hair isn't a help at all. In fact it's a hindrance. Because our man was undoubtedly wearing a wig."

"Well, that's been pretty obvious all along, hasn't it?" Frensham drawled.

"Yes," said Roger, swallowing slightly. "So what I want to ask you is, where could a man buy a wig round these parts?"

"Nowhere," Frensham said promptly. "He'd go to London."

"So I thought," Roger agreed. "And it's to London that we three are going tomorrow. Can you manage it, Frensham?"

"Oh, yes, I could, but—"

Roger looked at him. "You have your suspicions?"

"I have," Frensham agreed complacently. "But I'm not giving them. I prefer proof. Anyhow, I'll run you up tomorrow in the Bentley."

"I prefer the train," Roger said, so firmly that even Mr. Frensham was quelled.

They went on to discuss their plans for the next day.

But Roger was not to take the train to London after all.

On the platform itself, with the train steaming in, he suddenly smote himself on the chest.

"Look here, you two. I'm mad. There's an absolutely essential job to be done here and at once: trace the movements on that Tuesday of — you know whom!" He smiled slightly at Frensham. "Yes, I think I know what's in your mind. But there's no reason why you two shouldn't go ahead with that job. It's only a matter of going the rounds of the costumiers and asking if they've sold a longish black wig lately to a man with such-and-such hair. Eh, Alec?"

"Oh, rather. No reason why we shouldn't tackle that."

Roger jumped nimbly out of the path of a porter with an overloaded barrow. "Good. Then in you get. Oh, and Alec: take this spool to Scotland Yard first of all, see Moresby, and ask him to get it developed at once. Tell him I'll be ringing him up about it later. Yes, and give him this to go with it."

"This?" Alec said in surprise, taking the small framed photograph which Roger was holding. "Who's this?"

"Oh, young Meadows," Roger said easily. "I slipped it in my pocket yesterday. You never know. One other thing. If you have luck and trace that wig, ring me up at once at the Meadows' house. I've jotted down the number on the back of that photograph. I shall try and take a lunch off Miss Meadows, and I'll wait for a call — and catch the first train back you can," he shouted, as the train began to move off.

Roger was busy that day. From the station he took a taxi to the office of the Meadows' solicitor.

"I want," he explained, "a copy of the police statements on the whereabouts of all the interested parties at the time of the crime. The police are bound to have taken statements on that point. Can you get them for me?"

"I have it right here," replied the solicitor jovially. "Why? Got an idea, Mr. Sheringham?"

"I may have," Roger said with caution, and studied the list. "Miss Sheila Greyling, Miss Claire Meadows, Mr. John Frensham, Mr. James Meadows — h'm, all a bit vague, aren't they? Crime committed at 4.13 approx: Miss Claire Meadows alone at home, reading in garden; Miss Sheila Greyling and Mr. John Frensham lunched together in Bridport and spent afternoon on Worsley Moor — where's that?"

"About four miles away. Big tract, not unlike Dartmoor in miniature. Fine views."

"... Mr. James Meadows — yes — hullo! What was Greyling doing all alone in Hackney's Copse, whatever Hackney's Copse may be?"

"Yes, that's rather odd. Hackney's Copse is a wood belonging to one of Greyling's tenants. Greyling says he got a telephone message from the tenant saying a couple of elms there looked to him in a dangerous condition, and asking Greyling to meet him there at four o'clock to discuss whether they ought to be felled. Greyling went, but the man never turned up and says now that he never sent any such message."

"The deuce he does!" Roger was annoyed. "Why wasn't I told of this before? It's vital. Don't you see? It's the James Meadows alibi all over again."

The solicitor stared. "But why on earth should anyone want to get Greyling himself out of the way?"

"That's for you to find out," Roger retorted. "Or should have been. Now I must —" He thought hard.

"Who could have known Mrs. Greyling's whereabouts at 4.15?"

The solicitor shrugged his shoulders. "I suppose anyone. She was going to pay a call."

Roger thought again. "I want you to have a comprehensive enquiry made, at every garage within fifty miles of here, whether anyone hired a blue Morris Oxford saloon car on that date. Get all your clerks on half a dozen telephones. It's urgent."

"I'll do it somehow," the solicitor promised.

"I'll telephone you around lunchtime," said Roger.

He hurried out of the office, and told the driver of his ancient taxi to take him to the Meadows' house.

By luck Claire was in. Roger evaded her questions, hinted that he might be on the track of something, and hinted still more broadly that what he really needed on such a hot day was a rest and a long, cool drink. Yes, lager beer, already iced, was just what the system required.

He drank it with his hostess in the big, shady garden. Deliberately Roger kept the conversation light: so light that it was hardly surprising that amateur dramatics came up at last as a topic. In any case Claire seemed to notice nothing odd. She divulged that James was a minor member of it, with a surprising talent for rustic parts, but that she herself was not interested. No, none of the Greylings, or Jack Frensham, were interested either.

Roger finished his drink and sat up. "Miss Meadows, may I have half an hour alone in your brother's rooms — bedroom, study if he's got one, and even the attic?"

"You may, of course, but — the police have —"

"Yes, I know. But I'm looking for something that the police weren't."

Without more ado, Claire led him to her brother's bedroom.

His search took him nearer an hour than half, but it was successful. Not, however, that Roger showed his find to his hostess as he angled for, and obtained, an invitation to lunch.

During the meal he refused to say a word about the case, and chatted volubly on any subject that came into his mind. Claire obviously did her best to respond.

After lunch he asked to use the telephone, and put a call through to the solicitor.

"We got it for you, my boy," reported the latter jubilantly. "No trouble at all. Garage not ten miles from here hired out a car answering the description at ten-thirty that morning. And I'll tell you something."

"No," said Roger. "I'll tell you. The colour of his hair was —red."

"So you were on?"

"I was on," said Roger.

He went back to the drawing-room.

Twenty minutes later the maid announced that he was wanted on the telephone.

The caller was Alec, equally jubilant.

"Traced the wig all right. We split up to save time, and I hit the right place third shot. Fellow in the shop remembers distinctly, because the customer was fractuous, and look here, Roger, do you know —"

"Yes," said Roger. "He had red hair. Good. Come back at once, Alec, and meet me at Police Headquarters. I'm going there now. Yes, I've found something here. Oh, and bring Frensham with you, as a witness." He asked the name and address of the costumiers, and rang off.

This time Roger did not return to the drawing-room. He scribbled a note to the effect that he had been called away and hoped to have important news in a few hours' time and gave it to the maid to take to Claire. Then he went round to the garage, helped himself to Claire's own car, and drove off. On the seat beside him he laid tenderly the bright red wig he had found in a box at the bottom of a cupboard in Jimmy Meadows' bedroom.

He waited to telephone to Scotland Yard until he had reached the first town. Village telephones have not only ears but tongues.

"That you, Moresby?" he said, when the connection had been made. "You got a spool of films I sent you this morning? They've been developed? Good. You got the loose photograph too? Then will you send a man round to Narillon, theatrical costumier, in Wardour Street? Ask him if he can identify the man who bought a black wig there a couple of weeks ago, about which a large gentleman in an old school tie was asking this morning. Alec Grierson, yes.

Important? Yes, very. Ring me up as soon as you've heard at County Police Headquarters here."

Roger was not a fast driver, but he arrived at the County Police Headquarters in time to have an hour's earnest talk with the superintendent before the other two arrived from London. The superintendent was impressed, and went so far as to summon the chief constable. Even the chief constable was impressed.

In the middle of the impressed state came the telephone call from Detective Chief Inspector Moresby.

Roger listened, nodded with satisfaction, and gave the telephone to the chief constable. To the superintendent's raised eyebrows he said softly: "Identification not positive, but near enough. There would have been some other make-up, no doubt."

Ten minutes later Alec and Frensham arrived.

"Hullo," said Frensham. "Well, we've done the trick our end. I hope you have yours?" He laughed loudly.

"Oh, yes," said Roger. "I have. But it's the superintendent's trick now."

The superintendent did not waste time.

"John Frensham," he said, "I arrest you for the murder of Mrs. Vera Greyling on — here, Parker! Gravestock!"

But Alec had already tackled Frensham as he was diving through the doorway, and brought him down on the floor with a crash.

"IT'S QUITE SIMPLE," Roger explained to a bewildered and slightly bruised Alec, when Frensham had been locked safely away. "After all Frensham always had a big motive. Sheila Greyling is an heiress, but with the Greyling parents alive he stood no chance of inheriting even if he could persuade Sheila to elope with him. His plan of course was to eliminate them both by getting Greyling hanged for the murder of Mrs. Greyling. I expect the whole thing was suggested to him by seeing Jimmy Meadows on the local stage in a red wig, doing his rustic stuff. A red wig was a grand idea. Easy enough to filch from Jimmy's bedroom one day, and just as easy to replace, and a fine flaming beacon to mark a trail to the wrong man.

"His alibi wasn't too bad either, with the murdered woman's own daughter to back it up. Sheila Greyling admitted that they both felt sleepy after lunch and dozed. Actually she did more than doze. I imagine she had at least an hour's sound sleep, and I suspect a few grains of chloral hydrate in her after-lunch coffee as the cause.

"And that's all there is to explain. The man shouldn't have shouted so loudly at Mrs. Greyling, to attract the witnesses' attention. That made me suspicious at the start."

"But it beats me why Frensham himself suggested calling you in," Alec demurred. "You said yourself that would be idiotic if he was guilty."

"I'll explain that later," Roger said, in some confusion. "We must get off now and break the news to Miss Meadows that her brother will be free in an hour or two."

He made his farewells to the police and sought his car. When they were safely on the road he said: "Touching on that last question, Alec, I think the reason why Frensham called me in was that the local police were being too stupid. They couldn't, as Frensham aptly put it, see through the glass window he had put up for them. They arrested Meadows, you see, and never got beyond that, Frensham had laid such a pretty double trail too; even in the matter of alibis, Jimmy was meant in the end to be his nice little glass window. Unfortunately I saw a good deal further at the first glance, for the thing that stuck out a mile was that Greyling, whatever his temper, is far too much of an old school tie ever to do anything so outrageous as to make his wife die under the eyes of a dozen staring gossip-mongers. There's a lot to be said for the old school tie, in spite of the bearded ladies.

"Of course," Roger continued modestly, "Frensham gave me a great deal of help when he thought I wasn't doing well enough by myself. He found the number-plates for me, and I've no doubt he guided your footsteps to the costumiers, whom he couldn't of course visit with you. In fact I thought at times he was overdoing the helping hand, but his self-confidence was pathetic."

Alec nodded intelligently. "I get you. He thought you were smart enough to see through his first bluff, but he thought you were all too much of an ass to be able to see through his double-bluff."

"That," said Roger coldly, "is, in a crude way, no doubt the case."

"Mr. Bearstowe Says..."

FOR THE FIRST few months of the war Bloomsbury was able to carry on much as usual. Besides, to give a beer-and-sausage party, or even to attend a beer-and-sausage party, seemed a subtle defiance of Hitler and all his wars. That, at any rate, was the impression that Roger Sheringham was receiving at a party which he found himself unaccountably attending in the month of November 1939.

Roger did not care much for parties, even beer-parties; nor did he care much for Bloomsbury. For that matter Bloomsbury cared even less for Roger Sheringham. Either it knew him not or, if it did know, despised his best-selling capacities — and was inclined to go a few steps out of his way to let him know it In due course, therefore, Roger, tired of being snubbed, betook himself and his tankard into a corner and surveyed the smoke-wreathed hubbub with a surly frown.

Like gravitates to like. Into Roger's corner there imperceptibly edged a woman, obviously as lonely as himself but wearing in place of a surly frown a fixed and determined smile. Roger surveyed her. She was a somewhat faded lady, of middle middle-age, who had once been prettier than she was now. Her clothes were worn as wrong as even female Bloomsbury can wear clothes, but unlike theirs, were expensive. She was clearly out of place, and Roger decided that behind the fixed smile she was unhappy.

"Do you want to get away?" he asked suddenly. "I do. Let's go."

The lady started. She seemed unused to being addressed by strangers, even at a Bloomsbury party. "Go away?" she repeated vaguely. "Oh, no! I think it's wonderful!"

"Do you?" Roger said glumly. "What in particular?"

"Oh, well — everything. I mean, all these authors and — and poets and people. Oh, I do so wish I could write. Perhaps you write. Do you?"

"No," Roger said firmly.

"It must be wonderful to be able to, don't you think? Well, Mr. Bearstowe says he believes I could, if I could find a theme. Er — you know Mr. Bearstowe's work, of course?"

There seemed so much appeal in the question that Roger, rather to his own surprise, succumbed. "Of course."

She's in love with him, he thought without enthusiasm, as he noted the pleasure, singularly tinged with relief, or even gratitude, which at once illumined his companion's face. He wondered who this Bearstowe was, and why he was not looking after his own, as he prepared for the worst

He received it. A flood of Mr. Bearstowe promptly poured over him. "Mr. Bearstowe says..." Roger wondered how Mr. Bearstowe found time to say so much.

But all is salvage that falls into a novelist's dustbin. Fascinated, Roger began planning a short story. It would be called "Mr. Bearstowe says...", and it would be about — well, it would be partly about Mr. Bearstowe, of course.

"By the way, is Mr. Bearstowe here?" Roger asked. It is as well to have a working idea of one's characters' appearance.

"Oh, yes," the lady said eagerly. "He's over there." Her glance appeared to indicate a group of three bearded young men, one tall, one short, and one middling. There was nothing to show the height of Mr. Bearstowe. Roger could not decide whether he should be the tall, cadaverous young man, the short, bouncing young man, or the middling, might-be-anything young man.

There must be a triangle, of course. The faded lady's husband — "Of course my husband isn't much interested in that sort of thing," the lady supplied, rather wistfully.

"Of course not," Roger said with gratitude. No, of course the husband mustn't be interested. The husband must be a self-made man, who married a little above him and now thinks he married below him: a self-opinionated, self-satisfied man, who —

"You see, my husband doesn't care for me to go to concerts without him, and as he doesn't care to go himself —"

"Exactly!" — who rules his wife out of school as well as in, and won't let her go to concerts. Excellent. Probably one of those short, pompous little men.

"How tall is your husband?" Roger asked abruptly.

The lady looked taken aback. "How tall? Well, I don't really know."

"Oh, come you must know whether your husband's tall or short," Roger said impatiently. Ridiculous woman! It was important that the husband should be short, because then Mr. Bearstowe could be the tall, cadaverous young man.

"No, I think he's just about — average."

"In a country of dwarfs the average man is a giant," said Roger, inaccurately as well as inanely; but he judged that this was the sort of thing that the lady attended Bloomsbury parties to hear, and it seemed a pity that she shouldn't have at least one gem to carry away with her.

He was going on to supply more, out of sheer kindness, when his companion uttered a sudden exclamation and made a rush for the door. Through the doorway Roger just had a glimpse of a blond head throwing an abrupt nod in her direction, and Mr. Bearstowe passed — the secret still unsolved. All three young men had been blonds. "Gentlemen prefer to be blonds," Roger muttered sourly.

"Was that an epigram, my sweet?" asked a familiar voice.

"Crystal!" Roger exclaimed with relief. "Fancy seeing you in this bear-pit. And talking of bears, who is Mr. Bearstowe? You know him, of course. You know everyone."

"Michael Bearstowe? Yes. Well, I don't know quite how to describe him. He would be a dilettante, if he had any money. But he hasn't So he dilettantes on other people's."

"He's a sponger?" Roger asked delightedly. Oh, admirable, sponging, cadaverous Mr. Bearstowe, taking the wives of pompous average self-made men to concerts (wife paying)!

"I should say so. Why look so pleased about it?"

"Because it fits so nicely. Crystal, tell me more of this Bearstowe. My interest in him is insatiable."

"I don't know that there's anything more to tell you. He's the type who runs after the wives of rich men, and feeds them Culture and Literature in return for temporary loans. A literary gigolo, you might call him. I hear he's got hold of some groceress now and is toting her everywhere."

"Groceress, Crystal?"

"The female of a grocer. At least, I understand that the husband makes big noises in Mincing Lane. Isn't that where they groce?"

"No, I think it's where they drink tea and spit it out again. But this Bearstowe, Crystal — has he published much?"

"Nothing, that I'm aware of. Oh, yes, I believe he did have a short story printed in one of the cheap magazines once," said Crystal, whose job it was to know everything about everyone, and even a few things that they did not know themselves.

"It's perfect!" Roger said ecstatically. "I shall write the story this very evening."

Roger did not write the story that evening, or any evening; and within a week he had forgotten the very name of Bearstowe.

BUT MR. BEARSTOWE'S story was being written none the less, if by a different hand — and in a different medium.

She seems terrible upset, sir," said the station sergeant doubtfully. "Crying her eyes out already, and she doesn't even know the body's been found. I don't know whether she's fit to interrogate, sir."

"Well, try and get her to pull herself together," the superintendent said impatiently. The bathing is dangerous round Penhampton and one gets so inured to corpses after twenty years' police service that it is difficult to realise that the relatives are not equally hardened off. In his home the superintendent was the kindest of men, and loathed killing mice.

"You won't want to wait for this, Mr. Sheringham," the superintendent added to his visitor. "A woman come to report her husband missing after bathing. As a matter of fact, we've got the body already, but she doesn't know that. I'm afraid she'll go a bit hysterical when she does. They often do," added the superintendent with a sigh.

"No, I'll slide out," Roger agreed. "In any case, it looks as if the colonel isn't coming this afternoon; so —"

He broke off. The sergeant had returned already, with his charge. Roger, having no wish to intrude on the woman's grief, waited for them to pass before slipping quietly out. Then he caught sight of the woman's face and, after a moment of indecision, returned unobtrusively to his chair.

The woman was given a seat facing the superintendent's desk. She had pulled herself together bravely, but from the clenched hands on her lap it was clear that she was vibrating with nerves.

The superintendent made soothing noises. "Now, Mrs. Hutton, let me see — you're worried about your husband?"

The woman nodded, choked, and said: "Yes. He went out bathing this morning. I was to join him later. His clothes were on the beach, but — oh, I'm sure — I'm sure —"

"Now, now," said the superintendent mechanically, and asked for further particulars.

These took some minutes to obtain, but amounted to very little. Mr. Edward Hutton, described as a wholesale provision merchant with an office in the City and a home in Streatham, had been staying with his wife in the little village of Penmouth, some five miles west of Penhampton. He had left the house at about half-past ten that morning, telling his wife that he was going to bathe. Mrs. Hutton had arranged to join him about noon, but when she arrived there was no sign of her husband, though his clothes were behind the same rock that he always used for undressing purposes. Mrs. Hutton had called and searched, and then returned to her lodging. In the afternoon, being now thoroughly worried, she had decided to take the only bus of the day into Penhampton and report to the police.

The superintendent nodded. "Very proper, madam. Now as to your husband's description, can you give us some idea of his appearance?"

Mrs. Hutton leaned back in her chair and closed her eyes. "My husband is five foot seven — no, eight inches tall, not very broad, thinnish arms and legs, 34 inches chest measurement, rather long hands and feet, medium brown hair, clean-shaven, grey-green eyes, and rather a pale complexion; he has an old appendicitis scar, and — oh, yes, there is a big mole under his left shoulder-blade."

The superintendent could not restrain his admiration. "Upon my word, Mrs. Hutton, you reeled that off a treat. Very different from some of them, I assure you."

"I — I was thinking it out in the bus," the woman said faintly. "And — his passport, you know. I knew you'd want a description."

"Yes. Well." Surreptitiously the superintendent studied the description of the body now in the mortuary. It tallied in every particular.

With much sympathetic throat-clearing he proceeded to the distasteful task of warning Mrs. Hutton to prepare for a shock. He was very much afraid that in the mortuary now, if Mrs. Hutton would come along for just a moment —

He sighed again as the woman gave every sign of imminent hysterics.

"He's here already? Must I see him? Must I? Won't — won't the description do?"

It took five minutes to get her into the mortuary to identify the body.

But once there she regained her calm. A curious dead-alive look came into her face as the superintendent gently withdrew the sheet that covered the dead man's face.

"Yes," she whispered, tonelessly. "That's my husband. That's — Eddie."

And then Roger noticed a very curious thing. Like the others' his gaze had been fixed on the sheeted figure on the slab; but happening, by the merest chance, to glance round at Mrs. Hutton, he saw that her eyes were slightly closed. For all she knew, she might have been identifying a piece of cheese as her husband. He nudged the superintendent.

The superintendent understood and nodded back. "I'm afraid, madam," he said, as gently as he could, "you must *look* at him you know."

Mrs. Hutton started violently, opened her eyes, looked at the dead man in front of her, and uttered a horrible, hoarse scream.

For a moment Roger thought she was going into hysterics again. He jumped forward, as did both the superintendent and the sergeant, and between them they hurried Mrs. Hutton back to the office. The sergeant produced a glass of water, and within a few minutes the lady was able to stop sobbing and assure them that she was quite all right now, it was just the shock of seeing her own husband, actually lying there —

"Shock, yes," said the superintendent hastily. "Nasty thing, shock. I remember —"

When at last Mrs. Hutton got out her powder-compact, all three men heaved sighs of relief.

Roger, who had at last solved a problem which had been worrying him ever since he first saw Mrs. Hutton in the doorway, deemed it a good moment to introduce himself.

"Do you know that we've met before, Mrs. Hutton?" he said, with his best social smile.

She looked at him vaguely. "No. Have we? Where?"

"At a party. I didn't know your name, nor you mine, and I've been wondering why your face seemed known to me. Now I remember. It was at a deadly beer-party about two years ago, soon after the beginning of the war. Do you remember? In Bloomsbury. By the way, have you seen Michael Bearstowe lately?"

Mrs. Hutton jumped to her feet, her face dead-white. For a moment she gazed wildly at Roger, then she collapsed on the floor in a dead faint.

"That wasn't kind of you, Mr. Sheringham," said the superintendent reproachfully, when Mrs. Hutton had been finally tidied away into the care of the police matron. "I thought we'd got her round — why, she'd got her powder-puff out and all! — and then you go and do a thing like that."

"I didn't do anything," Roger said indignantly. "I only reminded her of a party we'd both been to and asked after an old friend of hers. Do you faint when people ask after your old friends?"

"You upset her."

"Apparently. But that's no reason for you to upset me. I might even try to upset you, in return. I might tell you, for instance, that the last time I saw that lady she was so vague that she couldn't tell me whether her husband was a tall man or a short one. Yet now she not only knows his height to an inch but his chest measurement too."

"Well, why not? She remembered it from his passport. She said so."

"They don't put your chest measurement on your passport."

The superintendent frowned. "What exactly are you suggesting, Mr. Sheringham?"

Roger laughed. "Now don't get official, Super. I'm not suggesting anything. I merely hand you a queer little discrepancy, and you can do what you like with it. But," Roger added thoughtfully, "do you know, I would like to have another look at the body, if you've no objection."

"Oh, I've no objection. But you won't find anything. The doctor's been over him already, and death's due to drowning all right. Still, have a look at him if you want I'm afraid I can't stay myself; I'm late already; but —"

Roger assured the superintendent that for nothing in the world would he detain him longer.

Roger did not have the mortuary to himself. There were two other men already there. The sergeant who had been appointed Roger's conductor, indicated that they were the police surgeon and the detective inspector in charge of the C.I.D. of the Penhampton police force; and he left him to them.

The sheet had been withdrawn from the body and both men were standing by the slab, gazing down. Roger joined them.

"Pasty-faced beggar, eh?" remarked the doctor cheerfully.

"Certainly no advertisement for Penhampton's Bonnie

Sunshine," Roger assented absently. He was remembering more and more.

Yes, and the husband was to have been a pompous, paunchy little bully, who wouldn't take his wife to concerts and wouldn't let her go by herself. Well, here he was face to face with the husband at last; and he certainly wasn't paunchy, and could hardly have been pompous. But that wasn't to say that he might not have been a bully, Roger thought, looking at the rather weak face and the indeterminate chin: the kind that bullies out of weakness instead of out of strength. Perhaps he was even that pathetic type, the artist *manqué* (his hands seemed to indicate the possibility), *manqué* and condemned to an office desk in Mincing Lane, and in consequence soured. Yes, and he had inherited the office-desk too, not achieved it; for this man had never made money, or anything else, if Roger knew faces. Well, it was a story, whichever way it went.

"Notice anything, Mr. Sheringham?" the detective inspector asked eagerly.

"No. Why?"

"I thought you were looking at him a bit hard."

Roger laughed. "Afraid not, this time. Except that Mr. Hutton wasn't as spruce as he might have been."

"How do you make that out, sir?"

"He hadn't shaved this morning."

"Sorry, but he had," the doctor corrected with a smile. "That cut's fresh, at the side of his mouth."

"Well, he wanted a new blade," Roger said feebly.

"Like most of us," the doctor agreed. "But if you're really looking for queer details, what do you make of his back?" He signed to the inspector, and the two of them turned the corpse over.

Roger saw that the skin on the back was badly lacerated from the shoulders to the small of the back, and the elbows were almost raw. "Barnacles?" he suggested.

The doctor nodded. "Rocks covered with them. And it was among the rocks that the body was found. Still —"

"1 see what you mean. If the body was washing about, why was it lacerated only in that particular area?"

"Yes, it's queer, isn't it? No doubt there's some simple explanation. Probably the man who found him pulled him in by the legs. That's all."

"No, doctor," put in the inspector. "The body was wedged

under a big rock at the side of a pool. Trewin, the farm-hand who happened to find him when he went down for a pail of sea-water, says he picked him up straight from the pool."

"There's an abrasion on the front of the right thigh, where he was wedged," supplemented the doctor.

"Yes, but that's natural," Roger said. "Those scratches aren't."

"And here's another thing. I've an idea those lacerations were made during life. There were signs of free bleeding — freer than I should have expected."

"Very interesting," Roger commented. "Very queer."

"Don't think there's anything wrong, do you, sir?" asked the inspector, hopefully.

Roger's reply was lost in the sudden entrance of the superintendent "Well, it seems we've caught a tartar," he announced, not without triumph. "Just had Scotland Yard on the phone. Caught me in the nick of time; another minute, and I'd have been gone. Seems this fellow was wanted by the Yard for black market stuff. They've got a warrant out against him, and they'd just heard he'd been seen in this vicinity."

"Well, fancy that," observed the inspector.

Roger stared down at the dead man. "You never know, do you? Still, that weak chin —"

"Yes, yes; criminal type, obviously," pronounced the superintendent. "Well, doctor, this is bound to raise the question of suicide. Any chance, do you think?"

"None that I can say. Of course, he may have swum deliberately too far out, but there's nothing to show it."

"Are you going to check up on Mrs. Hutton's statement, Super?" Roger asked suddenly.

The superintendent stared. "We'll make the usual routine enquiry at her lodging. Why, Mr. Sheringham?"

"I only wondered," Roger said mildly. "It would be interesting, for instance, if she took a bathing-dress out this morning, wouldn't it? Or if she left the house soon after her husband, and not at noon?"

"Why, Mr. Sheringham," said the detective inspector, whose job it would be to make these enquiries, "you don't think —?"

"I only think it might be quite an interesting case," Roger said.

AS HE TRUDGED along the coarse sand the next afternoon Roger wondered if he were wasting his time and energy. That Hutton had been murdered, he felt convinced; and the method was fairly obvious. But could the woman have done it? Physically, yes. But psychologically? Hardly. She was too vague, too woolly, too — too silly, poor woman.

Or did silliness not debar one from murder? Murder itself was usually very silly. Mrs. Hutton might not be the stuff of which strong, silent murderers were made; but mightn't she be a silly murderess? She was a hero-worshipper. How far would hero-worship carry her?

Roger's plodding feet seemed to be picking out a shambling refrain. "Mr. Bearstowe says... Mr. Bearstowe says..."

And suppose Mr. Bearstowe said, "Pick up your husband's feet when he's bathing and hold them up in the air for a few minutes, out of sheer girlish *elan*, and then I shall be able to marry your Mincing Millions."

Oh, Mr. Bearstowe was in it all right. Why else faint at the mere mention of his name?

Yes, and of course there was the evidence of guilt all the time. First she wouldn't look at her murdered husband at all; then, when she was made to, took one peep, turned pea-green, and screamed. If that wasn't presumptive evidence of guilt what was?

And reeling off the description in that silly way! Roger could almost hear the voice of tuition: "If they wonder how you've got it so pat just say you were thinking it out in the bus, or remembered it from his passport or something. They won't bother." And pat she certainly had got it like a child repeating a lesson. Mr. Bearstowe should have devoted more time to his artistic effects.

But the superintendent had smelt no rat. Roger thought the superintendent rather a foolish man. Now that inspector — Yes, there the inspector was, already. Then this must be the place.

The inspector was feeling a little guilty himself. "You know, I oughtn't rightly to be doing this, Mr. Sheringham. The super would be wild. He says it's a straightforward case of accident if ever he saw one, and you've got a bee in your bonnet about murder."

"I never so much as mentioned the word," Roger protested.

"No, but it was obvious what you thought. And I couldn't

but agree that there seems something fishy about Mrs. Hutton. More I think of it more it seems to me that she acted queer — very queer indeed."

"Have you checked up at the lodgings?"

"Yes, but more of a country house than lodgings. Must have been costing them a tidy packet to stay there. They've got money to burn all right those Huttons, in spite of the taxes and all. Still, her story's all right so far as it goes. She did leave at the time she said, and she didn't take a bathing-dress."

"Any signs of — worry?"

"No!" said the inspector emphatically. "I asked that specifically, and she was just as usual before she went out. Didn't answer her husband back when he laid down the law at breakfast as usual, or anything. But when she came back! Tears? Floods of 'em! And before he'd been missing long enough to make any ordinary wife do anything but curse about him making her wait for lunch, mark you."

"Umph! Remorse? I wonder." Roger felt a little puzzled. Bearstowe would hardly be the type to spring an unexpected murder on a foolish, possibly unreliable woman. He pushed the point aside. "Anyhow, where's the rock?"

The inspector pointed it out. The tide had gone down far enough for Roger, balanced precariously on slippery seaweed, to be able to inspect the crevice in which the body had been wedged. It told him nothing.

He gazed thoughtfully round on the broken, rocky shore, with little waves slapping whitely here and there and the seaweed waving in the pools.

"Well, sir, if you don't want me anymore, I think I'd like another word or two with Trewin. You never know. He might have noticed something."

"Do," Roger agreed. "I shall be poking round here for an hour or so if you like to pick me up on your way back."

But it did not take Roger an hour to find the thing which he had hardly expected to find. In only the third pool which he explored after the inspector's disappearance, shining merrily on a bunch of seaweed only a few inches below the surface, was a gold ring, simply asking to be found. Scarcely able to believe in his luck, Roger examined it. It was a man's wedding-ring, and the inside was inscribed, "E.H. — B.G. 18 November 1932."

Roger turned it slowly over in his hand. It was a chance

in a million. And yet what did it prove? That Edward Hutton had been murdered in that particular pool, and none other. Not very much. No hint as to who had murdered him, for instance.

Roger dried himself on his handkerchief, and sat down to await the return of the inspector.

He came an hour later, bursting with news. "The woman's in it all right, Mr. Sheringham. By a stroke of luck I found a man who was working in this field yesterday afternoon. He says he saw a woman on the beach about half-past three, and the description of the clothes tallies near enough."

"Mrs. Hutton didn't mention being on the beach then?"

"No, sir, she did not. But that's not all. There was a man with her."

"Ah!"

"You expected that, Mr. Sheringham?" asked the inspector, a trifle disappointed.

"In a way. Well, what did they do?"

"By the looks of it they came out of a little cave under the cliff here. I must have a look there later. The farm-hand thought they might be a larky couple, so he watched; but after a minute or two the man went back into the cave and the woman went off along the beach."

"Did you get any description of the man?"

"Nothing particular. Orange pullover, grey flannel trousers. Clean-shaven."

"Clean-shaven, eh? Yes, well, he would be, of course."

"Sir?"

"He had a beard last time I saw him, but beards are much too distinctive. Look here, Inspector, it's time I told you a few things. Sit down."

They found a rock and made themselves comfortable in its lee. Roger lit his pipe, and then told his tale.

"Mind you," he concluded, "there's no evidence that the man's Bearstowe. After all, it was over two years ago and she may have got a new hero by now. But it's worth making a few enquiries."

"I certainly will, sir. This alters everything. The super's bound to OK me spending a bit of time on the case now. And what are you going to do, sir?"

"Me? Do you know," said Roger, "I should awfully like

to ask Mrs. Hutton why she fainted at Bearstowe's name. I do so wonder what she'd say."

ROGER DID NOT put this interesting question, however. (For one thing was not sure that he had the moral courage.) Instead, he left Mrs. Hutton in peace and went up to London.

His objective was Crystal Vane, and he was lucky enough to catch her the first time he rang up her flat. Crystal was writing what she called one of her 'sob-articles' when he arrived, but she put it aside readily enough to answer Roger's questions.

Yes, so far as she knew the affair of Michael Bearstowe and his groceress had survived the war to date; Michael was on a good thing there, and it wasn't likely he'd let it go; no, he hadn't been called up — total exemption on some grounds or other, oh, yes, conscientious objector, naturally.

"Would you say that Bearstowe was utterly unscrupulous in attaining his own ends?" Roger asked carefully.

"If you mean, would he boggle at a little thing like seducing his groceress if it was going to pay better dividends?" Crystal began.

"No, no. Worse than that. Stick at absolutely nothing, I mean."

But Crystal's journalistic nose scented news, and Roger had to promise her the first chance when the story broke. Then they discussed the possibilities. In the end Crystal gave it as her opinion that Mr. Bearstowe was probably quite unscrupulous enough for murder if driven to it but it wouldn't be *like* him.

"I see," Roger said thoughtfully. "Then I wonder what did drive him. Something big, presumably. Money-troubles, do you think? They can be big enough, in all conscience. But what drove *her*? She doesn't look to me unscrupulous at all. It must have something even bigger. Love, I suppose. You know, there's something queer about this case, Crystal. It doesn't seem quite to fit?"

"Why do you suppose Mrs. Hutton was driven at all?" Crystal asked. "You say she was perfectly normal that morning. A woman of her type couldn't appear normal with her husband's murder in the offing."

"No. In fact she may not know it was murder at all, even now. Why shouldn't Mr. Bearstowe have said it was an accident, and she must just keep his name out of it for convenience? Yes! That explains her part much better. And yet — that excessive grief, for a husband she couldn't have loved? I don't know. No, it doesn't fit, somehow. I think I'll take a walk to Streatham."

But Streatham, it seemed, had nothing to tell Roger. Nor had Mincing Lane, where the offices of Hutton and Edwards were ominously closed. Enquiries as to Edwards showed only that there was no Edwards.

But at Cartwright Mansions, W1, where Mr. Bearstowe had a flat of surprising opulence for one with no means, the porter told Roger that Mr. Bearstowe was away on holiday; nor was it known when he would be back. Nor was it even known where he was; the porter thought, camping.

So that was one point established, at any rate, Roger considered, or perhaps two — or even three. At any rate, he might as well take them back with him to Penhampton the next day, little though they amounted to. What I want, Roger thought, is a couple of nice, juicy coincidences.

He got one at Paddington the following morning, when he ran into Mrs. Hutton by the bookstall.

Mrs. Hutton appeared confused, and dissembled her joy at the meeting; but Roger was officiously helpful, and gladly paid the excess fare over his third-class ticket for the privilege of traveling first with Mrs. Hutton. Mrs. Hutton could not escape without rudeness and she lacked the capabilities for that useful gift, which in this country is the prerogative of the Very Upper or the Pretty Well Lower classes.

But Roger learned little. The carriage was too full of people (with third-class tickets) to allow of intimate conversation, and Mrs. Hutton was obviously far too scared of her companion to respond to intimacy even had they been alone in the middle of the Sahara. In fact all Roger could learn was that Mrs. Hutton was very, very much on her guard. And why should she be that, if innocent?

As the train got into its rhythm, Roger listened to the refrain of the wheels.

"Mis-ter BEAR-stowe-says, Mis-ter BEAR-stowe-says..."

"You don't need to look at him when you identify him. Just keep your eyes closed and say it's your husband. They won't notice."

Had Mr. Bearstowe said that?

But why not look at a dear husband, so sadly and accidentally drowned? Is one frightened of a dead husband, that one cannot look at him? No, it didn't fit. Mrs. Hutton must have some guilty knowledge, even if she wasn't privy before the fact.

Roger looked at the faded, once-pretty face. Mrs. Hutton caught him at it, started violently, blushed unnecessarily, and looked away.

Dash it, Roger thought; the woman's as nervous as a kitten — Why? By the time the train reached Penhampton he still had not found the answer.

But if Roger felt that he had little to show for two days' work, that was certainly not the case with Detective-Inspector Brice. Almost before Roger had had time to ask for a cup of police-station tea, the Detective-Inspector had burst into his story.

"You were right, Mr. Sheringham. We've found Bearstowe. Got on his track, that is. He was camping on the cliffs, not a mile from the scene of the crime."

"Ah!" said Roger, and noted that it was now officially a crime.

"And about half-past one — that's a couple of good hours after the murder, by our reckoning — at half-past one he was seen by the farmer on whose land he was camping, he was seen taking his tent down. And he bolted for it, Mr. Sheringham. Packed his tent and things, all lightweight stuff, into the holder on his bicycle, and rode straight off. Didn't even wait to pay the farmer what he owed him for milk and such."

"I don't think I should pay too much attention to that," Roger murmured. "I should say that was fairly typical."

"Anyhow, he did. Now here's another point. When the farmer saw him, about half-past one, he hadn't shaved off his beard (yes, he still wore a beard; I found that out). When he was seen round about three o'clock, on the shore, he had."

"Ah!" Roger said again. "Yes, that's interesting. Sure of it?"

"Absolutely. The farmer was doing a bit of hedging, not fifty yards away. He says he could see Bearstowe quite plainly."

"How was he dressed?"

"The same. Pullover and grey trousers."

"Any trace of the tent or bicycle?"

"None. He must have hidden 'em before he doubled back to meet Mrs. Hutton, and afterward he picked 'em up and he's made off with them. We've put out an all-stations request for any solitary camper to be interrogated, anywhere."

"Quick work. Now here's another point I take it that your times are correct? What time does the doctor say that death occurred?"

"Round about eleven o'clock, he thinks. Anyhow, not before ten or after one. He was dead when Bearstowe took down his tent, if that's what you mean, sir."

"Yes, partly. And when he was taking down his tent, at one-thirty, Bearstowe had his beard. Less than two hours after he hadn't. Well, here's my point. How did Bearstowe get hold of a razor? Men with beards don't carry them."

The inspector beamed. "That question occurred to me, sir."

"I'm sure it did. I just meant if he had a razor with him, wouldn't that show that the murder was premeditated? If he hadn't it was probably done on the spur of the moment."

"Well, he hadn't," the inspector said with pride. "He got hold of one, and I can tell you where he got it from. Look at this schedule, please, Mr. Sheringham."

Roger looked. The paper contained a minute inventory of the belongings of the late Mr. Hutton, as left in his rooms; it was complete down to spare collar-studs. Roger ran his eye quickly down the column. A shaving-brush and soap were listed; there was no razor.

"I say, good work," Roger said warmly. "You mean Mrs. Hutton took it to him at three o'clock?"

"That's what she met him for, the second time," said the inspector, flushed with pleasure.

"The second time? Oh, I see. You mean, she met him first at twelve, and took instructions. Yes, of course." Roger drank his tea. "Well, that certainly seems to put the case in the bag, Inspector. So all you've got to do now is to find Bearstowe."

"Yes, and Mrs. Hutton," said the inspector, not without resentment "Gave us the slip yesterday she did, and got away to London. Went up to meet Bearstowe, for a tenner. We'll pick her up again, all right, but she may have tipped him off that — oh, there you are, sir."

"Ah! Mr. Sheringham!" said the superintendent genially. "Well, you were right, sir. I don't mind admitting it. And now we've got you and Mrs. Hutton together again. Yes, our chap picked her up at the station and brought her along. Didn't want to come, not a bit. What do you say, Brice? It's your case, but I think it's time we asked Mrs. Hutton a few questions. Eh?"

"I quite agree. Well, we'll see her in here. No, don't go, Mr. Sheringham. You were in at the beginning, so you may as well see the end." He leaned over the inspector's desk and pressed a bell.

In less than two minutes Mrs. Hutton was once again sitting on a police-chair confronting the superintendent; but this time it was a frankly terrified woman, and a police official who no longer spoke kindly. Roger looked at her, waiting like a cornered mouse for the spring of the cat, and felt rather sick. She was such a silly woman. Who but a woman of almost sublime silliness would bring her lover a razor with which to shave off his beard, but omit to bring shaving-brush and soap?

Suddenly something in his brain went 'click!' and he saw the whole thing.

He glanced quickly from the superintendent to the inspector, calculating his chances. No, there was not a second to lose. In another moment the superintendent might ruin the whole thing. He must charge in, and brave the wrath that would certainly come.

"Superintendent, may I ask Mrs. Hutton one question first?"

The superintendent looked surprised but gave permission, not very graciously.

Roger moved his chair so that he could look at the woman more directly. "Mrs. Hutton, do you mind telling me this: are you sure you really know what happened on Penmouth beach that morning?"

Mrs. Hutton's jaw dropped. Obviously she had not expected the question; equally obviously, she did not know how to answer it.

Roger followed it quickly with another. "Do you know, for instance, that *murder* had been committed?"

Mrs. Hutton started to her feet, prepared to scream, thought better of it, and fainted.

"Mr. Sheringham!" exclaimed the superintendent, in real anger.

Once again Mrs. Hutton was borne unconscious into the back regions.

"Listen, Super!" Roger pleaded. "The whole point was that Mrs. Hutton never knew that murder had been committed.

If you'd broken it gently, you'd have given her time to adjust herself to the idea; and she might have decided to help cover it up. Now she's had a bad shock — and she'll talk!"

"Humph!" The superintendent chewed his moustache, by no means mollified.

"We've been making a mistake from the beginning," Roger continued urgently. "A fundamental mistake. I've only just realised it. You see, this murder *was* planned. A long time ago, I fancy. A pit was carefully dug for us, and we fell into it. At first sight, I must say, it looks a terrific gamble, and yet — police procedure is so rigid. Yes, that's the clue. Police procedure is so rigid. Your own procedure protected the murderer, Super. He'd banked on it."

The superintendent raised heavy eyebrows. He did not look convinced.

"It was clever," Roger continued musingly. "He killed two birds with one stone, you see. That warrant for Hutton's arrest — he must have got wind of it somehow. By the way, was Hutton insured? I think you'll find he was. Yes, of course he must have been. Heavily. That's another thing Mrs. Hutton was intended to do: collect the insurance money. That was to be a tidy windfall for him to cash in on, you see, even if everything else went up the spout. Of course the bathing appointment was carefully arranged. Right time, right place, deserted beach and all the rest And then — up with his heels in some convenient pool, and what does it matter if his back gets scratched on the barnacles so long as his head stays under water? Nothing simpler! Then wedge the body where with any luck it won't drift loose for a few tides; and even if it does, what's the odds?

"Mrs. Hutton of course knew nothing in advance. That puzzled me from the first. How could such a foolish woman, however amiable, be trusted with murder-plans? Obviously not. And naturally, when she met him on the beach, he told her it was an accident. But what a convenient accident! It could be made to fit right in with their own plans. So he told her the tale and about the warrant and everything, and how the authorities would probably confiscate everything by way of a post-mortem fine except the insurance money, and why he must be kept out of it all, and what she must do. I expect he had some difficulty in rehearsing her, owing to floods of tears; that's why he didn't emphasise the importance of details as he should have done. And so, of course, she managed to give things away. She would. That was the one flaw in his plan, having to rely on poor Mrs. Hutton. But of course he had no choice. Lucky for us that he hadn't.

"So that was that And if things went right there was his future all nicely secured, and — his hated rival out of the way! Yes, I think he was really jealous. He must have been fond of Mrs. Hutton in his own way.

"After all, she suited him very well. Anyhow, he couldn't stand having a rival in her regard, so — exit rival! Hence those tears. She was fond of the rival, you see. Much too fond, in his conceited opinion."

"Now shall I tell you what suddenly gave it away to me? It was that shaving-brush and soap. How like Mrs. Hutton, I thought, to take her lover a razor to shave off his beard with and not take the shaving-brush and soap; and I wondered if even Mrs. Hutton could have been so silly. Well, of course she wasn't. The shaving-soap wasn't taken because soap doesn't lather in sea-water, so it would be no use. Ridiculous little point for such a case to hang on, isn't it? But the case does hang on it Because Mrs. Hutton wouldn't know a thing like that Therefore it wasn't she who left the shaving-soap behind, therefore it wasn't she who took the razor, therefore —"

"Then who did take the razor?" interrupted the superintendent "Of course, the murderer! Just as he brought that false beard to Penmouth with him, bought probably months ago. By the way, how delighted he must have been with that orange pullover. You see, any bearded face surrounding an orange pullover is just the same at fifty yards as any other bearded face surmounting —"

"Here, what's all this?" The superintendent looked his bewilderment "False beards? Orange pullovers? What do you mean, Mr. Sheringham?"

"I mean," said Roger gently, "that you shouldn't have relied on Mrs. Hutton's sole identification of her husband's body. You see, the body you've got in that mortuary isn't Hutton's. It's Bearstowe's."

What Roger Sheringham Did During the War

THE EXISTENCE OF *"The Bargee's Holiday"*, a short, short story that appears to be the last of Roger Sheringham's cases, was forgotten for nearly seventy years.

The story has only been published once before, on 18 February 1943 in a somewhat obscure British newspaper, the *North Devon Journal and Herald*. It seems likely that the story was specially commissioned by the newspaper from Berkeley, a 'local author', because its sole purpose is to emphasise the dangers posed by careless talk during wartime. In January, the month before publication of "The Bargee's Holiday", President Roosevelt, Prime Minister Churchill and representatives of the Free French Forces met at Casablanca to plan the Allied European strategy for the next phase of the war and the invasion of mainland Europe. The war against Germany and its allies was going well in North Africa and it seems likely that it was the intense speculation about when and where the European invasion would begin1 that gave Berkeley the idea for the story.

Then, as now, Devon was a largely rural area of southwestern England. In 1930, Berkeley and his wife purchased a rambling property called Linton Hills, hidden in 100 acres of dense woodland in what continues to be regarded as an area of outstanding natural beauty. With the oldest part believed to be over 400 years old, Linton Hills made the perfect country home for Berkeley who, for all his professed conviviality, was something of a misanthrope. According to Malcolm Turnbull in *Elusion Aforethought*[2], his biblio-biographical study of Berkeley – the house was "remodelled and expanded substantially" by the author although it remained "rather damp, dark and uncompromisingly 'basic'". It seems likely that the house and its estate provided the setting for

1   The invasion began in September with the allied incursion into Italy.

2   Bowling Green State University Popular Press, 1996.

Berkeley's 1930 novel The Second Shot, which was originally entitled *Murder at Minford Deeps*, a title redolent of
Berkeley's Puckish sense of humour and his tendency to
incorporate the names or real people and places in his fiction.

While it is far from a major work, *"The Bargee's Holiday"*
provides a charming coda to the Sheringham saga. Whether
or not it remains the *final* addition remains to be seen.

Tony Medawar and Arthur Robinson
December 2014

The Last Lost Case

AS ANTICIPATED, 'The Bargee's Holiday' proved *not*
to be the last of Sheringham. A second propaganda story,
'Hot Steel', was first published in the *Gloucester Citizen* on
27 April 1943 and in 2020 resurfaced in the third volume of
Bodies from the Library, an ongoing series of anthologies of
forgotten and unknown stories published by HarperCollins.

As well as being widely syndicated, 'The Bargee's Holiday' and 'Hot Steel' appeared in, respectively, the March and
July 1943 editions of *Defence*, a monthly magazine for the
Home Guard, Britain's war-time civilian army immortalized
in the long-running BBC television series *Dad's Army*. Given
their purpose, to raise awareness of the deadly consequences
of loose talk during the Second World War, it seems likely
that the stories were originally written with subscribers to
Defence in mind as well as newspaper readers in general.

With the discovery of 'Hot Steel', one can state with reasonable confidence that the Sheringham saga is now complete.
However, Anthony Berkeley Cox wrote many other stories
– under that name and under his best known pen-names,
Anthony Berkeley and Francis Iles. The best of these will
be brought together in **The Right to Kill and Other Stories** a new collection to be published by Crippen & Landru
in 2025.

Tony Medawar and Arthur Robinson
July 2023

The Bargee's Holiday

"IT'S A FACT! Every mornin' the blinkin' Sergeant calls us with a nice hot cup o' tea." The cheerful little soldier grinned round the railway carriage for applause. "Eh, Bargee? Ain't that the troof?" he appealed to his companion.

"Why do you call your friend 'Bargee'?" asked a comfortable-looking woman in one of the inside corners.

"For why? 'Cos that's what he was, mum. A blinkin'bargee. Swears like one too, eh, chum?"

"Was?" growled his companion. "Is!"

The little soldier instantly darted off on this new tack. "That's right. Now that's a funny thing. Wouldn't have thought the war'd make a shortage o' bargees, would yer? But it's the troof. Dahn where we are — can't tell you where, not even you, gent: that'd be careless talk, that would — but anyways, dahn that way there's more canals than roads, and blest if we don't 'ave to bring 'arf the rations up by water. And there's not enough bargees left to do the job, see? So we 'ave to do it ourselves, see? Old Bargee 'ere fancies 'e's back in civvies again; suits him dahn to a T. Eh, chum?"

The somewhat saturnine soldier was understood to growl that he wouldn't mind if they were proper barges, but them foreign things weren't no good to him.

As if at a cue the little Cockney amplified this observation. "That's right. Not only short o' bargees; short o' barges too they are. So we got to make do with some of the ones the Dutchies brought their Crahn Jools over in. Nice craft too, clean as paint and all ship-shape; but Bargee 'ere says they're too big for our canals."

The saturnine one growled something that might or might not have been assent.

"So I suppose you're both going to have a bargee's holiday and spend your leave letting someone else tow you?" tittered an elderly man opposite, inanely enough.

"Ten days' leaf!" sighed the soldier rapturously. "Coo, don't 'ardly bear thinking of, does it? An' I was beginning to think they was goin' to miss me out. I can tell yer, it made me 'eart jump clean into me mouf when I 'eard the Sergeant call my name out for the last batch — 'im as brings us our tea in the morning," he added with a wink. "Fact is, you see, old Rattlesnake — that's our Brigadier — well, 'e's got a personal dahn on the old Bargee an' me. Thinks I ought to 'ave been the bargee and him the garridge 'and before the war. But I told him straight, I did, I joined the R.A.S.C. to learn to punt, not to drive a blinkin' six-tonner: so —"

"I say," said Roger Sheringham suddenly. "What about careless talk?"

The little soldier stared. "Wot about it? I 'aven't told you nothink I shouldn't."

"You've told us you call your Brigadier 'Rattlesnake,' " Roger smiled. "What if a friend of his were listening?"

The little soldier grinned again. "I'll chance it, chum. Old Rattlesnake — 'is rattle's worse than 'is snake-bite."

And Roger, whose cousin had married an exceptionally pleasant man with the most inappropriate Army nickname of "Rattlesnake," grinned back.

It was early spring, and England was alive with rumours of an invasion of France at this point, that point and everywhere. In this electric atmosphere Roger paid a visit to the calm backwater of Franchard's bookshop. It was just one of those coincidences that the first person he saw, bending idly over a pile of blue-covered books, was that particular mild-mannered Brigadier known inexplicably to his troops as "Rattlesnake."

"I'm told," Roger said, "that your rattle is worse than your snake-bite. I hope Agatha can confirm it."

The Brigadier, suddenly addressed from the rear, started, recognised his assailant, and smiled a little vaguely. "Eh? Agatha? She's changing her library book upstairs. Eh? What did you say?"

Roger explained, and the two drifted into the usual stilted conversation of two men waiting for a woman. The soldier volunteered that he was snatching 48 hours' leave but didn't know when he would be able to take any more — if ever; and Roger sympathized fittingly.

"Shouldn't have thought there was much sale for these things now," he remarked, indicating the pile of continental guide-books at their elbow.

"No, but just like Franchard's, eh?" opined the Brigadier. "Don't recognise the war. Always sold guide-books, expect to sell 'em now."

"And, in fact, are selling 'em now." Roger leaned forward and deftly whisked one of the same books out of the soldier's tunic-pocket. "Unless, of course, you intended to shop-lift this one."

The Brigadier coloured and grabbed at the book. "Caught in the act," he conceded, with embarrassment. "Just happened to ... honeymoon ... sentimental memories... women, you know... thought Agatha would like."

"Careless lying," said Roger severely, "is just as bad as careless talk. I happen to know that you and Agatha spent your honeymoon on the Italian lakes, not in ... here, come into this corner!" He pulled the other into a small book-lined recess invisible to the rest of the shop. "Listen, Charles," he said rapidly. "I'm an enemy agent. Today's the 6th, isn't it? On or about the 20th we are going to invade — not France, as everyone expects, but Holland.

"Your brigade, trained already in the handling of Dutch barges, will take over all craft on the canals and be responsible for transport by water; others, presumably, will look after the road transport. After Holland, the plan is — here!" Roger broke off suddenly, not without alarm. "Put that silly thing away, Charles!"

But the Brigadier did not put his revolver away, and his manner was no longer mild. "This is serious, Sheringham," he said grimly. "You're coming with me to the War Office this minute — and if you can't produce a good explanation, it's going to be just too bad for you."

How did Roger Sheringham know that the invasion of Holland had been planned? How did he know the approximate date of the assault on the Dutch coast? The soldiers in the railway carriage had no idea they were "talking carelessly," for they were unaware of the significance of what they said, but they gave the whole invasion plan away. The Brigadier unconsciously confirmed a few details.

"Of course the men didn't realise what was happening," Roger was saying to an interested group at the War Office half an hour later. "But I gave you fellows credit for not being so stupid as to dump an R.A.S.C. Brigade down in a part of the country where they couldn't train properly. In other words, the handling of barges was their training; and now barges aren't sea-going craft and could never have made the journey over from Holland.

"That gave me an invasion of Holland, you see, nicely confirmed by the purchase by their Brigadier of a guide-book to that country — the significance of which he rammed home by a careless lie." Roger felt he owed something over that revolver, and was rewarded by the blush of mortification which his words produced.

"As for the date," he went on, not a little pleased with himself, "ten days means embarkation leave, these chaps were in the last batch. Charles was so busy he could only snatch 48 hours and didn't know when he would get any more — all the signs pointed to a date about a fortnight hence. Am I right?"

"That, Mr. Sheringham," said the senior officer gravely, "I must leave for you to find out. But I'll say this. I wish everyone who overheard something they shouldn't would come forward and report it as promptly as you have. If they did, we might be saved a lot of trouble and ... casualties."

Hot Steel

"ITLER WOULDN'T 'ARF give something for a sight of what you're lookin' at now,' bawled the little foreman.

Amid the deafening din of a huge munition works, Roger Sheringham could hardly hear the words. He grinned amiably and nodded, saving his larynx.

'Come and see what this lot's doin',' invited the foreman.

Roger looked round for his host, saw that he had not re-appeared, and followed his deputy towards a little group of half-naked men who were wiping the sweat off their foreheads with the air of something accomplished.

Some kind of a lull in the general din made conversation possible, and Roger learned that they had been forging the barrel of a six-inch gun. He said the appropriate things.

'And I expect Hitler would give something for the sight of that, too,' he added with a smile.

The burly man nearest to him wiped his forehead again. 'Well, sir, even 'itler must know we're making guns in England by this time.'

To Roger this seemed a very reasonable remark, but the little foreman appeared to find it highly humorous. 'Ah, it isn't the barrels,' he shouted. 'It's what's in 'em.'

'Shells, you mean?' hazarded Roger, relieved to find that the burly workman appeared just as bewildered as himself before the foreman's wit.

'Shells?' replied that humorist. 'No, wot I mean, it all depends if you know what you're lookin' at.'

"E's looking at a gun-forging, same as you are,' rejoined the burly workman, with an air of finality. 'Come on, mates.'

Roger was not sorry to be rescued at that moment by his host.

Arthur Luscombe at school had been a large, heavy boy, with a passion for imparting unwanted information in a ponderous manner. Now, as the managing director and virtual owner of Luscombe and Sons, he seemed to Roger to have altered very little. Leading his guest with measured footsteps towards his private office, he appeared determined on sacrificing his valuable time to pouring into Roger's reluctant ears just about everything anyone could want to know about steel, and a good deal more than most did.

'Austenite-alloy steels . . . low elasticity . . . manganese steels . . . toughness . . . resistance to abrasions . . . high-tensile alloy steels . . . gun-tubes . . . resistance to shock . . . nickel . . . chromium . . . molybdenum . . . you're not listening, Sheringham!'

'I am,' Roger protested, as they turned in the managing director's office. 'You were talking about steel, I mean,' he added hastily, after a glance at the other's face. 'You were saying that some—er—alloys were harder than others, and . . . and some not so hard . . . I mean, greater elasticity . . . yes, and . . . I say, though, wouldn't Hitler give something to see what I've just seen?'

The managing director's response to this artless query surprised its maker. It was with a positive start and a look of something remarkably like suspicion that he snapped: 'What exactly do you mean by that?'

'Well . . . er . . . nothing,' Roger returned lamely. 'As a matter of fact, it wasn't even original. Your foreman said it, so I thought—'

'Johnson had no right to say anything of the sort.'

'But it doesn't matter, does it?' Roger asked, still more surprised. 'I mean, munition works and so on . . . naturally Hitler . . .'

'Yes, yes. Of course. Naturally. Still, Johnson . . . However, it's of no importance. Now, I can just spare another ten minutes, Sheringham. Would you care to see our sidings? I have to go there myself in any case.'

'I should like to, above all things,' Roger said agreeably.

Five minutes later he was trying to look intelligently at long lines of railway trucks, but over which Mr Luscombe threw the complacent eye of proprietorship.

'Most interesting,' Roger said, doing his stuff. 'And I suppose this is the—er—raw steel, or whatever you call it. Where does that come from?

'Sorry, I can't answer that sort of question, Sheringham,' his host retorted, with (Roger thought) insufferable complacency. 'Official secrets, you know—Yes, O'Connor, what is it?'

Seeing his employer's attention distracted, the sidings foreman grinned sympathetically at Roger. 'Not that there's much official secret about it, sir,' he said, behind his hand. 'Anyone's only got to look at the labels on the trucks.'

Roger looked.

'Exactly. In fact, you get the stuff from Henbridge, wherever that may be—looks like a Government works.'

'Well, no, as a matter of fact we don't. We're getting our steel now from Allen and Backhouse, of Wolverhampton—this other label. That one's cancelled: some consignment from Henbridge to Allen and Backhouse, nothing to do with us.' The foreman saw Mr Luscombe returning, and hastily stepped back with an air of childlike innocence.

The rest of Roger's visit to the premises of Luscombe and Sons was uneventful. Indeed, it might very easily have passed out of his mind altogether. It is true that on getting home he had the curiosity to look up Henbridge in the gazetteer, and learned that it was a small village in the more inaccessible part of Cumberland, remarkable only as the site of the only coccodium deposits in England; whereupon he looked up coccodium in the encyclopaedia and gathered that it was a rare metal, resembling vanadium, but possessing certain unique properties, found only at Henbridge, in Cumberland.

It was just one of those coincidences, which so often do happen, which brought the name of Henbridge up in a conversation a few days later at Roger's club. It appeared that the man to whom he was talking lived there. Roger asked him about it.

'Used to be a grand little place—if you like 'em remote,' replied the other. 'Pitched up among the Cumberland fells and nearly a dozen miles from the nearest railway station. But it's all spoilt now. They've put up a huge great factory or something just outside, and the fells are covered with wooden huts. Just breaks my heart.'

'It seems queer,' Roger suggested, 'to choose a site a dozen miles from the nearest railway for a factory?'

The man snorted. 'But isn't it typical? Besides, that wouldn't worry them. They've brought the railway to Henbridge!'

'It certainly seems off,' Roger said mildly, and went away to look up trains.

'And you were as bad as any of them,' Roger was saying severely to a stricken Mr Luscombe a few hours later. 'Your works foreman was like a child playing with fire; couldn't help trying to be clever and drop hints that the stupid visitor wouldn't understand. He showed me there was some kind of secret going on; a simple remark of an irritated workman showed that the hands weren't in the secret, so it obviously wasn't a new hush-hush weapon; and then you gave me the biggest clue yourself.'

'I only told you a few elementary facts that you could have got out of any text-book,' protested the deflated remains of the managing director.

'It was the way you marshalled them. I know nothing of steel, but even I gathered that the hardest steels won't stand up so well to shock, and the ones that stand up best to shock have other drawbacks. You showed me that this fact, above all others concerned with steel, was most important to you. Naturally enough, perhaps, as one occupied in making gun-tubes, but there it was; the ideal steel alloy for a gun-tube had yet to be found, all the known ones lacked full efficiency one way or the other.

'Then your sidings foreman gave away that your suppliers have recently been changed, and I learnt that these suppliers are receiving consignments of what can only be coccodium. The inference is obvious. Experiments, using an alloy with coccodium to combine high resistance to both shock and friction have been successful, consignments of this coccodium steel are now reaching you, and are being tried out for six-inch naval guns. If Hitler had any idea of it, the works would be blown sky-high within 24 hours. So what?—And after all, why talk at all?'

'Look here, Sheringham,' pleaded the unfortunate man . . .

In the end Roger magnanimously promised to carry the matter no further. He decided that the managing director had learned his lesson—and it was quite certain that he would teach the others theirs.

Why Do I Write
Detective Stories?

WHY DO I write detective stories? Well, I wrote my first one *(The Layton Court Mystery)* for pure amusement, just to see if I could. That was a few years ago now, when detective stories had not reached the high standard expected of them today, and it was a common thing to read an otherwise good book in which one was irritated to find that a vital clue, which made the solution of the whole puzzle quite clear to the detective in charge, had been completely withheld from the reader till the end of the book. I was doing quite different work then, writing regularly for *Punch* and other humorous papers, but I was an eager reader of detective stories, and having been annoyed and disappointed in this way so often, I wondered whether I could not manage to write a story in which the reader should know just as much as my detective, and yet not be able to detect quite so well as he could. The book happened to sell just about twenty times as many copies as any of my previous ones, so I just bought a new typewriter and got down to it in real earnest That is why I am still writing detective stories today.

I'm glad the idea did occur to me, because detective stories really are fun to write. All the time one is having a game with the reader-to-be, trying to trick him into thinking evidence is important which has no importance at all, giving him quite fairly the really important evidence but in such a way that he will miss its significance, and generally doing one's best, as one says in England, to lead him down the garden path. Of course the idea of giving the reader all the available evidence is an old one now, and no detective story which does not do so is considered worth anything at all. In fact it is the first rule of the English Detection Club, of which Mr. G. K. Chesterton is President and of which I was the first Honorary Secretary, that no detective writer is eligible for membership who willfully withholds vital information from the reader — but detective-story fans would be surprised to learn what big-selling names have been excluded from the club under this rule!

The reason why detective stories are so popular is simple enough. They are, after all, only a glorified puzzle; and everyone enjoys a puzzle. To read a detective story as it should be read is really a test of intelligence; in fact one might say that whereas the ordinary novel appeals only to the emotions, the detective story appeals to the intellect, which surely should be the more important People, highly superior people, occasionally say to me, in their highly superior voices: "Oh, yes? But of course, I *never* read detective stories." I try not to point out that in this admission they are confessing that they have not got the necessary brainpower which a detective story demands.

How long can the detective story expect to maintain its present popularity? Always, I think, provided that it moves with the times. That is, so long as those who write them will recognize that the convention of yesterday will not suit the requirements of tomorrow. In other words, the days of pure puzzle story, without living characters, an interesting setting, or some kind of resemblance to real-life are over. Already, without sacrificing the puzzle element, authors are paying far more attention to character and atmosphere. Already the detective story is becoming altogether more sophisticated. Its development on these lines is, I think, inevitable. The detective story of the next decade will be not the infant prodigy of literature that it has been hitherto, but a real, true-to-life novel with a detective interest And this, I submit, is just what it should be.

The Body's Upstairs
By AB. Cox

(With apologies to Anthony Berkeley)

SO AS THE matter was urgent I decided to consult the only private detective I knew personally. I did so the more readily because I knew that among all the World's Greatest Detectives he was (according to his publishers) the World's *Greatest* Detective.

The World's *Greatest* Detective received me kindly, buffeting me several times on the back with hearty, if somewhat painful, bonhomie. I told him my trouble.

"I see," he nodded. "Very awkward. Read this letter out to me, while I drink my beer." He produced two enormous tankards from a cupboard and filled them from a barrel which was standing handily in a corner of the room.

Between gulps I read the letter:

"Dear Cox: — I am getting together the Christmas Number of L.O.[1] now, and want something from you to fill up an odd corner. About 1,200 words, and as soon as you can. Glorious weather, isn't it? Yours, R.S."

Roger Sheringham disposed of the contents of his tankard in one sustained effort. "Yes," he said. "And you say you actually did And an idea for this article?"

"I did," I agreed sadly. "A marvelously original idea, giving me scope to be as gay, as Christmassy, as witty as I liked."

"Witty?" said Sheringham suspiciously. "Are you witty? There's not room for two witty people in the same place, and I'm usually considered the witty one."

"Yes, yes," I said hastily. "Of course. No, I'm not really witty. I meant, facetious. They often get mixed up, don't they? At least, by their perpetrators."

Sheringham's heartiness became tinged with gloom. "And by one's audience. I have even been accused of facetiousness myself. In print. Some people have no sense of sparkle."

"Or of hearty humour," I hastened to agree. "But what about this idea of mine? Time's getting short, and I shall never find another."

1 *London Opinion*, for which this parody was probably written.

"You want me to trace it for you? My dear chap, of course. Child's-play." He buffeted me several times again on the back, reassuringly but excruciatingly. I tried to dodge, but his aim was unerring. "Have some more beer?"

"I still have some, thank you."

Sheringham refilled his own tankard, and we settled ourselves in two large leather armchairs.

"Now this missing idea of yours. When did you have it last?"

I considered. "I remember having it while I was shaving yesterday morning. Then when I got into my study after breakfast to put it on paper I couldn't find it."

"You looked everywhere?"

"Everywhere I could think of. My notebooks, my blotting-pad, the walls in the bathroom — yes, everywhere."

"At what time did you discover its loss?"

"I made an exact note of it for you," I replied, not without pride, knowing how careful Great Detectives are about that sort of thing. "It was ten-seventeen precisely."

"And you were shaving at...?"

"About nine-twenty."

"Say nine-fifteen. So it disappeared between a quarter-past nine and a quarter-past ten. I see. You realise that's an awkward time. A good many people are about just then; the milkman, the butcher, the gardener's boy for orders, the postman. Any of them might have taken it Have you interrogated them?"

"Well, no. I was hoping that you ..."

"That is not necessary," Sheringham returned with dignity. "Those are not my methods at all. I leave those rule-of-thumb ways to the official police, who have no delicate perceptions at all. *My* methods are mainly psycho-thera-peutical."

"Indeed?" I replied interestedly.

"Certainly. Beer, brag, and brains, are what I rely on for my astonishing results. Beer loosens the tongue, the tongue loosens the brain, and — well, there I always am. For instance, as regards your milkman, your butcher, your gardener's boy, the first question I always ask myself in connection with a suspect is, is he psychologically *capable* of the crime? There is no need to waste time in personal interrogation. Is your gardener's boy a *potential* London-Opin-

ion-Christmas-Number-idea-kleptomaniac? Unhesitatingly
I tell you, no."

"Thank you very much," I replied gratefully.

Sheringham rose and re-filled his tankard. "And so with
the rest of them. And that leads us to the deduction that your
idea has not been stolen at all. *It is still in your own possession.*"

"Is it?" I asked, a little doubtfully.

"Certainly," Sheringham replied sharply. "You have mis-
laid it, that's all. We will now try more direct means for
discovering it I shall employ the psycho-analytical method
of the association of opposites. Do any of the following words
directly not remind you of your idea? Mistletoe, Christmas
Pudding, almonds and raisins, ice, snow, Christmas presents, New Year resolutions, Hark the Herald Angels, turkeys,
calendars, holly, mince pies, step-ladders, Good King Wenc-
eslaus, waits, diaries, the weather, Christmas cards —"

"No, no," I cried, "I said, my idea was *original.* It wasn't
on any of the old, hackneyed themes. It was brilliant, novel,
scintillating —"

"Have some more beer," said Sheringham, as he rose to
replenish his own tankard.

"Not a single one of those words fails more than any
of the others to remind you?" he resumed disappointedly.
"Then we must try another of my methods. And this one,"
he added modestly "practically never fails." He drew out
his watch and consulted it closely. "I shall now talk to you
for three and a half hours without stopping. This will allow
all the submerged portion of my unconscious to rise to the
surface, so that, listening intently to my own words, I shall
give myself a brilliant notion or two towards the solution
of your case."

"Do I have to listen too?" I asked.

"It's usually done," Sheringham replied, in somewhat
hurt tones. "And anyhow, if this was in one of my books
you'd have to read me. Besides, I talk most amusingly and
extremely wittedly. I think you'd better."

"Very well," I agreed.

Sheringham began.

It was, however, considerably less than three and a half
hours before his exclamation of acute dismay woke me up.

"I must postpone your case after all," he cried. "I know
how urgent it is (yes, I know these editors too), so I'll ring
up at once; but they can't send before six o'clock."

"What's happened?" I asked anxiously.

"The barrel's run dry!"

"And in any case," he added, "I doubted from the beginning whether one would be enough. This is a three-barrel problem at least Come again tomorrow evening. By that time I shall have solved it for you."

I went sadly away. I could not share his confidence.

I wish I could remember my idea. It was such a brilliant one.

A Checklist of the Sheringham and Moresby Mysteries

by Anthony Berkeley Cox

Novels

The Layton Court Mystery. London: Herbert Jenkins Ltd, 1925, as by "?"; New York: Doubleday & Co., 1929. [Sheringham)

The Wychford Poisoning Case: An Essay in Criminology. London: W. Collins Sons & Co. Ltd, 1926, as by "the author of The Layton Court Mystery"; New York: Doubleday & Co., 1930. [Sheringham)

Roger Sheringham and the Vane Mystery. London: W. Collins Sons & Co. Ltd, 1927; New York: Simon & Schuster, 1927, as *The Mystery at Lovers' Cave.* [Sheringham and Moresby)

The Silk Stocking Murders: A Roger Sheringham Case. London: W. Collins Sons & Co. Ltd, 1928; New York: Doubleday & Co., 1928. [Sheringham and Moresby]

The Poisoned Chocolates Case: An Academic Detective Story. London: W. Collins Sons & Co. Ltd, 1929; New York: Doubleday & Co., 1929. Expanded from the short story "The Avenging Chance." [Sheringham and Moresby; the novel also features ABC's other amateur detective, Ambrose Chitterwick |

The Piccadilly Murder. London: W. Collins Sons & Co. Ltd, 1929; New York: Doubleday & Co., 1930. [Moresby and Chitterwick; Sheringham is mentioned but does not appear]

The Second Shot London: Hodder & Stoughton Ltd, 1930; New York: Doubleday & Co., 1931. Expanded from the short story "Perfect Alibi." I Sheringham)
Top Storey Murder. London: Hodder & Stoughton Ltd, 1932; New York: Doubleday & Co., 1932, as *Top Story Murder.* [Sheringham and Moresby]

Murder in the Basement London: Hodder & Stoughton Ltd, 1932; New York: Doubleday & Co., 1932. [Sheringham and Moresby]

Jumping Jenny. London: Hodder & Stoughton Ltd, 1933; New York: Doubleday & Co., 1933, as *Dead Mrs. Stratton,* with introductory note "Concerning Roger Sheringham." [Sheringham]

Panic Party. London: Hodder & Stoughton Ltd, 1934; New York: Doubleday & Co., 1934, as *Mr. Pidgeon's Island.* (Sheringham)

Trial and Error. London: Hodder & Stoughton Ltd, 1937; New York: Doubleday & Co., 1937. [Moresby and Chitterwick; Sheringham is mentioned but does not appear |

Short Stories

NOTE: The details given are of the stories' first known publication. Stories with an asterisk are collected in *The Avenging Chance and Other Mysteries from Roger Sheringham's Casebook.*

*   "The Avenging Chance." *Pearson's Magazine,* September 1929. A slightly longer version appears in *The Roger Sheringham Stories,* introduction by Ayresome Johns. London: Pledge Limited Edition, Thomas Camacki, 1994. This version is used in this collection. [Sheringham and Moresby]
*   "The Story of a Perfect Alibi." *Radio Times,* 1 August 1930. Revised version, as "Perfect Alibi," in *Evening Standard* (London), 11 March 19.53. The revised version is used in this collection. (Sheringham)
*   "The Mystery of Horne's Copse." *Home and Country,* January-December, 1931 (Serial in 12 parts). (Sheringham and Moresby)

* "Unsound Mind." *Time and Tide,* 14 and 21 October, 1933 (2 parts). (Moresby)
* "White Butterfly." *Evening Standard,* 28 August 1936. (Sheringham and Moresby)
* "The Wrong Jar." *Detective Stories of Today,* ed. Raymond Postgate. London: Faber & Faber, 1940. (Sheringham and Moresby]
* " 'Mr. Bearstowe Says ...' " *The Saturday Book 3,* ed. Leonard Russell. London: Hutchinson, 1943. |Sheringham|

"Direct Evidence." *The Roger Sheringham Stories,* introduction by Ayresome Johns. London: Pledge Limited Editions, Thomas Camacki, 1994. (Sheringham]
* "Double-Bluff." *The Roger Sheringham Stories,* introduction by Ayresome Johns. London: Pledge Limited Editions, Thomas Camacki, 1994.
* "Double-Bluff" and "Direct Evidence" concern the same murder but develop differently: "Double-Bluff" would appear to be the later of the two and it is therefore the version included in this collection. (Sheringham]

"Razor-Edge." *The Roger Sheringham Stories,* introduction by Ayresome Johns. London: Pledge Limited Editions, Thomas Camacki, 1994. A previously unpublished early version of "Mr. Bearstowe Says..." (Sheringham]
* "The Bargee's Holiday". *North Devon Journal and Herald,* 18 February 1943
* "Hot Steel". *Gloucester Citizen,* 27 April 1943

Plays

Temporary Insanity. The Roger Sheringham Stories, introduction by Ayresome Johns. London: Pledge Limited Editions, Thomas Camacki, 1994. Adapted from *The Layton Court Mystery.* Apparently never performed. (Sheringham]

Red Anemones. The Roger Sheringham Stories, introduction by Ayresome Johns. London: Pledge Limited Editions, Thomas Camacki, 1994. Broadcast on BBC Radio *(Plays by The Detection Club),* June 1 and 8, 1940. The play was adapted from "Razor-Edge." The order of writing, therefore, was probably the short story "Razor-Edge" (unpublished during Berkeley's lifetime), followed by the script "Red Anemones," followed by "Mr. Bearstowe Says ..." We have chosen the latter, as

Berkeley's final version, to be included in this collection. {Sheringham and Moresby]

Miscellaneous

* "Concerning Roger Sheringham." Included in *Dead Mrs. Stratton,* New York: Doubleday, 1933, and some later reprints. A biographical note on Sheringham.

Unfinished fiction

In *The Anthony Berkeley Cox Files: Notes Towards a Bibliography,* Ayresome Johns records four fragments of works featuring Sheringham.

The first comprises the opening pages of a chapter of an unnamed novel. In this Sheringham and Alec Grierson are at the breakfast table, discussing cricket and the deaths of two people by gas poisoning within two years of each other. The second is also the opening section of a chapter of an unnamed novel; on this occasion Sheringham is breakfasting alone when he is visited by one of his nephews.

The third fragment is also an untitled typescript of the "opening chapters of a Roger Sheringham mystery novel" (sic); one page was reproduced on the back cover of *The Anthony Berkeley Cox Files: Notes Towards a Bibliography.* However this has since been identified as the opening chapters of an early draft of "The Mystery of Horne's Copse," which is included in this collection and was discovered by Arthur Robinson in 2000. The final fragment is the initial chapters of an early version of *Roger Sheringham and the Vane Mystery,* possibly prepared with a view to serialisation.

In the introduction to *The Roger Sheringham Stories,* Johns notes the existence of a six-page typescript entitled "Seaside Story" which would appear to have been the outline for a novel, based in part on the plot of "Razor-Edge" and which, initially, was to have involved Sheringham. Johns goes on to give details of the developing plot and speculates that the novel might have been published, without Roger Sheringham and under a new pseudonym. However, he concedes that there is no real evidence for this.

Parodies

"The Clergyman's Daughter" by Agatha Christie. *Partners in Crime.* London: W. Collins Sons & Co. Ltd., 1929; New York: Dodd, 1929. The heroine of Berkeley's *The Silk Stocking Murders* (1928) had been a clergyman's daughter. (Sheringham is referred to but does not appear)

"The Conclusions of Mr. Roger Sheringham" by Dorothy L. Sayers. *Ask a Policeman.* London: Arthur Barker, 1933; New York: Morrow, 1933. In *Ask a Policeman*, a round-robin mystery by members of the Detection Club, John Rhode wrote the first part, describing the murder of a newspaper owner. Helen Simpson, Gladys Mitchell, Berkeley, and Sayers wrote further chapters, offering their own solutions. Each author's chapter features another's detective. Thus, Berkeley's chapter gives Lord Peter Wimsey's theory while Sayers contributes a chapter in which Roger Sheringham proposes a solution. Sayers ends her chapter by suggesting that Roger is wrong again, with Moresby Apparently about to refute his solution. (Sheringham)

"A New Denouement" by Christianna Brand. *The Poisoned Chocolates Case.* San Diego: Mystery library, 1979. Specially written for the Mystery Library reprint; Brand presents a further solution to the problem of *The Poisoned Chocolates Case.* (Sheringham does not appear)

* "The Body's Upstairs" by A. B. Cox (sic). *The Roger Sheringham Stories,* introduction by Ayresome Johns. London: Pledge Limited Editions, Thomas Carnacki, 1994. No earlier publication has been established. (Sheringham |

NOTE: The most complete published bibliography of Cox's work appeared in the modestly subtitled *The Anthony Berkeley Cox Files: Notes Towards a Bibliography,* by Ayresome Johns. London: Ferret Fantasy, 1993.

A fuller bibliography of Cox's published works is available on the Web at http://home.lagrange.edu/arobinson/coxbibliog.htin

Crippen & Landru publishes first editions of short-story collections by important detective and mystery writers.

This is the best edited, most attractively packaged line of mystery books introduced in this decade. The books are equally valuable to collectors and readers. *[Mystery Scene Magazine]*

The specialty publisher with the most star-studded list is Crippen & Landru, which has produced short story collections by some of the biggest names in contemporary crime fiction. *[Ellery Queen's Mystery Magazine]*

God Bless Crippen & Landru. *[The Strand Magazine]*

A monument in the making is appearing year by year from Crippen & Landru, a small press devoted exclusively to publishing the criminous short story. *[Alfred Hitchcock's Mystery Magazine]*

Crippen & Landru
Lost Classics

Peter Godfrey. *The Newtonian Egg.* 2002.
Craig Rice. *Murder, Mystery, and Malone.* 2002 eBook, $8.99
Charles B. Child. *The Sleuth of Baghdad.* 2002.
Stuart Palmer. *Hildegarde Withers, Uncollected Riddles.* 2002
    eBook $8.99
Christianna Brand. *The Spotted Cat.* 2002
Raoul Whitfield. *Jo Gar's Casebook.* 2002.
William Campbell Gault. *Marksman.* 2003.
Gerald Kersh. *Karmesin.* 2003   eBook, $8.99
C. Daly King. *The Complete Curious Mr. Tarrant.* 2003 eBook
    $8.99
Helen McCloy. *The Pleasant Assassin.* 2003
William DeAndrea. *Murder – All Kinds.* 2003
Anthony Berkeley. *The Avenging Chance.* 2004
Joseph Commings. *Banner Deadlines.* 2004 eBook $8.99
Erle Stanley Gardner. *The Danger Zone.* 2004 eBook $8.99
T. S. Stribling. *Dr. Poggioli: Criminologist.* 2004 eBook $8.99
Margaret Millar. *The Couple Next Door.* 2004
Gladys Mitchell. *Sleuth's Alchemy.* 2005
Philip Warne/Howard Macy. *Who Was Guilty?* 2005 eBook
    $8.99
Dennis Lynds writing as Michael Collins. *Slot-Machine Kelly.*
    2005
Julian Symons. *The Detections of Francis Quarles.* 2006
Rafael Sabatini. *The Evidence of the Sword.* 2006 eBook, $8.99
Erle Stanley Gardner. *The Casebook of Sidney Zoom.* 2006,
    eBook $8.99
Ellis Peters. *The Trinity Cat.* 2006
Lloyd Biggle. *The Grandfather Rastin Mysteries.* 2007
Max Brand. *Masquerade.* 2007
Mignon Eberhart. *Dead Yesterday.* 2007
Hugh Pentecost. *The Battles of Jericho.* 2008
Victor Canning. *The Minerva Club.* 2009
Anthony Boucher and Denis Green. *The Casebook of Gregory
    Hood.* 2009
Vera Caspary. *The Murder in the Stork Club.* 2009
Michael Innes. *Appleby Talks About Crime.* 2010
Phillip Wylie. *Ten Thousand Blunt Instruments.* 2010

Erle Stanley Gardner. *The Exploits of the Patent Leather Kid.* 2010, eBook, $8.99
Vincent Cornier. *The Duel of Shadows.* 2011, eBook, $8.99
E. X. Ferrars. *The Casebook of Jonas P. Jonas.* 2012
Charlotte Armstrong. *Night Call.* 2014, eBook, $8.99
Phyllis Bentley. *Chain of Witnesses.* 2014
Patrick Quentin. *The Puzzles of Peter Duluth.* 2016, , Clothbound $29, eBook $8.99
Frederick Irving Anderson . *The Purple Flame.* 2016, Clothbound $29, Trade Paperback $19
Anthony Gilbert. *Sequel to Murder.* 2017, Clothbound $29
James Holding, *The Zanzibar Shirt Mystery.* 2018, Clothbound $29
Q. Patrick. *The Cases of Lieutenant Trant.* 2019
Erle Stanley Gardner. *Hot Cash, Cold Clews.* 2020, Clothbound $32, Trade Paperback $22, eBook $8.99
Freeman Wills Crofts, *The 9.50 Up Express.* 2021, Clothbound $32, Trade Paperback $22, eBook $8.99
Stuart Palmer. *Hildegarde Withers, Final Riddles?* 2021, Clothbound $32, Trade Paperback $22, eBook $8.99
Patrick Quentin. *Hunt in the Dark.* 2021
William Brittain. *The Man Who Solved Mysteries.* 2022, Clothbound $32, Trade Paperback $1922 eBook $8.99
John Creasey. *Gideon and the Young Toughs.* 2022, , Clothbound $35, Trade Paperback $20, eBook $8.99
Pierre Very. *The Secret of the Pointed Tower.* 2023, Clothbound $32, Trade Paperback $20
Anthony Berkeley. *The Avenging Chance and Even More Stories (Enlarged with Two Stories).* 2023, Trade Paperback $19, eBook $8.99

SUBSCRIPTIONS

Crippen & Landru offers discounts to individuals and institutions who place Subscriptions for its forthcoming publications, either the Regular Series or the Lost Classics or (preferably) both. Collectors can thereby guarantee receiving limited editions, and readers won't miss any favorite stories. Subscribers receive a specially commissioned story as a gift at the end of the year. Please write or e-mail: Orders@crippenlandru.com for more details.

Printed in the USA
CPSIA information can be obtained
at www.ICGtesting.com
LVHW091553311223
767720LV00061B/1412

9 781936 363803